ROCKY FRONTIER

BOOK 1 OF THE ESSO TRILOGY

JADEN FARQUHAR

PART I

1

―――――

orning on ESSO-3, the three workers descended into the cave.

Laurence was walking behind Eric and Ken, his coworkers for this job, who were chatting away. The two of them had been working the job for months, while Laurence was new to it. Jobs were always based on one's skills on the ESSO[Eh-So]-3 Colony, and they changed quickly based on the demand. Laurence's skillset was in increasing demand these days.

The cave they were in was pitch-black and well underground. It was a wide open area with mostly jagged gray rock. They had to watch out for the occasional ice patch. The ceiling was maybe 30 feet above them. The three were shining lights from the helmets of their environment suits to see. Space suits, really, they were similar to traditional space suits. With added padding on areas including the shoulders and chest. The environment of ESSO-3 may as well have been outer space, the atmosphere was thin, nights were 14 hours long while days were only ten, the planet was mostly rock and ice. One of ESSO-3's only redeeming factors was its fresh water.

"Laurence, you've been pretty quiet." Eric said. "By the way, can I call you Larry?"

"We're supposed to use our full first names." Laurence replied.

"Nobody follows that rule. I'm calling you Larry." Eric said. So that was his name for the rest of the night.

"So, why don't you guys give me a recap of the job." Larry said.

"Ken?" Eric said.

"Sure thing." Ken replied. "So as you know, this dark, dreary looking cave is actually teaming with life. You see those icicle looking rock formations, hanging from the top of the cave? Those are stalactites, and the microbes we're looking for like to live up there on them. The ones that help us decontaminate the water from all those heavy metals and radioactive stuff."

"I've got all the climbing gear," Ken added. "When we find a suitable spot, we'll set up on one of those cave walls. We set Eric up with his harness, bring out the cable, and we belay, meaning we hold onto his cable and give him slack. Then Eric can climb up and get to the stalactites."

"I've got gecko hands," Eric said, grinning. He held up the special gloves, which were lined with small fibers on the palms and fingertips. "They make climbing pretty damn easy."

"Just keep your eyes open, that's your job." Ken said. "But you already know all this stuff."

Larry nodded and smiled. "I like hearing it back. Sounds like a good job."

"Ok then..." Eric replied.

They came across a wall of jagged rock, and shined their lights to see a massive stalactite directly above them.

"Here's a good spot. Set me up guys." Eric said. Ken set down a large grappling hook device and shot out a cable that flew up to the top of the cave wall. It hooked onto some rock jutting out two or three feet from the top of the cave, with a loud echoing thud. The cable hung down, a thin sturdy wire only a few inches thick. Ken grabbed the cable and hooked it to the belt of his suit, and he held out the climbing harness he was carrying and gave it to Eric, who strapped it on. The two did this all with extreme efficiency.

"Alright, let's go." Eric said. Ken gave him a thumbs up. Eric shined his light onto the wall and identified a good flat rock face a few feet above him. Eric leapt up like a monkey, taking advantage of ESSO-3's light gravity. It had 70% of the baseline level for a planet. Eric clasped onto the flat face of the wall, and his gecko hands started going to work. He would pull off each hand lightly, pulling the palm up first and then the fingertips, and then he would press his hand flat against the wall to stick. Using this technique, Eric could scale the wall in minutes. He did not need the cable to climb, that was just so Ken and Larry could catch him if he fell.

He reached the top of the wall. "Give me some slack." Eric said. Ken loosened his grip. Eric then turned himself around and leapt. He landed on the stalactite, his hands and feet tightly clasping the base stem of the rock structure. The three workers had earpieces in, so they could hear Eric loud and clear as he panted, slightly out of breath.

"Impressive." Larry said.

"Ha ha," Eric said. "You wish you could do that Larry." Eric reached onto his belt and pulled out his sampler. It was a hybrid tool that was a rock drill, but also had a built-in compound microscope. Eric drilled into the stalactite, careful not to drill anything loose, as small debris flew out.

"Yep, this one is teaming with the little bugs." Eric said. Once he had collected his samples, Larry and Ken could carefully pull him down using the cable.

The three workers continued on with this job for hours. As they did, they carried on some discussions.

"I just don't see why a guy like you, who's only been assigned on ESSO-3 for what, six months, gets to carry a gun." Eric said. "I've been here 11 months. Ken's been here 17. I think I've earned the right to defend myself."

"Meritocracy." Ken said. "Which you support, Larry?"

"Yes I support it. The Boss's system makes sense. If you're going to give out guns, give them to as few people as possible. So give them to the most qualified, not the people who have been here the longest."

"Easy for you to say," Eric replied.

"Guys, I'm just glad robots aren't used for doing jobs like this." Ken said. "A robot who could do what you do, Eric? Would be way too smart to trust." For a moment this ended the conversation. Then Eric pushed further.

"So because Larry here can press a changing light on a computer screen faster than anyone else, he deserves that kind of power, of being armed?"

"Reaction time is genetic, Eric, if we get into trouble Larry is the best equipped of the three of us to spot it first."

"Why are you backing him up?" Eric responded. "No offense, I mean. But I believe in trust, Larry. Trust takes time to build."

"Well I believe in science," Larry said. "It's a well known fact that you can't truly trust anyone on ESSO-3. Humans weren't built for ESSO-3. Cold, dark isolation. This planet is known to make anyone go off the rails. Makes us just as bad as robots." Larry continued, "the Boss knows this, it's not that he's biased against anyone, he just takes precautions."

"I only wonder," Ken replied, "Is it that the planet makes us crazy? Or that only the crazy come here willingly?"

With this, the conversation ended. They carried on with their work in silence, for what felt like an eternity. Far less jovial than during that first stalactite they'd started on. Ken broke the silence.

"Larry, you know what happened with the robots, 50 years ago?" Ken asked.

"I mean, they got too smart, too *self-aware*. We scaled back everything to do with them. Only use 'em for basic tasks now," Larry said. "And for some idiotic reason we sent them out into the universe, to places like here, to explore for us. Still don't know what happened to all of them."

"Yeah that's the stuff they teach in school. What's funny is all the stuff they don't tell you about it."

"I guess so."

• -   -

"Alright, after this, we'll do one more for today." Eric said. They stood under a massive, thick stalactite, the biggest one yet. It had sheets of ice on it.

"Careful with that one, Eric." Ken said.

Eric did his thing, he climbed up and jumped onto the stalactite. He balanced precariously on the slippery structure. This time he had landed at a bad angle. He was drilling into the thick, trunk-like rock. Just then, Larry heard a strange rattling noise from his earpiece. A metallic clanking. It was getting louder.

"You guys hear that?" Larry asked.

"Hear what?" Eric said.

"That weird noise." Larry paused for a moment. "Ken, can you keep that wire steady for a bit?"

"Sure."

Larry kept his head light on Eric, took out a hand light and shined it across the ceiling of the cave. He spotted a strange, metallic object. It appeared to be a set of legs. Its body was small, a thin mess of armored plating with a few circuits sticking out. It was a four legged object, moving effortlessly on the ceiling, and it was sprinting towards Eric. A robot.

Without a word, Larry drew his handgun and traced the path that the creature was moving along. With one eye closed, he fired three shots immediately at the robot. One shot landed and pierced one of its wiry legs. It let out a high pitched, ear piercing screech, and leapt forward.

"What's going on!" Eric yelled.

"Eric, I'm lowering you down now." Ken said. "Jump!"

Eric unstuck his hand and prepared to jump. His foot slipped on an ice patch and his whole body came down. His sampler fell out of his hand and plummeted down. Eric stuck his left hand on the stalactite at the last second, and held onto the tip of it by that one hand.

"Quick, just let go, I'll bring you down!" Ken yelled.

But it was too late. As Eric looked up, the robotic spider was already on the stalactite. He saw one of its legs poised, with a sharp blade at the end.

"No no no!" Eric cried. The robot sliced through his cable.

Several sharp stalagmites pointed up from the ground below him. His left glove was now all that stood between him and a 30 foot drop.

Larry quickly sidestepped so that Eric was not in his line of fire. The robot was crawling down the stalactite. Larry opened fire, six more shots within seconds, the explosive sound echoing throughout the cave. At least four of the shots careened through the robot's body. The robot tried to retreat back up the stalactite, crawling backwards, but it had taken too many hits. On the fourth hit the robot suddenly collapsed, as if it went limp. One of its legs came loose and it flipped over, dropping like a stone.

Eric's hand was slipping out of his glove. That singular device holding him up. There was nothing Ken could do, the severed cable had slipped loose. No one else had climbing gloves, and even then, there was no time. Eric's palm had already slipped out, he was holding onto the glove with his fingertips.

Larry's hand shot to his earpiece, when all he could hear was Eric's deafening, chilling scream, as he plummeted down to the ground.

2

_____

The Infirmary, much like most other buildings in the Colony, was a mix of fabric and tarp-like materials and solid metal. Steel beams held up the integrity. In the early days of the ESSO-3 Colony most structures utilized polyesters. But as more shipments of people arrived, among the supplies that came with them, and among the most heavily requested by the colonists, were these solid construction materials. There was no safety and no guarantees with the weather. The wind was brutal and often kicked up debris. And there was always the possibility of more sinister, more unnatural attacks on the Colony.

As Larry entered, Eric was laying on a mesh cot, Ken standing over and talking to him. At one remark Eric laughed so wildly, it seemed clear to Larry that Eric was still under the influence of a few drugs. Most notably, there was a stump where his right arm used to be. Indoors, people wore thin, skin tight, all black outfits instead of their bulky environment suits.

Eric's fit snugly around his body, but the right sleeve hung loose beyond the stump. Larry had seen this, Eric had his arm penetrated by a stalagmite from the fall. But the rest of the mission, carrying Eric to the surface, the screaming, the tension, was all a blur in Larry's memory.

Before being allowed in, Larry had to be washed down. The whole place was heavily sterilized, it smelled of ammonia. Contamination could be a real problem with the micro-organisms on the planet. Larry waited patiently just outside the operating space, until one of the two doctors present gave him the okay, as they shuffled through the place carrying out tasks. Ken shook Eric's left hand before heading out. Eric maintained a warm smile on his face. Ken gave Larry a curt greeting as he left, simply muttering "Larry," dryly.

Larry approached Eric, whose warm somewhat delirious smile faded to an expressionless gaze.

"How are you feeling, man?" Larry asked.

"Oh, I'm great!" Eric said. "Just a little fall. It's not like I lost anything important, right? Right." The room stirred. Larry looked at one of the doctors. Even through a surgical mask, he could sense the discomfort. Larry persisted.

"I can't imagine what you're going through right now Eric."

"You're right about that, Larry." Eric stared him down, but Larry was unfazed. "The pain is better at least, I can say that."

"Good, I'm glad for that."

Eric's eyes wandered to Larry's handgun. Larry carried it at all times, even indoors. He had a holster on his indoor outfit. What Eric said next, he enunciated slowly and deliberately, his voice trembling a bit.

"I could have *really* used one of those." Eric said. Larry said nothing. Eric went on, "You're a good shot Larry, a really good shot. But 30 feet away? That is tough even for you."

Larry took a moment, crafting his response.

"It's an unfortunate world Eric. I agree with you on that. I'm truly sorry about your injury." And the last touch he added, "No one could have done that job like you."

Eric sighed, and then laughed a bit. At first it appeared to be humility. Then Larry realized it was because someone else had entered the room. Not just anyone else, but the Boss himself.

He wasn't a particularly tall man, he was short. Middle-aged, while most of the colonists were in their 20s. A few of the colonists were even in their late teens. He had a big thick beard, something else unusual for colonists.

"Eric Wisen," the Boss said. "Laurence Atkins," the Boss added offhandedly.

"Franklin Howe." Eric said.

"How are you doing? How's the arm?"

"It's....better. Better sir."

"Good. Excellent." Franklin Howe, referred to as the Boss in third person, but always by name to his face, grabbed a crate from a corner of the room. One of the shipping containers the Transport Vessels used, lying around. He pulled it up to Eric's cot and sat on it. Larry remained standing, not saying a word.

"Eric, I'm going to give you the hard facts. Try not to look so distraught," Franklin Howe said. Eric nodded. Just about every trace of Eric's earlier sarcasm was gone.

"The surgery, the time off, the artificial arm the roboticists are cooking up for you, it's all gonna be very costly."

"How much?" Eric asked.

"A quarter."

"A quarter of my final pay cut?"

"Resources are sparse these days. But you know that. You knew the risks when you signed up for this program. It pains me, believe me, but on the job injuries are costly, we're running an operation here." Franklin Howe said. "16 months of your service left, I hope your luck turns around Eric."

"A quarter of my cut," Eric repeated, this time to himself. "Jesus."

"Hmm." Franklin Howe said. "You'll probably never be able to do your harvesting job again with an artificial limb, that's for sure. We'll have to figure out something else for you. We can't really have four people on that cave assignment, it just doesn't make sense. We'll find a suitable replacement. In the meantime, just rest up."

Eric put his sole remaining hand to his face and groaned. Larry then spoke up, surprising both of them.

"He should keep the caving job with me and Ken." Larry said. "He has a good rapport and works well with Ken, I've seen it. I'll switch roles with him."

Franklin Howe gave Larry a puzzled look. "Your job is security. Eric doesn't have a gun."

"But Eric can use his experience to mentor me for climbing and harvesting, and he can help Ken belay. Clearly the robots can crawl on ceilings now, so nowhere is truly safe. The climber is the most vulnerable, so they should have a gun. It's easier than shooting from 30 feet away."

Franklin Howe pondered it, and nodded. "I guess you've at least rationalized it. Sounds like a lot of extra work for you, on top of your other job - driving, was it? - Anyway, I expect you and Eric can figure it out."

"Got it," Larry said.

"Gentlemen," Franklin Howe said, and he left. A doctor

hurried over and moved the crate the Boss was sitting on back to its place.

"A quarter of my cut." Eric said again. "And he tried to transfer me too. Least you had the decency to stop that, huh Larry. I applaud that."

"You're *welcome*, Eric." Larry said. "I'll leave you be now, I've got work to do. Goodbye."

Eric said nothing.

Larry walked away. As he exited the Infirmary, he heard Eric loudly yelling. "Hey! Now that they're gone, can I get more painkiller!" And once again the busy shuffle of doctors.

• - -

The driving job was Larry's day job. Driving around a glorified shuttle bus, miles across the barren surface of ESSO-3. The vehicle was essentially a buggy, with thick rims and an open top. It somewhat resembled an SUV, an old four-wheel drive vehicle Larry remembered from his 20th century history classes. Their vehicle was bulky, not the most maneuverable, but it could transport six people back and forth, with two back rows of three seats each. Those were six people in addition to him and his colleague Stephanie, the repair engineer. So that was the job. Carry people, tools and some supplies back and forth between the various mining sites surrounding the Colony. These little pockets of Civilization were all that stood between the Colony and the vast open terrain of a very sizable planet.

Larry drove across large open plains of gray and dark rock. Dust and debris kicked up constantly from the wheels. There were massive mountains in the distance. During the day, the sky was a deep pure blue with plenty of clouds. At night, jet black. Right at the start of his route, Larry always drove past a massive frozen lake, with a little natural rock bridge cutting between its two massive sheets of crystal-like ice. There were glaciers on ESSO-3; ice was the planet's defining feature. As for life, the colonists had found nothing more complex than microbes. Nothing organic, that is.

The air on ESSO-3 was even somewhat breathable. Somewhat. Anyone unfortunate enough to have a leak in their suit would start to get dizzy and faint within a few minutes. As Eric did, Larry remembered, in those brief blurry moments after his big fall. Most workers wore similar suits, including security, scientists, laborers, etc. Engineers like Stephanie had slightly bulkier suits, carrying around tools and utilities with them. A lot more than just Eric's (recently broken) multi-purpose sampler.

After Larry's encounter with Eric and the Boss earlier in the day, he did most of his job without saying a word. Until, nearing the mine that was their destination, Stephanie got some words out of him.

"So what made you late today? That's not like you." Stephanie said.

Larry, who had been simply taking in his surroundings and drifting, cleared his throat. "Well, you heard about Eric's accident, right? I was on assignment with him. I took some time to see how he was doing."

"Yeah I heard Eric lost an arm. Something like a 30 foot drop? Even with ESSO-3 gravity he's lucky not to be dead." Stephanie said.

The news had not yet spread around that it had been a robot responsible for Eric's fall, though Larry imagined plenty of people suspected it. With recent events, more sightings of them lately, professionals didn't just drop like that by chance. Well sometimes they did, but that's not what people like to believe.

"Poor guy is losing a sizable chunk of his final pay." Larry said.

"It's tough. But it's no travesty," Stephanie said. "I've worked with some of the people who build the robotic limbs. It takes a lot of time and energy. Not to mention the actual operation. Someone has to front those resources lost."

"Agreed."

"I'm sure Eric didn't agree with that though, right?"

"Yep. How'd you know?"

Stephanie laughed. "I used to work with him. And his little right hand man Ken. All they do is complain about the way things are run. Freedom this, freedom that. It's all about freedom to them."

"True. I do sympathize. If Eric was allowed to work some overtime, he could cut down on some of what he lost. I had to volunteer to switch jobs with him, *just* so the poor guy could keep his assignment. Now I'm doing that exerting cave harvesting stuff."

"Oh please. The last thing we need is someone like Eric overworking himself, getting even more emotionally volatile than he already is. And if he was armed, God, he'd probably shoot someone."

"But is it not hypocritical that the Boss lets me work double time but not Eric?"

"You have skills. Driving, good aim, good hearing. That basic stuff that you can't just study. Intelligence is the most important thing, obviously, but somewhere in that list you've got the second and third best skills for sure. You're versatile, you should be fully utilized."

"I totally get the Boss's logic. I'm just a little sick of special treatment, is all." Larry replied. "Also, are you calling me stupid?" Larry added lightheartedly.

"I'll put it this way, it's not your job to be smart, and you're still smarter than that idiot and supposed 'scientist' Eric." Stephanie said.

They were now driving up a small mountain. Doing so was easier on ESSO-3, less gravity weighing you down. But the driver had to be careful about their traction and not slipping. In the early days the colonists had carved out paths in the mountains, and smoothed out the terrain at parts for driving. It was a great manual job for anyone short of work back in the day. Back when work was extremely abundant.

A movement in the corner of Larry's eye caught his attention. Keeping one hand on the wheel, he reached towards his holster, only to find it was debris crumbling off a large rock structure in the distance. A jagged peak, eroded by wind and weather. One of the toughest parts of the driving job, the unease of being open and exposed.

"Larry, what are your goals right now?" Stephanie asked.

"Sorry?"

"Your goals. I write all mine down."

"Yeah well I'm not you Stephanie."

"Okay, but you're taking on the extra work. Right? You're not getting paid more. I don't get the why behind it. What are you going for right now Eric?"

"Eric?"

"Larry, I mean." Stephanie said.

"Extra work is great to keep me busy. Keep me sharp."

"Sure. But what's the point?"

"What's the point of anything, Stephanie? What's the point of ESSO-3?" Larry said. Stephanie was somewhat taken aback. Larry sighed. "Work keeps me busy. It gives me a purpose. Is that not all I can ask for?"

"If you say so." Stephanie said. And that was the end of that line of questioning.

After a lengthy drive, they arrived at their designated mine. A large open pit mine, where people with vehicles and tools were extracting minerals, ores, and salt. No automatic machines, everything was person operated. Except for a primitive computer system to keep track of all the workers and their timeliness.

Most of the resources would be offloaded by bigger vehicles than Larry and Stephanie's buggy. Their job was personnel. Drop people off, return to base to do their secondary jobs, and come back for pick up. And that's what they did. Fuel inefficient? Yes. (Though the vehicles ran on battery power that the colonists referred to as "fuel"). But energy was one thing the Colony had plenty of, manpower was much more important. Allowing people like Larry and Stephanie to fully utilize their skills in other assignments as well.

Six miners, men and women covered in dust, undoubtedly with sweat as well inside their suits, loaded the vehicle after another hard day at the job. A long drive back, with laughter and banter in the back seats. Stephanie engaged with them too. Larry simply drove, silent.

And as they finished up their job, Larry would be able to return to his quarters relatively peaceful and undisturbed. Something he wouldn't be able to do for a long, long time thereafter.

3

L arry was restless. But "restless" was an extreme understatement. Every chance he began to fade into unconsciousness, he was yanked back and left dazed. In the images flashing in his head, which he could only assume were dreams, he was being smothered. Whether it was by crashing waves in an ocean storm, as he struggled to stay afloat, or smoke all around him as he tried to escape a fire. Or of course, the vacuum of space, strangling the air out of him.

Larry finally thrust awake. All of the images in his head vanished, and he was sitting up on his bed, gasping. He looked around, confused, until the fog began to clear and he remembered where he was. It was the night after his visit to Eric in the Infirmary, and his job with Stephanie. He was in his quarters, trying to get some sort of sleep amidst his busy schedule.

And when the fog fully cleared, he cringed. Because the root of his restlessness, the crashing waves and the smothering smoke, all derived from one sensation; a ringing in his ears.

Everpresent, high frequency. It was just intense and pervasive enough to drive him crazy. Covering his ears helped him alleviate the sound somewhat, but the minute he fell asleep it jolted him back awake. So he decided to get up and turn on the lights. Back home, he might've been able to say "Lights" and some sort of (primitive) computer would comply and activate the room's lights. And then he could specify "dim," or "bright," or any percentage amount that was a multiple of ten. But on ESSO-3, there was no taste for such an overly complex system. A physical light switch worked just fine, without all the moving parts. Less chance of something going wrong.

So Larry flicked the light switch and took a look at his quarters. Two adjoining rooms, a few desks, a few padded chairs. Gray Walls, gray everything. A hard floor. The first room had a table, a few homely items and gadgets. The second room was the bedroom, with all the personal items. And there was a small airlock with a glass barrier between the front door and the first room, giving a buffer between ESSO-3's relatively toxic air, and the comfortable back-home air within the quarters. Given that the ear assault was not going away, Larry put on his environment suit and went for a walk.

• -   -

The ringing was still present outside, a fact that made Larry's heart sink, but at least things felt a little less claustrophobic. Larry made his way from his quarters, a few rocks crunching beneath his feet. ESSO-3's nighttime. For a moment, if one just looked straight up at the night sky, the deep dark filled with stars, the planet didn't feel so alien. The nighttime sky, the window into the rest of the stars above, unimaginably far apart, it was universal. Then to look back down at the gray rocky wasteland of a surface, and nothing for miles out but ominous mountains, was like a punch in the gut.

Larry walked straight ahead, surrounded by a few rows of quarters. The quarters at Main Colony were sectioned off into a couple different areas, but each area housed dozens of them. Dozens of these individual four-walled, rectangular, identical looking buildings, one floor two rooms. Quarters Area #1, the one part of the Colony that was totally polished, everything was uniform here. Larry frankly wished it wasn't.

As he stepped past these identical buildings, they really evoked nothing in him. He felt nothing. It wasn't like the ESSO-3 residents would come out once a week for communal activities, or parties, or (if you went back in the history books) church service. This was no suburb or town. Everyone had their own schedules and places to be, at their respective times. Larry didn't even know offhand who lived in the quarters adjacent to him. It was just a few dozen workers being housed in their chambers, to recuperate for the next day's tasks.

Sure, he knew a few neighbors, Rodney from Agriculture, Aisha from the mines, who was also a part time driver. It wasn't like he was stopping to say hi to them. Nor were they to him, not after maybe the first week here.

Everything felt open and spread out. As Larry cleared Quarters Area #1, it took him a good five minutes to close the distance to the next building on his left, the Agricultural Facility. Also known as Hydroponics. The structure was two parts: a large, rectangular, steel beamed foundational building, and a lengthy tarped section extending out which housed the crops.

This was a relatively cool breeze. Larry only had to wipe his helmet once from dust kicking up. Nights when the wind picked up, Larry had seen tarp structures like that rattling violently. It was no wonder solid materials were so requested, soft materials made everyone uneasy.

Larry also knew, from Rodney of all people, that the tarped section wasn't even where the real food miracles happened. It was a good bunch of highly genetically modified crops, wheat, corn, and other starches. They essentially lived on droplets of water. They generated high amounts of produce quickly. And they could handle the most barren, bitter soil around. They may as well grow in the vacuum of space.

"That'll be the next breakthrough, wait and see," Rodney had said.

But the real food miracle happened within those big steel-beamed walls. The lab section, where chemists whipped up proteins, lipids, all the good parts of the diet that kept everybody going. It wasn't transmutation, but just about. All the chemists needed were a few good living cells, transported cryogenically just like the humans, and from there they could go to work. From there all they needed was energy and resources.

Larry walked by this great structure with a smile on his face.

"You're a good listener pal. Now screw off," Rodney had said. And Larry had done just that. Screwed off for five weeks in fact, five weeks since he'd talked to his old pal Rodney.

Past Hydroponics, Larry came upon one of the workshops on his right. Workshops were small buildings, no bigger than if two quarters were lined up together. Perfect spots for engineers to house equipment, work on smaller gadgets, or just organize their things. Stephanie had told him about that stuff. To Larry's left was Quarter's Area #2. He walked on past these spots, paying them no mind.

Finally he came upon the Water Treatment Plant. Out on a hill in front of him. The place where water was made safe for human consumption. The crops could probably take it raw, but just in case they couldn't they got clean water as well. The Water Treatment Plant towered over a river below. Past that river was nothing but open rocky plains, vast, with the occasional large patch of glistening ice. Past that, nothing but the distant mountains and the horizon.

Larry came in closer and closer, to the edge of everything man-made. He started to walk up the hill. As he looked up, out in front of the building there were two white figures. Night guards. At first Larry stopped in his tracks, he wasn't supposed to be out here at night. It probably wouldn't have been too serious an offense, but to Howe, every offense was a lot more than nothing. But when Larry saw the two men both leaning casually, facing each other, having a conversation, he carried on with no worry.

Back down the hill and over to the edge, where there was a small cliff, only around 20 feet up maximum, overseeing the river, Larry walked right up to the edge and stared out at the horizon. He took deep breaths. His eyes scanned the scene out in front of him. He planned on being there a while, getting lost in that view. When something made him drop to his feet. Immediately. Something that caught his eye.

• - -

Larry was prone, careful not to hit his helmet against the hard rocks which were right in his face now. Watching over the cliffside, down at the river, he gazed at what was going on. At the river were piles of waste, created by the workers during the

day. Main Colony had no time or extra space for waste management. Everything got dumped occasionally, but as rarely as
possible.

Toxic chemicals along with general debris had to be filtered
out from the river by the workers. They had a process. What got
left over is what made up those big piles. Down by one of the
piles Larry saw a white figure crouched behind it. Holding
some sort of tools, Larry couldn't make out from the distance,
interacting with the disgusting pile. Larry watched intently,
shifting his clunky helmet every so often. He could feel goose-
bumps even in his suit. He felt exposed.

The figure dug through meticulously, selecting certain
samples and packing them away. Their hands worked quickly.
Larry could not make out anything identifying about this
person. They weren't carrying any special equipment. It was
way too far to make out a face, even if the face wasn't buried in
its nasty work. No, there was no telling who this colonist was
from that distance.

Larry had to make sure he couldn't be spotted. He backed
up slowly on his elbows and knees, still watching the figure, but
shifting as much as he could. He tried to move his head down
further, but his helmet got in the way. He also tried to keep
jagged rocks from pressing against his knees. Larry backed up
until he could only half-see the river and that mysterious
distant figure.

Larry took his eyes off for only a second, but as his eyes
came back to that spot, he was sure the figure had looked in his
direction. He could feel it. He hoped he hadn't been spotted. As
he looked back, the white figure was still scrounging through
the toxic waste.

• -   -

Larry backed up more and slowly made it to his feet. He turned around and began to pace back. Walking all the way from the cliff, back to the hill, and past that in a straight line. He took one absentminded look back at the Water Treatment Plant, but he wasn't being watched by the guards. Nor by that other trespasser. Now he could feel the bitter cold all around him.

Larry made his way back to his quarters and retired for the night.

4

Back in the Infirmary, this time for himself. Larry had made himself an appointment. He was sitting on one of the cots.

"So, random ringing, in your ears, most prominent at night." The doctor said.

"That's right." Larry replied. "You're sure there's nothing wrong with my hearing?"

"Correct." The doctor said. She had run all the standard hearing tests on Larry, his hearing was not only good but exceptional. No damage visible to the inner ear, no tinnitus, everything was healthy. There was an increasingly uncomfortable expression on the doctor's face, as Larry continued questioning.

"Could it not be some kind of head damage, I hit my head or something?"

"Doubtful." She replied. "Do you even remember hitting your head?"

Larry shook his head.

"How about medication. Someone slipping me something? Something in the water, maybe?"

"Look, Larry, I think you're dodging the most plausible answer. The ringing is in your mind."

"You're saying I... that I might be going crazy?"

"Hallucination is a possibility. Do you have a history of psychosis in your family?"

"No." Larry said.

"None at all?"

"No doctor." Larry said firmly.

The doctor sighed. She looked down for a moment. She looked drained, there was barely any color in her face. Her name was Grace Sullivan, Larry knew that. Head Doctor, basically the only doctor there who wasn't a part-time field medic. Field medics being those who accompanied workers or drivers on missions. Grace was in charge of the Infirmary at the main site of the ESSO-3 Colony. Home base. A lot of responsibility, and plenty of work for her in a place like this.

"Look, you don't seem like the delusional type. So it's most likely just stress," she said. "You're probably just working too much. It'd be a good idea to file for a transfer of position to Mr. Howe, if you can." Grace said.

Larry shook his head. "Working is the only thing that keeps my mind off it."

"Well... I can give you something to help you sleep. Wait here." Grace went to a nearby cabinet and pulled out a syringe device. It was compact, it fit in the palm of her hand. The barrel was a red, opaque material. She walked back and handed it to Larry.

"What's this?" Larry asked.

"Sedative. Give a big push for half a second to give yourself a dose."

"Where do I spray?"

"Here." Grace took Larry's left wrist, and turned it over so the palm faced up. Larry still had his environment suit on, minus the helmet. There was a small flap in the center of the wrist, a black material, in contrast to the rest of the arm of the suit's white color.

"You ever wonder how the field medics administer things when treating people on duty? Just lift the flap and jam the syringe in there, right on a vein. It's resealable so don't worry about leaks, just don't keep it open for long."

Larry nodded. "Not bad." He felt the plunger of the syringe with his fingers and pressed on it lightly. It did not budge. He surmised it took a decent amount of force to administer the drug. That was good, it made it hard to mess up the dose. Larry found it funny that this was the opposite of his gun, which had a trigger pull as light as a feather. He supposed this was for the best, a gun better give out as many "doses" as it takes.

"One spritz can take the edge off, if you're really in pain." Grace said. "Two spritzes should only be done at your quarters, it'll knock you out quickly if you can't sleep. There are at least a month's worth of doses total."

"Sounds manageable."

"Oh, and don't even think about trying to use it to kill yourself. Three spritzes is the max before it auto locks for a little while. When you don't show up to work the next day, everyone will know exactly why." Grace said. She laughed, pointing at Larry's holster. "You'd probably lose that too."

Larry scowled. "Yeah no. That's not me."

"Alright. Well that's all I can do for you," she said.

"Understandable. Thanks for the medicine. I'll hang in there." Larry replied. He stashed the syringe and left the Infirmary. He now had two things to hold onto at all times.

· - -

The Boss's Office. Just a bit smaller than a usual quarters unit. Though Howe had his own one of those as well. Just like with his quarters, and most of the other buildings at the Colony, Larry had to enter through the airlock and remove his environment suit. Doing so had become second nature by the first week of being at the Colony.

The Office had no furniture, only a big desk at the back, facing right where you walked in. That was where Howe sat, in a big chair, going through reports and briefings, as was his job. He had a tablet from which commands were sent out remotely, one of the limited examples of computer electronics being used at the Colony. As Larry walked up to Howe's desk, Howe gave him a stern look. Larry stopped just a foot in front of the desk, and Howe waved at him offhandedly. Larry caught the hint and took a few steps back.

"Laurence. Got something to tell me? And you couldn't have just made a report?"

"Yes."

"Fine," Franklin Howe sighed. "Make it quick."

"Okay," Larry said. "So I figured this was an important Security matter."

"Get on with it."

"Right. Last night, I was walking at night, when I came across something suspicious."

"Just wandering at night?" Howe said. He snickered. "Trying

to wear yourself out, get someone hurt on a security detail, cause you hadn't gotten enough sleep?"

"That's beside the point. Trust me." Larry said. There was a short, heavy eye contact the two made, but then Howe seemed to relax a bit. "Alright. I'll let that slide. On with your story."

"I was by the Water Treatment Plant. I saw someone doing something, harvesting. They were digging through the hazardous waste and minerals that get filtered out of the water, the piles of it by the river. I believe they got a hold of harmful chemicals."

"Was there not a security detail watching that place?" Howe asked. "I know I assigned one."

"They were clearly slacking."

"I see." Howe said, nodding slowly. "I see. You know what a person could do with chemicals, right?"

"Make poison?"

"Exactly. You and I think alike. That's why I can't stand working with some of these folks, like the scientists. Security officers got common sense."

Larry smiled.

"Look," Howe went on. "It's pretty obvious I'm not the most popular man around here. Plenty of idiots disagree with my ways. And I'm a big target. If someone wants to murder some-one, just going by logic, it's most likely me. This matter needs to be looked into."

Larry shrugged. "What would you have me do?"

"Investigate. I know you're more of just a hands-on employee, but you're closer to... closer to *them* than me. Ask around. Although frankly, you don't seem like the sociable type."

"I'm plenty sociable." Larry said.

"You don't seem sociable." Howe laughed. "But no matter. Just dig around, ask questions. See if you can come up with some names of people who got it out for me. That's all you can do. Meanwhile I'll stay vigilant and keep security close."

"It'll be hard to find specifics, but I'll see what I can do," Larry said.

"Exactly. The most important thing here, we gotta make sure no one else finds out about this. I don't want ideas being put in other people's heads. Only you and me know about this poisoning threat. Got it?"

"Got it." Larry said.

"Good. Now get going."

Larry extended out his hand. Howe looked confused for a moment, and then half-heartedly shook it. Larry then turned and left the office without another word.

• - -

By early evening Larry was free, and he still had time to take care of business. On his way back to his quarters, he decided to turn and make his way over to the Water Treatment Plant, not too far. At this time there were still some active workers busy over by the actual building, and over in the distance standing on a small rock-hill were two men Larry recognized as Security. Day shift, no doubt. Two men in white environment suits talking to one another. Larry made his way over to them. As he approached, they didn't turn to him until he was just a few feet from them. Their smiles faded. The one on the right, his name was Alfonso, began talking.

"Ah. I know you," he said, looking at Larry. "Laurence. The most boring security guy I ever worked with."

"How long'd you work with him?" the one on the left asked.

"Two weeks. Brief assignment, he was a freshie. Dumb as a rock too."

They both began laughing. Larry was silent.

"It's just a joke, calm down." Alfonso said, putting a hand on Larry's shoulder.

Larry forced a chuckle. "Fair enough."

"So what's your business here, man?" Alfonso asked.

"Night shift," Larry said, "I need to talk to them. I thought they'd be here by now."

"Oh, okay. Yeah, they should be here in a few minutes."

"That's fine." Larry said.

• - -

In actuality it was a full half hour before the two night shift guards arrived. Larry had to make small talk for a long time, though bringing up the incident with Eric's arm got conversation flowing. It was no secret plenty of people in the Colony had heard about the incident, news was spreading. And everyone was curious.

As they finally did arrive, the two night guards strolled over to where Larry was, shaking the hands of Alfonso and Alfonso's colleague, and taking their spots. The two day guards walked off, heading back to their quarters. The night guards now standing in their place were named Geoffrey and Finn. It was Finn who did most of the talking.

"What's the matter with you? New? Day shift's over." Finn laughed.

"No, I'm not on this shift," Larry replied. "I'm just here to ask you guys some questions. If you don't mind."

Geoffrey turned to Finn who shrugged. "Alright." Finn said. "Ask away."

"Last night on shift, did you guys see anything strange?" Larry asked.

Finn and Geoffrey looked at each other and snickered. "Nothing far as I can tell." Finn said.

"Well, I mean I came by last night. Could you tell?"

"Can't say I remember that."

"Of course not. You guys weren't paying attention last night. You were slacking."

Finn got closer to Larry, uncomfortably close, and stared him down. Finn was quite a few inches taller than Larry, and had broader shoulders. He was plenty intimidating. He was one of *those* kinds of security guards. The other kind though, Larry's kind, were far scarier. And Larry knew that Finn almost certainly knew this, which was why Larry didn't back down. Larry's kind wasn't big and tough, but he could nail you from 50 feet away right between the eyes if he wanted to. He could do it very quickly.

"So what if I was?" Finn said. "Howe's too tight with his rules anyway. Runs this place like old Stalin, from the history books. You know, Stalin?" He turned to Geoffrey, who only looked confused. Finn scoffed, muttering "Ah forget it," as Larry responded.

"Look, all I'm saying is you missed something last night. A colonist, I don't know who, doing.... well I mean to say me, uhh I was the colonist, me sneaking right by you. Just keep an eye out, okay?"

"Okay, fair enough man," Finn said.

Larry cleared his throat. "So, you don't like Howe, huh?"

"Nope."

"Me neither. His rules are ridiculous, he overworks us." Larry then turned his face to a scowl and raised his tone. "My coworker, Eric, got injured doing brave work. He couldn't even get compensation."

The two night shift guards shook their heads. "It ain't right." Finn said.

"Damn straight," Larry replied. "Say," he started, almost whispering (despite there being no one around). "I actually think Howe should get replaced. How many people do you think would agree with that?"

Finn looked puzzled, and then laughed. "Boy you really got nothing better to do, huh? Well you're lucky I'm bored." Finn lowered his tone. "Look, obviously the workers and security guards, us lower class, or whatever the hell they think of us, don't like him. It's the fancy engineers and doctors who back Howe, from my experience."

"Ah," Larry said. "Those damn people think they're better than us."

"Exactly." Finn replied. "And by the way, your buddy Eric, I've met the fella. He's no dummy. Only scientist I've met who agrees with us guys on the problem of this Colony. The four letter problem."

"Got it." Larry said. "I'll have to ask him about it."

"You do that, buddy. Now, haven't you got somewhere to be?"

"Yeah, I'll get out of your hair," Larry said. "See you guys around."

"Yeah whatever." Finn replied.

Larry walked off, as Finn resumed his conversation with Geoffrey. After several minutes, Larry looked back, in the distance he could still see the two night guards chatting away, paying no mind to their jobs. Larry shrugged and headed back to his quarters, where he was ready to rest up. To at least give the sleep medication a try. Though he had a feeling the ringing problem would stick with him for a lot longer these coming nights.

5

Eric was finally back to work at the harvesting job, handling belay along with Ken, as Larry once had, and instructing Larry on his own former role. Climbing the walls, drilling into stalactites. Larry was a quick learner. Eric gave Larry all sorts of tips such as "use one smooth motion to peel the climbing glove off the wall, like a wave" and "when jumping off a cave wall, don't hesitate at all. If you hesitate you'll never get yourself to go through with it." Or more often, short, unsolicited tips such as "you're doing it wrong," and "go faster!" Regardless, Larry appreciated the good tips, even with the outbursts of pure impatience.

They had also received a new sampler, out of Eric's salary, for Larry to use when collecting the microbes. Larry kept this hanging on his waist opposite his holster. It was a bit awkward but Larry could manage. As Larry scaled another wall in preparation for a jump, Eric went on about his new robotic arm. A sleek, black right arm that was a few inches longer than his natural left arm. It was thin and cylindrical, with shoulder, elbow, hand, and all five fingers as well.

"It's a good arm, don't get me wrong." Eric said. "Functionality is great. But there are no sensations."

"So when you touch things with it, you don't feel anything?" Ken asked.

"That's right. I can use my brain and move the fingers, rotate the thing all sorts of ways. But when I touch something that's cold, or hot, or smooth, or scaly, there's no difference." Eric sighed. "Sometimes I have trouble picking things up with it, cause I can't tell if something's in my grip. When I put my other hand - my real hand - on the arm, I also feel nothing. It feels like touching something that isn't me."

"That must be difficult." Larry said, grunting as he climbed.

"It can be. But hey, as a scientist, it's an interesting experience. And the thing looks pretty badass."

Larry leapt out onto a stalactite. Every time he did, even though Ken and Eric could catch him at any moment with the belay, he still felt his heart drop a bit. It was certainly not an easy job, but Larry was managing it well. While not easy it was simple, and Larry appreciated that. As he pulled out his sampler to drill, he kept up conversation.

"So Eric, you're a little infamous here on ESSO-3, I'm finding." Larry said.

"Infamous? What are you talking about?"

"Well, some people know you for the ideas you express. About the Colony, and the running of things."

Eric laughed. "If that's what you call infamy. People knowing that I have common sense."

"You get what I mean."

"Lots of people agree with my views, Larry. That the Boss's cold, overly robotic way of thinking, it's no good. I'm just known cause I'm not afraid to say it. It's not like I have followers, just people in agreement."

"And I find a lot of what you say compelling." Larry said. He paused and thought about how to proceed. "So... you think you're gonna do anything, with all those people in agreement? Maybe push for some sort of change?"

"If I was going to 'do anything,' as you say," Eric replied. "Why would I tell you, Larry? You haven't earned my trust at all."

"Eh, give him a break Eric." Ken said.

"Why should I? You're talking about the guy who once said he believes in science over trust. Talking like that to someone who *is* a scientist."

"He also saved your life from a robot though. And advocated to keep you on this assignment," Ken said. "Yeah, he sucks up to the Boss, but it sounds like he's just doing his best in a broken system."

"Hmm... well that's true. A good first step, let's say. I'll give him 20% for that." Eric replied. "You hear that, Larry? You've earned 20% of my trust."

Larry chuckled. "Well alright then," he said, carrying on with his work.

• -   -

Back in his quarters later that night, Larry laid on his bed, fingers over his ears. He held the syringe in his hand ready to knock himself out, ready to go. He held it for a while. Eventually, he heard banging on his door. Larry put away the syringe, walked across the room with little enthusiasm, and opened the airlock door. The protocol for someone coming into your quarters, which wasn't too common on ESSO-3, one waited for the person on the inside to unlock the door, then to clear the airlock, and then to give them the verbal good to go. "Come in," or "What do you want," and usually a bit of hostility for the guest interrupting their cherished down time. And this is exactly how Larry did it. In came Stephanie in her environment suit. She stood in the airlock behind the glass, wiping dust off her chest and arms.

"Stephanie?" Larry said. "Why are you here? How did you know where my quarters are?"

Stephanie gave him a painted smile. "Work! Isn't that exciting?"

"Just tell it to me straight." Larry replied.

Stephanie cleared her throat. "Fair enough. Look, the Boss radioed in and told me which quarters were yours. We have a special, urgent rescue assignment."

Larry nodded plainly. He started putting on his environment suit. Meanwhile, Stephanie arranged some of her engineer's tools, and double checked what she had. While Stephanie's movements were quick and forceful, Larry did everything smoothly. Larry was ready to go within five minutes.

"Tell me about the assignment," Larry said.

"A driver and engineer crew, like us, were transporting workers. They were attacked on their way back by robots. Now they're stranded out on their route. They need us to drive out there and go help them."

"Sounds reasonable. Anything else?"

Stephanie shook her head. "Not a ton of details."

Larry gave his weapon a quick inspection. "Well alright then, Let's get moving."

• -   -

The wheels of the buggy pounded the rocks beneath them, as Larry drove at full speed. Slamming through the harsh night-time wind that the arid surface provided. The roaring wind almost drowned out the ringing in his ears for Larry. Almost. The whole situation at least made it easier to take that off his mind. It also made it so Larry and Stephanie had to practically yell to hear each other.

"You didn't tell me you shot a robot." Stephanie said. Larry did not respond.

"Larry."

"Oh... yep. During the cave job with Eric." Larry replied.

"You said Eric fell."

"He did. I didn't lie."

"Well now the engineers get to have a look at the thing you shot."

"Well I bet you can't wait for your dissection." Larry said. And he left it at that.

"Probably why the Boss wants you for this robot mission now." Stephanie muttered to herself. The buggy skid over a patch of ice. It was a bumpy ride for both of them. But Larry just kept his same position, leaning forward, unphased, while Stephanie was agitated by the bumps. Stephanie leaned her head to the side and looked at him inquisitively.

"What's wrong with you?" Stephanie asked. "You look like you're in pain."

Larry did notice he was wincing. In the environment suit he couldn't cover his ears.

"It's nothing. Just a long day."

"You can tell me things, Larry. We don't have to just be all professional all the time." Stephanie said. She followed up with. "Ah forget it. Just let me know if you want to talk."

"Thanks for the offer." Larry said.

• -   -

As they arrived at the site of the rescue, they saw a damaged buggy similar to theirs but with a tire having fallen off, a few parts missing, and an engineer working on the engine in the front of it. There were six workers hovering around the broken vehicle, one person standing quietly to the side, and one sitting leaning against the side of it, hardly moving. As the workers spotted Larry and Stephanie they waved.

"Stephanie, why didn't we bring a doctor?" Larry asked.

"They already have one. We didn't have much time for coordination." She replied.

As they pulled up, the tires came to a screeching halt. Stephanie stepped out of the buggy while Larry turned off the engine. The workers came up and crowded around Stephanie, greeting her. One of them gave her a handshake. Another gave her a hug.

"You know these guys, Stephanie?" Larry asked. One of the workers finally gave a look at him.

"The Chief Engineer?" The worker replied. "Who doesn't know her?"

"Is he armed?" Another one asked Stephanie.

"Of course," she said.

The engineer of this stranded crew, his name was David, came and showed Stephanie to the damaged vehicle, where he began pointing out repairs to be made. Larry went up and put his hand on Stephanie's shoulder.

"What are you doing? We should just leave their buggy and start driving people back. Come back for it in the morning." Larry said.

"That's not the mission, Larry." Stephanie replied. "These things don't just come and go, and the Colony doesn't have any to spare. We're gonna repair it."

"She's right you know." David said. "The robots attacked us for parts. We fought them off but they might just come back. There might not be a buggy left by the time we come back in the morning, if we leave it."

"Ok, fine, you're right. But shouldn't I start driving people back now? Don't you have another security guy to keep the lookout? That guy over there who's just sitting there," Larry said, pointing at the man who was leaning against the buggy, just six feet in front of them.

The additional person, not the six workers nor David nor the man sitting against the buggy, but the one standing quietly off to the side, now approached Larry and chimed in. She was a field medic. "Hey driver, Larry's your name? Well we've got a driver-security guy too, the one you're pointing out. And just so you know, he's blind."

"Blind?" Larry said. "What the hell are you talking about?"

Now Stephanie's attention was caught as well. "A blind security man?" She laughed.

"Blind-*ed*, I should say. The robots did it to him. Both eyes. He's been all catatonic for the past hour ever since."

"I saw it happen." David the engineer added. "Our guy was shooting at the robots. One of the things shined these intense green lasers right at the poor man's eyes, for just a few seconds. He started screaming, firing like crazy, and he tripped over himself. The robots were running away, but the damage was done."

"There was nothing I could do for him." The field medic said.

"Jesus. That's horrifying." Stephanie said.

Larry took a moment to process this. "Avoid looking at them, got it." he said. "Well that's it then. Let's get going."

• -   -

Stephanie and David worked on repairs for the next 30 minutes. The six workers simply chatted with each other. Larry and the field medic stood together and gazed into the distance forebodingly, keeping the lookout. They stood by the Blinded Security Man, who still did not say a single word. He groaned a few times. Larry quietly worked through the details of his plan, should the robots return. The field medic shook her head and sighed.

"Isn't it crazy that they can blind people now? How do we know anything of what to expect?" She said.

"Yeah. We were all briefed to know a little about those things, how they sort of evolve, change over time. Improve themselves. But now we've actually seen it." Larry said.

"Yeah, hard to believe they were apparently sent here docile. When people sent them out some half a century ago."

It was true. The robots originally had rounded features. They were harmless, even cute-looking. And they had no weapons.

"Well." Larry said. "We just have to stay vigilant with what we do know."

"Very matter of factly put, Larry. Aren't you afraid?"

"Terrified."

"I guess you just don't let it show, do you?"

As they talked, Stephanie and David were both bent under the buggy, repairing an axle. The six workers were inattentive as well. But Larry spotted a few specks in the distance. Specks growing ever-slightly larger, that weren't there before. They were coming.

Larry quickly pointed in the distance. "There they are. I'm certain. Time to get ready."

The field medic did not argue. She went over to the group of six workers and gave them the word, and they all went and sat behind the buggy in a row, facing away from the oncoming threat. David peaked out from under the vehicle.

"Hey, don't do that." Larry said. "Stay under the whole time without looking. I'll tell you if they get too close."

"Right." David replied.

"You better know what you're doing!" Stephanie said.

Now it was just Larry and the Blinded Security Man standing between the robots and the vehicle. They were still far in the distance, but close enough now that Larry could make out the shapes. Three small figures that resembled the spider-like creature Larry had shot in the cave. One large shape that resembled nothing Larry had seen up to this point.

Larry went over to the Blinded Security Man. The man's gun had been dropped in his previous fight, and set down right next to him thereafter. Like Larry's gun, and all others carefully distributed by the Boss, it was sensitive to the weight of the hand, so that only the owner could fire it. So it wasn't much use for killing robots now. But Larry delicately placed the gun in the Blinded Security Man's hand anyway, wrapping the man's finger around that feather-light trigger.

"Look, I know you've been through a lot, but you need to be ready for this right now." Larry said.

Larry held the man's right arm, the one with the gun, and lifted it so it pointed out towards the horizon. "You've probably got good hearing like me. You were placed Security after all. When you hear them getting close, start firing in their general direction. Doesn't matter about hitting them."

Larry also had a mirror that was a few inches wide, which Stephanie gave him from the damaged buggy. That part of the trap was her idea. He slid this mirror into the Blinded Security Man's left hand, and led the hand up to one of the man's eyes. Since the robots' features were lean, basically built for survival like Darwinian Evolution, Larry hoped they would not be advanced enough to deduce his trap.

"Did you get everything?" Larry asked.

The Blinded Security Man spoke for the first time in hours. His voice was so quiet it was nearly inaudible. But Larry heard it. "Yes."

Now that everything was set in place, Larry ran to his position. Several yards away from the buggy, off to the side, the tire that had fallen off the buggy had been propped up by the workers. Larry hid behind it as cover. And now, Larry waited.

• - -

Larry could finally hear the stomping of metal legs on the rocky ground audibly as the robots approached the buggy, charging at full speed. Crouching and hunched over, under nothing but a propped up tire, he felt utterly exposed. One of his gloved hands gripped the thick rim of the tire, the other held his weapon. He held his breath as he prepared for what he was going to have to do. Held his breath until the furious stomping was practically on top of him.

Sure enough, the Blinded Security Man came through. Larry heard several gunshots in a row going off wildly. He clenched up, frozen for just a second, but by the seventh gunshot he willed himself to peak over the tire. As he did, he saw a bright green laser reflecting upwards off the Blinded Security Man's mirror, into the night sky.

Now Larry stood up fully. He could see the whole scene. The Blinded Security Man leaning against the buggy firing his gunshots, and there were two lasers set at him simultaneously, one of them blankly hitting his other eye. Clearly the robot could not tell that eye was already shot, with whatever sensors, or internal processing, or who knows else it was using to see its surroundings.

Larry traced the two radiant green lasers. He now saw the charging robots clearly. Three of them were spider-like, same as the one he had dealt with in the cave. The four thin wired legs. The armored plating and metal pieces of its tiny body. The haphazard loose circuits sticking out of it. These spiders were around two feet tall, around the size of a dog.

The fourth robot was leading the pack, and it was entirely new. It moved with four legs similar to the Spiders, but its front legs were much larger than its hind legs. It also had a larger body, and thicker plated legs. Its shape resembled that of a gorilla, except with no head. It had two cylindrical pointers on top of its shoulders that looked like small telescopes. Those were the source of the two green lasers. The gorilla robot was the only one with these devices.

Larry aimed carefully, his hand trembling from adrenaline. Tracing his hand along at the moving target, a skill he had trained again and again, just like when he had shot at the spider-like robot in the cave, he fired a shot that tore through the gorilla robot's shoulders, puncturing both of the pointers. The lasers instantly shut off. Larry yelled out in exhilaration.

"I got the lasers!" Larry shouted at his colleagues at the buggy.

After getting shot, the gorilla robot stopped in its tracks and recoiled. The spiders stopped as well. The whole group now refocused on Larry, the man behind the tire, the immediate threat. They charged him.

Larry was ready. The robots were now in his direct field of view, and he could look straight at them without getting blinded. He opened fire, spraying them down systematically. First he fired several more shots at the gorilla robot, landing most of them in the body and legs. This artificial monstrosity, which would no doubt be the alpha were this a pack of real organic animals, was brought down. It collapsed on the ground as its body was torn apart by bullets. The spiders kept coming. Larry switched the spray one by one, unloading. The spiders were harder to hit, but he needed only to land a few shots. Larry brought the first one down, and then the second, just as they closed in. As the last one got within ten feet, he landed one shot in its leg, before he pressed the trigger and heard only a small click. He was out. The last spider descended upon him.

The spider leapt at Larry with full force. He instinctively

dropped his empty gun and grabbed his tire with hands and feet, falling backwards onto the ground. He landed hard on his back, lifting the tire into the air above him with all four limbs. Even with ESSO-3 Gravity, the tire was extremely heavy. The spider landed on top of the tire and stretched out two of its long bladed legs, slicing furiously at Larry while also tearing up the rubber rim of the tire.

"Help! I need help!" Larry cried. He could feel the combined weight of the tire and the robot absolutely straining his muscles. They felt like they were on fire. Larry held on, through swinging and slashing, yelling for help. This went on, the determined robot's blades reaching just inches from Larry's body. Until, through both the tearing and yelling sounds, Larry could faintly hear the whine of a buggy's electric motor. The spider must have detected it too, because it leapt off Larry's tire, landing forward on the ground beyond Larry's head. Free of the robot's weight, Larry leaned to the side and dropped the tire on the ground beside him, and rolled away to his side.

As Larry looked up, catching his breath, he saw the buggy he had arrived in, no more than a foot in front of where his feet had been, with Stephanie behind the wheel. He stared for a moment in confusion, before Stephanie shouted "get your gun!"

Larry, with his arms and legs still feeling as though they had been crushed by a machine press, spotted his gun on the ground and grabbed it. He quickly reached for another magazine, a couple were stored compactly near his holster, and reloaded the gun. The spider had whipped back around, and it jumped onto the hood of the buggy, causing Stephanie to recoil back. Larry once again opened fire, destroying the robot with several shots at point blank range. It fell off the hood of the vehicle and attempted to crawl away with partial leg function. Larry fired at it until it stopped moving.

And then he fired at it some more. He emptied his whole second mag into the thing.

Stephanie got out of the buggy and came to him. "Larry," Stephanie said, as Larry kept shooting. "Larry!'"

Larry clicked the gun several times after it was out, and then threw the gun at the ground, slamming it.

"Woah, what?" Stephanie said to him. "What was that?"

Larry was panting hard. He did this for 30 seconds. Stephanie gazed at Larry. A look that didn't come off as her being intimidated, more so almost warning him. Warning him to stop being extremely uncomfortable. Larry took the hint. He sighed, and then he chuckled a bit. "It's nothing. That was intense is all."

"Okay then," she said. And her look disappeared, into a smile. "Wow, that was something."

"Yeah. Hey, our plan worked." Larry said.

"It worked well."

• - -

They drove back to the damaged buggy, which at this point was almost fully repaired. They brought back the missing tire with them, driving past a group of robot carcasses. As they returned, the workers, the field medic, and David the engineer came out of hiding. The Blinded Security Man simply sat leaning in his same spot.

"Wow, good work you two, good stuff," David said. The others murmured in agreement. "What was your name again?"

"Larry." Larry replied, knowing who he was referring to.

"Well, I can't speak for the others, but I'll remember you going forward." David said.

Stephanie and David finished up the final repairs, and the two buggies drove home together in the waning hours of the night. A successful mission, and good work. Two things Larry could appreciate.

6

They drove back to the Colony, Larry still reeling from the adrenaline of the fight. Nighttime turning to morning, Larry's next job would soon be starting once they got back. At this point the ESSO-3 Sun could almost be seen on the horizon, just below it. Larry looked over at Stephanie.

"Hey, remember earlier you said you'd be there if I wanted to talk?" he said.

"Sure," she replied.

"Well I've got a problem I think you could help me with. Could you meet me at my quarters tonight?"

Stephanie looked a bit confused. "I'm busy, you know."

"Please, it's important." Larry said. "Trust me, I understand time is valuable."

Stephanie nodded. "Alright. If it's that important, I guess we can discuss it over dinner."

When they arrived back, Larry, Stephanie, and the rest of

the group they had just rescued, the Blinded Security Man was walked by their field medic to the Infirmary. Though with no particular rush or urgency, there seemed to be little optimism for the man's injury. Larry wondered what would happen now to that man, stripped of his sight probably for the rest of his life. On the job injuries were somewhat common, but for most things short of death there were usually remedies. Or at least some way for the worker to adapt, use what skills they had left. The engineers could whip up an artificial leg or arm, like in Eric's case. And the doctors could usually find some drug to alleviate a disease, ache, or pain. But eyesight, nobody could whip up artificial eyes. That man might just spend the rest of his days sucking up the Colony's resources, at the expense of his final pay, until the next soonest scheduled transport home, months from now.

As for the rest of them, the six workers went on their way, while Larry, Stephanie, and David went to go see the Boss.

• - -

"Ah, hello you three." Franklin Howe said, as they entered his office.

"Franklin Howe." Stephanie said. She stepped forward.

"Looks like the mission was a success. Good job," he said.

"Yep. If a bit understaffed."

"Doesn't seem like it. You pulled it off, didn't you?" Franklin Howe gave her an artificial smile. Reminiscent of the one Stephanie gave Larry back when she first described the frantic mission to him, Larry noticed. He would think two people so close to each other in the chain of command would be more warm in their interactions, maybe have a better rapport. Then again, this was ESSO-3.

"Affirmative" Stephanie replied.

"And I think that is a testament to your leadership skills, Chief Engineer."

"Thank you. We came here to discuss a....disturbing new development."

"Of what sort?" Franklin Howe asked.

"The robots. They were using some kind of intense light weapons. To blind people. There was already one casualty of this when we arrived."

Franklin Howe gave a heavy sigh. "You're right, that is disturbing. How did you fight this?"

"We used distraction." Stephanie said.

"I had to be quick and accurate, and shoot the blinding weapons to disable them first," Larry added. "No time for hesitation."

"I see." Franklin Howe said. "Well, we'll have to brief everyone to keep their guard up, not much more we can do."

"The engineers and I can work on visors for the helmets that may filter strong light." David said.

"That would take an exorbitant amount of time and resources," Stephanie said. David shrunk back a bit, but then Stephanie added, "But, far as we know, the robots only seem to use resources when absolutely necessary. Which means they are starting to at least get annoyed by us humans. We have to be ready for them."

The Boss nodded. "Precisely, your logic is sound," he replied. "Well, get on it, with the visors. Prioritize field workers. As for now, you three probably have work to do. Get going."

The three of them exited the office one at a time, using the tedious airlock that came at the entrance of every building. As Larry was about to head out last, the Boss stopped him.

"Laurence, how's your special work for me coming? Found any leads?"

Larry simply said, "Still working on it," and left.

• -   -

In the evening after a whole day at work, Larry was sitting in his quarters on his bed with his head in his hands, as he heard banging on the door just like the night before. Routinely as ever, he made his way to the front door, cleared the airlock, and gave Stephanie the verbal go ahead. Stephanie entered with an infectious grin on her face, and began taking off her environment suit

"Good Evening." She said.

"Good Evening." He replied. "Thanks for coming."

Dinner was of course rations. Rations allocated to each worker, from the limited things they could grow in the rocky soil in controlled environments. And the slabs of cultivated protein the biologists could miraculously put together in the lab. There was a rotation of "fancy" rations the colonists got, not purely efficient, but of course a limited effort for mental health, to keep life from becoming a completely routine drag. They sat at a table in their skin tight black indoor outfits, and Stephanie brought out a fancy ration.

"Charming setup," she remarked. "So what's up? What did you want to talk about? Because you look a little unhinged these days at work."

"Don't worry," Larry laughed. "I don't plan to kill anyone or something,"

To his surprise, Stephanie actually laughed at this as well. "I believe you. But you realize I'm not a doctor, right?" She said.

"I went to the doctor, but it didn't help much, I just got sleep medicine," Larry said. He sighed. "It's not the typical, depressed and homesick kind of thing. Not at all. It's this ringing I'm having."

"Ringing?"

"Ringing in my ears. It just shows up randomly. At night by myself, or at times with other people. I hear it constantly."

"That sounds... annoying"

"It's more than annoying. I can't get sound sleep with it going on. I can't think. Sometimes I can't even tell if I'm sane. And it's not going away." Larry said. "The doctor even said I might be psychotic. I know I'm not."

Stephanie fidgeted a bit in her seat. Larry was completely still and stiff.

"Why ask me about it though?" she asked.

"I think you can help me," he replied. "Those earpieces we use in our environment suits, to communicate, have you ever repaired one of them?"

"Yeah."

"So the thing can pick up sounds, and play them out in your ear, right? If you could tinker with mine, boost the range of frequency the thing picks up, and amplify the sound it puts out... maybe when there's ringing I could see if it's really picking up a physical sound."

Larry realized how exasperated he sounded as he said this. Stephanie pursed her lips, and thought of how to respond.

"Look... you really think there's a ringing going on, every so often, from some mysterious source, and you're the *only* one, of over a hundred colonists, who can hear it?" Stephanie said.

"I have more sensitive hearing than most colonists. It's part of why I'm Security."

"Ok, sure, that's true. But still, it doesn't sound very likely at all."

"I know, I know. It sounds improbable. But, if you help me do this, I can know for sure next time I hear ringing whether it's real, or in my head. At least I'll have that certainty."

She sat and thought about it for a moment.

"You know what, sure. You seem to trust me enough, Larry. So I'll do you this favor."

Larry sighed, this time out of relief. "Thank you Stephanie."

• - -

For about 40 minutes thereafter, Stephanie tinkered with the earpiece from Larry's environment suit. As an engineer she carried some of her field tools on her suit, and she was able to use those for the job. She worked on the small delicate device, a black piece that was no more than an inch and a half long, with surgeon-like precision. As she worked, she was the one who was chatty.

"I noticed you don't have any pictures on display in your quarters. No family you're missing?" Stephanie asked.

Larry cleared his throat. "Nope."

"Interesting." Stephanie waited for a response. When no response came, she pressed. "Bad relations? Or maybe you just don't really have much family."

"You love to pry, don't you?"

"No need to be rude."

"Just an observation." Larry replied. "Also, I don't think

most people who have loving friends and family come to an ESSO Colony."

"True."

"So I'd rather not talk about my family."

"You don't like to talk about your past, or your future." Stephanie said. "Just an observation."

"Sure." Larry said. "Why don't you tell me something about you, Stephanie."

"Okay." Stephanie replied. "I always liked school, I was a good student."

"Of course."

"I used to tinker with things as a little kid. With my dad. He was an aerospace engineer."

"And Mom?"

"Mom didn't like me," She laughed. "See this is conversation, Larry. I finished your thing." She held up the little black earpiece in her palm, screwing back in a small plate on the back. "Should pick up any sort of high pitched signals and fill your ear with it. Don't say I didn't warn you."

"Got it," he said.

She handed him the earpiece and stood up. "I have places to be. Like my bed. I gave you an hour of my time. I think you owe me one for that."

"If you say so. But seriously, thank you."

And with that, Stephanie went and put back on her environment suit and walked out the door. Larry put in his earpiece, went back to bed, and began to drift.

7

H is thoughts were a blend. Eagerly, he drifted away for the first time in so long. Everything began to clear away until there was nothing inside. Nothing. All he could feel was his breath. And soon he was surrounded by a cold blur. It was surreal, not fully shaped, but it was blueish. Ice, maybe? All around him. But not like the bitter ice of ESSO-3. More like the cryosleep, all those days ago, that final day he left to start this new chapter of his life. Quietly taking him away. But the colors around him began to melt. Slowly at first, the blue hues around him faded white. And then from white they turned to red. Suddenly it was fire, burning all around him. He couldn't breathe. He gasped.

Larry's eyes fluttered open. The ringing, just like those times before, had yanked him back to consciousness. But this time it was different. In his left ear the pressure he could feel on his eardrum was pounding; it was about as light and as subtle as a brick falling out of the sky. His fingers clutched the earpiece in his left ear, which he had almost forgotten about, and ripped it out. Now the pressure on his left ear(and his right) was still present, but the original intensity was replaced with a comparatively surface level unease. Larry took a deep breath.

His left hand fumbled on the bed for the missing earpiece, which he found, and then held in his trembling palm. He carefully placed it back in his left ear. The moment it made contact the ringing became twice as loud, twice as invasive. He pulled it out, and once again the sound dipped back to just a subtle noise. The earpiece was picking up the sound, a sound that was clearly very palpable and present outside Larry's head, and amplifying it. The ringing was real.

· -   -

Carefully clutching the earpiece in his hand, while the painful but manageable ringing persisted in his ears, Larry came to the vehicle lot. He had quickly gathered his environment suit and gun and left his quarters. He now stood several feet from the place where he and Stephanie parked and took out the buggy every long day of work. There were a few other similar vehicles right next to his, each with their own electric charging station, with big thick cables that linked back to the main power supply in the Colony. The vehicles were actually stored out in the open, covered with just a tarp. They were built to withstand the extreme weather and temperature 24 hours a day.

Larry knew that what he was about to do was absolutely traceable. Stephanie would notice the amount of power drained from the buggy's battery the next day. If Larry recharged the vehicle, that unauthorized recharge would be logged in the power supply's primitive computers, a report would undoubtedly go to the Boss. This was far more consequential than simply sneaking around the Colony on foot at night when he couldn't sleep.

But the first thing Larry had noticed as he stepped outside his quarters, putting the earpiece to his ear every so often (and cringing every time), was that it got louder outside. This was a phenomenon he originally thought he had imagined. So now Larry was following the sound, every time it got just a little louder.

Larry loaded himself into the buggy, wiping dust off the wheel with his gloved hands. The engine gave a soft whine as it came on, soft enough not to overpower the ringing, and he took off.

• -   -

The next few hours he spent acting driven and autonomous, hardly thinking. It was cold all the time on ESSO-3, but at times like this deep into the night, the cold penetrated the suit, and one could feel the icy chill in their bones. This was one of those nights. Tires struggling and scraping over dry rocks, the quiet whine of the engine, dry wind slapping the front plate of the vehicle and Larry's entire body above his waist. And ringing. Those were the four sounds of the night.

Larry would drive forward for about five minutes, put in the earpiece, and listen for subtle change. It either got louder, which meant go forward. Quieter, which meant turn around. Or little noticeable change, which meant a 90 degree turn. If he caught himself starting to drift off from exhaustion, flashing the headlights a few times gave him something to do. Or knocking gently against his helmet with his hand. Or a few other strange rituals he came up with for himself. Occasionally the sound would disappear entirely for a few brief moments, leaving Larry nothing to do but shake in place and stare out at the emptiness around him.

He knew he was getting close when he didn't even have to use the earpiece anymore to pick up the changes in the ringing. It was glaring now. His ear strained and his head throbbed. That was when he spotted it. Way off in the distance in front of him, several miles from the Colony at this point, with nothing but rocks, wind, and darkness all around him. Out on the horizon in front of him, there were movements. Almost like shadows in the dark. But they were real and palpable, he could tell. He drove forward.

• -   -

Robots. Flustering about in the dark. A cluster of them, at least seven. There were at least five spider-like ones moving about, and two of the gorilla-like ones, just the same as the one Larry had fought the other night, the gorilla that had blinded their guy. These robots were out in the open, but there were piles of metal and parts scattered about the place, and there was a rough perimeter. There was one *thing* Larry spotted, lying in at the top of a pile of metal and scrap and wire and circuit, Larry could make out parts of two legs and a body that was only half complete. It looked like a dissected insect with its guts hanging out.

These creatures were carrying around parts and pacing about frenetically. Larry saw this all while hiding behind a nearby mound of rocks. He had left the buggy a few hundred

feet away, to avoid drawing attention, and had crept up carefully to this gathering to get a view.

He was using both hands against his helmet to cover his
ears, the ringing was so loud. He could now tell what was
making the horrible sound, more of a beeping, one of those
strange amalgamated machines all about the place. He decided
he would refer to this place as the camp.

At the center of this camp, which all the activities of these
gleefully manic robots seemed to focus around, was a tall
pointed structure. It was around 20 feet tall, with a large tree
trunk like base protruding to a thin pointy top. There was a big
cable sticking out of the tree trunk looking bottom piece. One
of the spider creatures hooked onto the cable and pumped
some sort of fluid into it. Suddenly, the thing jittered and
backed away from the structure, as there was a small burst of
fire underneath it, and exhaust coming out of it. This happened
in just a brief second. This structure was a rocket.

Larry's eyes wandered to another spider-like robot, which
was on the perimeter of the camp right in front of the rock
Larry was hiding behind, facing toward the rocket. In a quick
motion it walked in a circle, turning around towards Larry's
direction. The creature twitched, and suddenly crawled right at
Larry. Larry ducked his head under the rocks and sat with his
back against them, panting. He drew his gun and got ready to
shoot. He heard the pounding of metallic legs on rocks, as it got
even louder than the constant ringing. Out of the corner of his
eye he saw the thing just a few feet to the left of him. But then
the imposing legs just kept moving forward, past Larry.

Larry sighed in relief, quietly. He was still being careful not
to make a sound or sudden movement. But given his fight last
time, shooting at the robots from the side as they charged at the

Blinded Security Man, him having taken them by complete surprise; combined with this moment right here, where the robot had marched right past him, he concluded that the robots must not have peripheral vision. Or it was terrible quality if they did. Must not have been the biggest thing on their survival checklist, he supposed.

But this spider was still moving out in the distance, way past Larry. He wondered where it was going, there were no objects out in that direction, aside from his buggy several feet away. And then Larry realized, that must be it. The thing had spotted his buggy, somehow, and given what had happened to David's crew earlier, Larry concluded, his ride home might be looking at getting dissected by this spider-thing very soon.

Fighting the urge to shoot and alert every (borderline) living being in the camp, Larry crouched to his feet and sneaked forward, following the spider. Larry had to practically jog on his feet to catch up with the robot, but he made sure to tread lightly. Gun drawn, he shadowed the spider for a few hundred feet, looking back occasionally at the camp to make sure nothing else spotted him. Far as he could tell, the other spiders and the couple of gorillas were busy piling things onto and crowding around the rocket, as if it were some sort of altar.

As the spider closed in on the buggy, Larry still dozens of feet behind it, the spider poised its bladed legs and leapt onto the front of the vehicle. Larry sprung into action, shooting the spider to pieces before it could damage his ride home.

Larry didn't even bother to turn around. He knew those thunderous shots would set off the robots back at the camp. Larry sprinted to his vehicle, as pairs and pairs of metallic legs pounded in the distance. Larry pushed a sharp metallic leg of the dead robot that was still on his hood out of his face, and hopped in the driver's seat. Looking straight ahead, he could now see several spiders and a gorilla in hot pursuit. There was a suitable gap between them and him, but the robots were closing it fast. Larry hit the throttle and for a brief second drove toward the aggressive stampede of robots. Only to take a sharp right that screeched the tires, in order to turn around and head in the opposite direction. Back to Civilization, away from the camp. Larry drove for half an hour straight before even feeling safe to let up a bit.

• -   -

Returning to civilization was not the part of this whole nighttime excursion Larry had thought much about, but it turned out to be pretty difficult. Having navigated entirely by the ringing of his ears to get to where he was, with a focus purely on moving forward, he hadn't followed any sort of concrete directions at all. So he spent the next hours driving the open ground for miles, plowing ahead and praying to find some branch of the Colony. Fatigue was the biggest understatement one could use to describe his state.

By dawn, Larry had finally stumbled across another buggy heading en route to a mine, filled with workers. He did not approach their vehicle, but he simply passed by and headed in the direction they were coming from. He was far enough away to only just make out the looks of confusion and suspicion. The early morning sun at his back, with the harsh winds having let up slightly, Larry made his way back on the brink of collapsing from exhaustion.

• -   -

It was now midday, a buggy from another job was pulling into the vehicle lot having dropped off workers, with all the usual remaining passengers, a field medic, an engineer, plus one extra: Stephanie. The vehicle pulled into a charging station right beside Larry's buggy. As the medic and engineer hurried off to their next assignments, Stephanie approached Larry's buggy. There she found him passed out, his helmet resting against the steering wheel of the vehicle. His suit dirty, covered head to toe in dust. Stephanie shook him awake.

"We need to go see the Boss...right now," Larry mumbled.

"I already wrote you up," Stephanie said. "I had to do another job with those guys I was just with, so as not to waste time. So I guess you took a midnight drive?"

"Yes... I used the earpiece... I traced the sound. Remember the ringing I talked about?"

"Okay, so you took the buggy off-shift to chase sound? Larry, what in the world."

"Look, I found robots. *Multiple* robots. We have to go see the Boss now."

• -   -

Larry and Stephanie once again entered Howe's Office, hurriedly taking off their environment suits at the airlock. Franklin Howe sat in his chair giving a look of confusion and disapproval, as the pair approached him.

"Well I just read your report about Laurence commandeering a buggy, Stephanie. And now you two are skipping work. This better be important." Franklin Howe said.

Larry, expecting Stephanie to talk first, waited, until Stephanie nudged him rudely. Larry, still hardly awake, launched into his story. Starting with the ringing, and then telling them about the camp, the several robots he had discovered crawling around the place. And most importantly, the tall structure he had found at the center of the camp, the rocket.

"Hold on wait a minute," Franklin Howe interrupted. "Rocket? You're sure this thing the robots had built was a ship."

"I'm very sure," Larry said. "Not just because of its shape. It had thrusters, for sure, and it ran on some sort of gas fuel rather than electricity."

The Boss grunted and scratched his head. "What in the world could they be using it for? They can't get out of the star system with a conventional rocket. It just isn't doable."

"Maybe to use on us as an attack." Larry said. "Who's to say they don't know about the Colony? They could load it with explosives and use it as a missile."

Franklin Howe nodded. "Definitely a possibility. We need to prepare some kind of defenses."

"Doubtful, actually," Stephanie said. Larry and the Boss both looked at her. "The robots aren't a military, their primary goal is survival. We've established this."

"You don't think they see us as a threat to their survival?" Larry shot back.

"Of course they do. Because we'd wipe them out if we had the chance. But they can't afford to pile all their resources into inefficient weapons. Why do you think they don't use guns? Blades that double as tools, blinding lasers that are basically just sensors on steroids? That's way more efficient and useful."

"So what do you propose it is, Stephanie?" Franklin Howe said.

"Maybe it actually is just a rocket," she replied. "Maybe it's for transporting things. Resource Collection. Perhaps they have some sort of... space station."

Franklin Howe's eyes widened. "A space station? Right above us? There's no way. One of the Transport Vessels would have seen it, a pilot would have surely said something."

"They're not on the lookout for anything, far as I know," she said. "They just pull into the system quickly, and land people on the planet. They could have missed something."

"What you're suggesting..." Franklin Howe began in a somber tone. "Is way out of the realm of *everything* we've known the robots to be capable of building up to this point in time. Far as we've known there are only a few stragglers out there. And they build with scrap. Never have I even heard of an organized camp all the time I've been on ESSO-3. Up until now."

"Then you had better get one of those scientists to use a telescope and check what's in orbit, Howe." She replied.

Franklin Howe shook his head and grimaced. "I'm much more inclined to believe Laurence's theory. It's much more sane-"

"I'm your Second in Command, doesn't that mean anything? You should listen to me," there was rising aggression in her voice.

"-But I'm going to look into your theory too. See, I was getting to that," he said, with a sarcastic smile.

The anger evaporated from Stephanie's face, replaced with a smile. "Well, glad we're on the same page. If you'll get on that, Larry and I will go do our overdue job for today."

"Very well. Excellent work bringing this to my attention you two."

With those pleasantries, Stephanie left the office, and Larry followed her without another word.

8

About a week later, during a shift of Larry's work with Eric and Ken, Larry and Eric were contacted via their earpieces by the Boss to attend a mandatory meeting, in the Infirmary of all places. So the two of them marched out of the cave that was their job site right away, leaving Ken to clean up the supplies and grumble about the disruption.

"You have any idea what this is about?" Eric asked on the way.

"Probably what me and Stephanie came across. Robot stuff. You'll probably be briefed pretty soon," Larry replied.

"And you didn't even invite me? Damn buddy, I'm hurt."

They arrived at the Infirmary, except as a cleared out space. No medical staff buzzing around. Standing in the middle of the room were four people. Franklin Howe, Stephanie, Doctor Grace Sullivan, and a fourth man Larry didn't know. Howe and the Doctor were talking amongst themselves. Stephanie was talking to the other man, clearly in a friendly manner, and

Stephanie was laughing. As soon as Larry and Eric entered the room, Stephanie shot Eric a dirty look. Or perhaps Eric did to Stephanie first, Larry couldn't tell.

"Morning Eric,"

"Quint," Eric replied.

"Ah, they made it. Everyone is here," Franklin Howe said. "Let's get started."

The medical staff had laid out six crates in a circle for everyone to sit down on. Larry and Eric went ahead and took their seats. Eric rested his organic left hand in his robotic right hand. He winced as he accidentally squeezed his palm too hard with the robotic hand for just a second, and then eased up.

The Boss went on. "Throughout the week, I assigned a special job to one of our scientists who has an interest in astronomy. I told him to watch the sky in intervals for any strange objects orbiting ESSO-3."

Stephanie cleared her throat, and Franklin Howe backed up his story to include earlier events.

"This was after Laurence over here, a security worker and driver, stumbled across what was essentially a base for several of the robots, what he called a 'camp,' with the robots building a structure resembling a rocket. Stephanie suggested this could indicate the robots having far more advanced structures built than we previously thought, such as a space station. The conjecture was correct, my sky-watching scientist spotted it."

"Woah hold on, you're telling me those things can construct buildings now?" Eric said. His voice genuinely faltered.

"Apparently they have been for some time," Franklin Howe replied. "This structure is very large. Several hundred yards wide, the scientist estimated."

The room was silent for a minute. Everyone seemed to be

processing what he had just said. Franklin Howe went on. "As you all know, this sets a new precedent for the threat of these robots. Once just a vague oddity, with a few of them showing up just a few times a year. We always knew they were intelligent, we always knew they could build more of themselves. But building on this scale, we never imagined. We have to assume this means war."

There was more processing, more worried looks on everyone's faces. Larry was attentive.

"Okay, first of all, what do you suggest about the Station?" Quint asked. "Are you gonna have the engineers build a missile or something to shoot it out of the sky? Have a pilot guide one into the thing?"

"That's one possibility," Franklin Howe replied. "But not what I'm leaning towards."

"We need to take the opportunity to learn about this, not just blow everything up! For our own sake," Grace chimed in.

"Definitely," Franklin Howe said. "Which is why I brought you all here. The Chief Engineer and I discussed this beforehand, as First and Second in Command, and we agreed to this plan. We decided boarding the Station would be a better strategy than blowing it up from afar. That way, we can learn more about the nature of our enemy. We assembled the four of you here as the crew."

Stephanie nodded in affirmation. The four of them, Larry, Eric, Quint, and Grace, all exchanged looks with each other.

"This is way, way above my paygrade," Eric said.

"Who cares about pay if the robots drop on us from orbit?" Quint shot back.

"Exactly," Stephanie said.

Eric put his hands up and smirked. His robotic arm made a

creek that was just audible as he did this. Audible for Larry's hearing, at least. "Fair enough, got me there."

"You'll all get bonus pay for this. I don't want to hear about that issue again," Franklin Howe said sternly. "Anyway, you all play a vital role in this mission. Laurence here is one of our more accomplished security officers. He'll drive us to the Shipyard and be with us for protection. And his experience with fighting the robots will be useful. Grace as medic, because in this highly unusual environment we're getting into, I trust none of the field medics with only their basic training. The Doctor definitely may need the skill to improvise. Quintin is our most skilled pilot; he will get us to the Station and back safely. In addition he is Security, making his skillset invaluable. Eric, the Colony's Head Scientist, can help us interpret what we find."

Larry spoke for the first time in this conversation. "What happens if one of our E-Suits is torn in space? That sounds deadly."

"Laurence, my point still stands," Quint said. "That's just the risk we have to take."

Every time one of them referred to him as Laurence, Eric looked at Larry with his lip curled slightly. "Hey I'm sorry," Eric said. "You're saying it's just the four of us going? Couldn't we use an engineer?"

"My wording was misleading I suppose." Franklin Howe replied. "All six of us are going."

"You?" Eric said. Larry and Grace were equally surprised.

"Yep. Who knows what we'll find up there. Maybe a link to other robot structures, if there are communications being sent out from the Station. Maybe we'll get some insight into their plans, their future goals. Or maybe we'll find weapons, pointed right at our little Colony down here. Whatever we find, imme-

diate executive decisions might have to be made. There won't
be time for a process, I'll make decisions on site."

"Say we all die," Eric followed up. "Four senior officers,
essentially. Who's gonna be left to run things on the Colony?
Yeah there's Head of Energy Distribution, Head of Agriculture,
whatever else, but you're taking a lot of leadership people into
danger."

Larry's main field, Security, didn't have a chief or head officer. That was because Security was a straightforward job not
needing specialized management. In Security matters, officers
reported directly to Franklin Howe himself. It was just the way
things were run.

"Does Quint seriously have to repeat himself again? How do
you not get it?" Stephanie said. "If we don't do this mission,
there *might not be* a Colony, in the near future."

"I don't know, Steph, maybe if we actually allowed people to
arm themselves, and set up some defenses, the place would
have a fighting chance!" Eric said. At this point they were
shouting at each other.

"Everybody just calm down, this is unproductive," Grace
said. "We're going on the mission, Eric, that's been established.
And we need everyone here."

"That's enough from you Eric," Franklin Howe added,
redundantly.

"Alright, alright," Eric said.

"To reiterate," Franklin Howe said. "Quint is piloting us to
the space station, you will all play your roles, I will lead. This
goes above everyone's scheduling or assignments, obviously.
Any additional questions?"

"When do we leave?" Quint asked.

"Now."

The six of them, now crewmates, walked together in their environment suits to the vehicle lot. They all went forward as a group, but really they were in pairs. Stephanie talking with Quint, the Boss talking with the Doctor. Larry and Eric lead the pack, but they were not a pair like the others. They hardly interacted with one another. The one thing Eric said to Larry was, "If we run into anything, try not to miss any shots, okay?" To which Larry simply nodded.

These subdivisions were maintained as they got into Larry's buggy, and Larry drove out to where they needed to go. The others chatted away in the back of the vehicle, while Larry just drove, and Eric looked to be contemplating, occasionally fidgeting. The Shipyard was the farthest of the established Man-made sites outside the Main Colony. It was in the opposite direction of the mining site Larry drove to for his usual day job with Stephanie.

Stephanie had handed them all special visors the engineers made. These were to hopefully protect their eyes from any blinding weapons the robots tried to use, like the green lasers used by the gorilla robot Larry and Stephanie had encountered. There were only these six prototype pairs available so far, everyone else in the Colony was going to have to wait. Wearing it would make it a bit harder for Larry to see clearly, but only a bit, and he figured it would be worth the hassle.

And there was one other thing the Boss was carrying, a large gray case he held in his lap during the vehicle ride. A box that rattled in the Boss's arms. No one had commented on this when they were walking to the buggy; no one commented the whole way there.

• -   -

About 40 minutes later, they pulled into a vehicle lot similar to the one at the Main Colony, but smaller. They had arrived at the Shipyard. Desolate, empty, everything covered in dust. There was no charging station that they came to, not one hooked to a power source anyway. Rather, a collection of disposable box-like batteries, half as tall as the vehicle, left in a pile at the lot. Dropping these off every so often was much more efficient than sending power out this far.

The Shipyard barely had any actual structures, and no barrier separating it from the outside world. This had obviously been set up early into the Colony's days, without much thought, and with very little regard for security. Back then, all there seemed to be for outside security threats were single-celled organisms, and only a rumor of a few harmless, probably not even still operational robots. Relics of a bygone era.

But the other reason for its openness was the sheer size of the vessels it housed. Several of them, lined up relatively neatly. They were different variations of the same base design. A large thick body with a pointed nose. Four massive engines on the sides, a pair at the front and a pair at the rear, for vertical landing and take off. 60-80 feet long. Sleek and black, of course. At least when built they were. Now they were more of a worn gray with patches of that smooth black. The size and weight of these titans easily matched a building each.

These were the conventional ships utilized for Interplanetary Travel, called *Orcas*. Each one had its own make, model number, and story behind it, but to the colonists each one was simply an Orca. Large, sophisticated, ruthless; two pairs of aggressive engines each. These ships could travel to nearby planets within hours, and cross a solar system in just a few days. The once meek, vulnerable shuttles humans used for space travel had been replaced with these ships, navigating the gaps in the night sky the way the sea predator for which they were named prowled the oceans, with all the confidence of an apex predator.

But even at these impressive speeds, it would take the Orcas centuries at top speed to cross the unfathomable light years of space that were interstellar gaps. Which is why there was another class of ship the Colonies utilized for Interstellar Travel, the Transport Vessels. These were the vessels that arrived at the outskirts of ESSO-3's Star System, in intervals of around twice a year. Orcas docked on the Transport Vessels, which brought lucky colonists who had served their full time the ride home. As well as deploying new Orcas loaded with fresh workers, and fresh supplies, to land on the planet on schedule. Once they finished these tasks, the Transport Vessels reversed course. All the way back seven light years, that unimaginable distance, to reach home. If the Orcas were apex predators of their Star System sized ecosystem, the Transport Vessels were like a deity that watched over the ecosystem from above. Their power was unmatched.

As the crew of six arrived in their buggy, which was more like an insect of the ecosystem, they boarded the Orca of their choice hastily. The inside of the ship was long and straight filled with seats lining the sides. The only other room was a cargo hold in the back, a sizable room with piles of crates. It also had four cryo-stasis chambers. These weren't for the sake of sleeping during travel, the usual journey in the Orcas lasted only a few days maximum. Spending all that time in the cramped space was painful but doable. In the Transport Vessel cryosleep was used for the journey, which lasted not days but a decade. But in the Orcas, the cryo-stasis was for medical reasons. Were someone unfortunate enough to be injured, or discover they have a disease while in space, if all other options fail, freeze them for the time being. Such was standard protocol, of which Doctor Grace Sullivan was fully familiar, of course.

As they boarded the ship, Stephanie went to the Cargo Hold. She brought out a pair of thick gray boots, with several metal rings on the underside, that were each no more than an inch thick. "Magnet boots," she said. "So we can walk on the Station in zero gravity. They're not perfect, they're slow and sluggish, but they're suitable. Everyone take a pair." One by one they grabbed their pairs.

Quint took the pilot's seat, the second seat next to him remained vacant, and Larry, Eric, Stephanie, Grace, and Franklin Howe all took their spots as passengers. The engines of the Orca roared, and the whole ship shook from the vibrations, as they ascended into the atmosphere.

9

Quint took them through the upper atmosphere of the planet, nothing but the pure blue sky getting rapidly thinner, until they reached orbital height. The Orca got them here within minutes, the whole while Larry's ears railed from the thunderous sound around them, and his body nearly buckled from the pressure of liftoff. Some of the others groaned uncomfortably, made faces, or closed their eyes, most notably Grace. To Larry, this was just a continuous reminder that already, before they had even fully left the planet, they had entered a domain fragile humans were never designed to be in. One slip up, one tear in his suit, or one mistake in procedure, and that could be the end of his life.

They reached orbital height and the Orca's engines cut out. The pressure subsided, and everyone took deep breaths. Larry looked at Quint sitting alone at his piloting chair. Beyond Quint, Larry could see through the large front window, the only window on the ship, the blackness of space. The horizon of ESSO-3, the planet in all its glory on display, a massive dark blue sphere with looming gray clouds and gray surface. There were no oceans, but there were massive light blue patches, glaciers. And above the horizon way out in the distance, the ESSO-3 System's single canary yellow star. At orbital height in front of them, everything was clear, except for a few visible bits of man-made space junk. But these were sparse.

Larry undid the buckle holding him in his seat, and immediately felt the weightlessness. He pushed off from his seat and floated to the front of the ship, where he grabbed the second seat next to Quint. Everyone else remained in their seats. Larry held onto his new seat and maneuvered himself around, and buckled himself into it.

"Laurence," Quint said. "Pretty view, isn't it?"

"Definitely," Larry said.

"Best part of being a pilot." Quint said. "So why'd you come up here?"

"I'm ready to watch what comes next. I'm curious."

"Ah, excellent." Quint turned to the other four passengers behind him. "Don't get too cozy, we're gonna get going now."

The Boss gave him a thumbs up. Quint engaged the throttle. There was an array of levers and controls in front of Quint and Larry, which Larry trained his eyes on. They flew forward, towards that big yellow star in the distance, over the horizon. As they crossed the horizon, the ship's movement matched the curvature of the planet, and it felt like they would descend back into the sky at any point. The surface of the planet retreated underneath them as they traced the orbit, until a massive object came over the horizon. Their target.

The station was as formidable as Franklin Howe had described. This foreboding, looming, oddly shaped mass was suspended in the vacuum in front of them. Hundreds of yards big. It was asymmetrical, with a centerpiece and three branches around it. Its overall shape resembled a large, distorted knucklebone.

It looked unnatural to its surroundings, like a tumor. Larry looked back at his fellow crewmates, sensing the unease in the room, as the Station grew and grew as they got closer to it. Right away Larry noticed some form of movement on the outside of the station, he couldn't make anything out, but there was movement. At the tip of one of the three big branches.

They came within about a hundred feet of the Station. They could now see large metal tubes running along the side of it, going off in different directions for hundreds of feet. Most of the Station was made of the same twisted uneven plates and scraps as the robots themselves, with only a few spots of uniformity. The part they came upon, the centerpiece, they could see four other structures sticking out of it. They realized these were not parts of the Station, but docked rockets. 20 foot long rockets, just like the one Larry had seen at the camp.

"We're close enough now, looks like they don't have any ranged defenses or anti-aircraft guns," Quint said.

No one reacted. Franklin Howe simply muttered, "Good."

"I'm taking her in to dock," Quint said.

The engines ignited. They got closer and closer to the centerpiece of the Station, as Quint used a series of quick engine bursts to keep them on course. Quint skillfully maneuvered the Orca, getting to around 30-40 feet from the Station. From there they could see the Station from around a 30 degree angle. The four rockets on the side facing them were mounted on these four black rings, which were docking ports. There were two more empty ports on the side facing them, to the left of the other rockets.

"You ever seen all-purpose docking, Laurence?" Quint asked.

"Can't say I have."

"Well this Orca can stick onto most ports, even those lousy ones the robots made. Watch and see."

Quint pulled in the Orca up to a few feet from one of the black rings on the Station. He turned on a screen on his control panel, showing the back of the Orca where docking happens. After over a minute of careful micro-bursts from the engines, matching the movement of the Station as it orbited, Quint pulled a lever forward and the Orca latched onto the Station. The ship shook slightly as this happened. Some dust fell from the ceiling.

"Hold on everybody, let me make sure it's secure... got it!" Quint said.

"Nice Job Quint!" Stephanie said.

"Good work," Franklin Howe said.

"Wow, didn't expect to get this far," Eric muttered.

Quint spun around in his seat to face them, still strapped in like the rest of them. "The docking is secure. We can board whenever now."

Larry took a deep breath. Stephanie began to fidget with her thumbs, Grace put her head in her hands, Eric looked silently at the ground. The reality was now sinking in, what was about to happen, and what they were about to go do. Franklin Howe cleared his throat.

"Alright everyone. None of us know exactly what we're

about to venture into. Keep your eyes peeled, stay close. Laurence and Quintin, you see anything, you shoot. Period. We can't take any chances. We go in, we find what we need, we get out. Any questions?"

There were no questions, only nods. The crew unstrapped themselves from their seats, and one by one went through the adjacent room, the Cargo Hold. Larry and Quint followed behind, pushing off from their seats and floating over. There were several crates floating inside the Cargo Hold. Stephanie was the first to use her magnet boots to stick onto the ground. By putting her feet inches from the floor, the magnets kicked in and stuck comfortably. It took effort, but she could pull a leg up and unstick it from the floor, in order to take a step forward. If she did this with both feet at once and brought them above that five or six inch threshold from the floor, she could float weightlessly again.

The other five quickly followed suit. The magnet boots were hardly used during the transport flights that first brought the colonists to ESSO-3, the only outer space experience for most of the colonists, because they were burdensome and unnecessary, and most of the time was spent in cryosleep. So it took Larry, Eric, Grace and Franklin Howe a few minutes of practice before they were ready to go. Now all six of them stood at the airlock at the end of the Cargo Hold, which led to the big circular opening on the other end where the ship had docked.

Quint going first, followed by Larry, one by one the crewmates of the Orca climbed through the circular opening and boarded the Station.

• - -

The first thing Larry noticed was a bright shade of red filling his vision. For a moment it was like he was getting blinded in real time. Then he realized this was just the color of the light of the room. The tunnel, more like. It was a long gray tunnel, only about eight feet wide, with a series of red lights running down the center of the ceiling. It was shaped like a hexagon. About three quarters of the lights in view were red, the others were not on. The six of them stumbled around in their magnet boots briefly, before marching down the long tunnel as a group.

They stopped as Stephanie inspected the first of the lights they came across that wasn't emitting anything.

"Guess the robots were too lazy to finish the job." Eric laughed.

Stephanie held a hand up to the light. "No, this light's functioning, it's just not visible," she said. "Maybe they don't see the full visible light spectrum. Maybe they see their own spectrum, something lower wavelength. Something that includes infrared."

"Interesting," Grace said.

When they reached the end of the tunnel, it simply branched off into more tunnels in all three directions. The tunnels were inconsistent, some were wider than others, some were taller than others. All had a hexagonal shape and uneven plates on the walls.

"Where to?" Stephanie asked.

"Let's first get some bearing on how many more ships they have," Franklin Howe said. "We can head to the other side of this Centerpiece part of the Station, the part that wasn't visible from our ship, and see if they have any more docking ports."

"So straight ahead then," Quint said.

"Yes."

They forged ahead through the tunnel heading forward. Which lead to another tunnel. And so on. They had to make a few turns along the way, the path was windy and nonsensical, but they managed to keep going generally the same general direction. There seemed to be hardly any air. But Larry could tell there was some, because he could faintly hear the buzzing of the repetitive red lights. And the loud planting and unsticking of magnetic boots. Still, robots didn't need oxygen, so he imagined some parts of the station might be total vacuum. By the time they got around to the tenth of these tunnels, the ceiling was so low that Quint, the tallest among them, had to duck his head constantly.

At the end of this part there were a few metal beams and other construction parts blocking a passageway. Eric stepped forward and grabbed onto the biggest beam, which leaned against the wall at a 45 degree angle, with his robotic arm, and struggled to lift it.

"Help me get this!" Eric said.

Larry stepped forward and lifted from the base of the beam. His gloved right hand slipped a bit, and he caught himself an inch before touching a sharp piece of metal. Larry froze for a moment. *One tear and that could be the end.* This was a solemn reminder, he couldn't be too careful.

Larry returned his hand to the beam and kept pushing. Quint joined from the other end. Together they hoisted it up and laid it flat on the floor. Eric panted.

"I hope this place is finished enough that we can actually walk through it," Eric said. The others quietly agreed. Stephanie took out a gadget with a blinking red light, which she called the tracker, which blinked about every ten seconds. She showed everyone.

"Good thing we have this, it'll help us get back," Stephanie said. "The light blinks faster when you're closer to the receiver. Which is on the ship of course."

The blinking red light was difficult to see with all the red light around them. But luckily for them it was not impossible, just difficult. "I should've picked the color green," Stephanie laughed.

They carried on forward. After several more of these slightly varying tunnels, they came across a room. It was large, the ceiling was about ten feet tall. Quint relished finally being able to stand up straight again. This room didn't look too dissimilar from the rest of the Station, aside from a series of large machines taking up the space. They were prisms, and they appeared basically identical to one another. As the crew took a closer look, the prisms were lined with circuits. Stephanie shined her head light so she could see better, and analyze them.

"These have to be.... computers," Stephanie said.

"There are so many of them. And this is just one room," Grace said. She looked at Stephanie with a look of horror. "You don't think there's.... something greater than one of those spiders or anything else.... running the show. Something a lot more intelligent."

Stephanie hesitated. "It could just be data storage. Maybe they have a lot of plans but they aren't very smart, just brute force processing power."

"Hope so," Grace replied.

They moved forward, but Quint stopped, staring at one of the prism-computers. He drew his gun and pointed at it.

"Quint?" Franklin Howe said.

"Maybe we should damage a few of these, hit the robots where it hurts," Quint said.

"Bad idea, what if they have some sort of alarm," Eric said. "Isn't that right Stephanie?"

"Yeah, why take the chance," Stephanie said.

"Fair enough," Quint replied, leaving the prism alone.

They came to the next room, it started off as another computer room, with the prisms on the sides. But this room was longer, wider, and at the far end was something else. In the far corner, its limbs spread out across the floor. Some wires coming out of its head, plugged into one of the prism devices. One of the spiders. Larry spotted it first.

"Nobody move," Larry said.

"I see what you mean," Quint said. The two of them paced forward cautiously. They crossed the row of computers as the others waited behind. As they approached the creature, it did not move, it only twitched slightly. The two of them closed in with their weapons drawn.

Once they got within no more than ten feet, the robot sprung to life. Its legs flailed around wildly for a moment, and it charged at them haphazardly, ripping out its own wires as it ran. Larry and Quint unloaded, firing shots into the spider and killing it before it could get close enough to leap at them.

Larry heard two clanks from behind him, that sounded like something landing on something. He and Quint spun around. The two rows of computers in this room almost leaned up against the wall, but there was still space between them and the wall on each side. Two spiders had emerged from these claustrophobic spaces, had sprung themselves and landed, digging their limbs into the ceiling, one on each side. Despite zero gravity they were agile, showing no signs of sluggishness. They first faced Larry and Quint, but then immediately angled themselves at the other four crew. Two pairs of blades each poised at the rest of the crew.

Larry and Quint both shot at the one on the right first, Larry's shot hitting first, before Larry realized his mistake and switched to shooting at the one on the left. It had already leapt through the air by the time Larry was shooting into it. Franklin Howe, Stephanie, and Grace all ran to Quint and Larry (as quickly as they could with magnet boots), as the spider from the left swung at Eric with a blade as it landed. Eric was quick, he was able to duck his head and dodge the thing. But his leg twisted and he fell back on his rear, his feet stuck firmly to the ground. Quint had shot the robot on the right to death, but the one from the left had now landed at the entrance of the room, and it rapidly angled itself around to face Eric, looming over him.

The spider stuck its two hind legs in the floor, which was thick enough to support this, and stood on them like a bear. It raised its two bladed limbs high in the air. Eric rolled to the right as one of the blades thrusted into the floor where his head was. Just after this, the robot was pelted with shots from Larry and Quint, until it tumbled backward and stopped moving. Eric once again was panting. "Always me with these things," he said. But the other five were occupied. The shots that killed this spider had come from three guns. Everyone turned and stared at Franklin Howe, who held out a smoking, silver gun in his hands. It was an antique, a double action revolver. Three of them stared at Howe. Quint simply reloaded his gun, not caring much, admiring the empty magazine which floated weightlessly in front of him.

As Eric got to his feet and marched over to the rest of them, he saw what the commotion was about, and his eyes widened.

"What the *hell* is that you're holding," Eric said.

Franklin Howe laughed, fitting a few bullets from his hand into the cylinder of the gun. "A personal item, collector's item, I brought with me to ESSO-3. Thought it'd come in handy. Quint knew."

They turned to Quint, who grinned at them. "What'd you think was in that big case he was carrying?"

"We're not allowed to bring guns as personal items," Larry said. "Not even an 'antique.' How'd you manage?"

"I came long before you all, during a looser time of ESSO-3. Like the Wild West," Howe said.

"Before rules many of which you yourself implemented," Grace remarked.

Everyone now turned to the elephant in the room. Grace looked away, pretending pointlessly to be disengaged, but the rest of them stared right at him. Right at Eric, whose demeanor wasn't angry, but sober. He pointed a heavy finger at Franklin Howe. The words trembled as he spoke.

"Hypocrite! I was on my ass, about to get impaled by a robot, moments ago. I *lost* an *arm,* to a robot. A sacrifice I made, because of your rules. Which you don't even follow turns out."

Larry saw Stephanie, who did not reply, simply distancing herself from the whole situation.

"Stephanie? Quint? Larry? Can any of you, his lackeys, explain that? He distrusts others, but expects us to trust him blindly." Eric said. He enunciated the next three words very clearly. "Drop the revolver."

Everyone in the room already knew what was about to be said next. "I'm not dropping a damn thing," the Boss replied coldly. "We can discuss this later, right now we need every gun we have. We can get technical about it later."

Eric said nothing. At this point, there was little else he could do. Quint was smug the whole time, Stephanie uncaring, Grace staying out of it. And Larry said nothing as well. "Let's get going," the Boss said. And that's what they did.

10

They were relieved to find more of the familiar tunnels in the path ahead; at least they knew what to expect for the time being. But there was little talking. Grace looked to Larry to break the silence, as they lagged slightly behind the other four.

"Sleeping any better these days, Larry?" she asked.

"Hardly," Larry said. Then he smiled. "But at least now I know why."

These tunnels had fewer twists and turns, and instead led straight for the next 15 minutes. Until they came across a dead end. From the distance they could see a wall blocking their path ahead. As they approached, this ominous barrier became clear. It appeared to be a door. A large, smooth sheet of metal bolted into the wall. But it had no handle. As they came close to it, they noticed a small opening in the wall to the right of the door.

"I bet this opening here next to it is a port," Stephanie said.

"Yeah," Larry said. "It looks just like what one of the spiders was plugged into before it woke up and attacked me and Quint."

"So that's how they recharge, I guess?" Quint said.

"Could be," Stephanie replied. "They could also be uploading or downloading information. I bet one of the robots could plug into this port right here and open the door."

"But there haven't been any doors before. For the entire Station up to this point," Larry said. "Why have one now."

Stephanie thought about it for a minute. "Airlock?"

"To what?"

"Let's find out," she said.

"How?"

Stephanie again took time to think. "What if we went back to the computer room, dragged one of the robots we killed over here, and plugged it in."

"Stephanie, dragging one of those things could take hours," Eric said. "And if the robot is dead, how would it still be able to open the door?"

"We've seen them twitch for a while sometimes after they die. Maybe their complex functions are destroyed, but the basic ones could still be intact."

"Sounds like a stretch." Eric replied.

"If it's the only way forward, that's what we'll do," Franklin Howe said. "Stephanie, lead the way."

So the crew of six marched back the way they came, back through the repetitive tunnels, all the way until they reached the computer room again. As they entered, they came upon an uncanny sight. The prism-computers were still in perfect shape, the room was identical to how they'd found it, but for the remains of three spiders. One had its limbs sprawled out on top of one of the prisms, the one Quint had killed. One was by the corner to the right, with its ripped wires still stuck in a port. And one was by the opposite entrance, laying belly up, its wry legs still twitching erratically.

"That's the one we grab," Stephanie said. "It appears to still have limited functioning."

They walked over to the robot, and Larry lifted one of its front legs, a long, thin and with a very sharp blade at the end that must have been a foot long. Larry grabbed at the joint of the leg, which jolted slightly when he touched it, but he held on firm. Three others, Stephanie, Grace, and Franklin Howe, grabbed the other three legs in the same fashion. Eric carefully side-stepped around the body of the creature, pressed up against the prism-computers so as not to be on the receiving end of a blade jabbing out from a twitch. Eric came around to the back of it and grabbed onto the creature's small compact body, lifting with both hands. Together they hoisted up the carcass and began to heave it. Quint stood in front of the pack with his hands free so he could shoot in case of danger.

"Alright," Stephanie said as she grunted. "Take each step forward in unison."

And that's what they did. For at least half an hour, they hauled this robot forward, all lifting their magnet boots and then planting them firmly for each step whenever Stephanie said "Step!" Eventually they got into a rhythm and she stopped saying it. The legs hardly fit and had to be bent to go through the tunnel, the robots certainly hadn't left extra space in their construction, but it managed to fit. Quint simply idled for most of the time as they struggled, but they agreed this was warranted. Slowly but surely they made progress. Until they came up upon that dead-end door once again. Once they came up to about three feet from the door, they laid the robot down gently and all sat down for rest, and took deep breaths.

"Good work everyone," Franklin Howe said, panting like the rest of them.

"Good work Quint!" Eric said. Quint simply shrugged.

Stephanie sidestepped around to the robot's head, and with Eric's helped they tilted it slightly to the right. As she had noticed before, there were a few exposed wires coming out of the head, which were now bent and sprawled across the floor like loose spaghetti. She grabbed the one she recognized and pulled it forward, carefully straightening it out. She held it up to the port next to the door, and it was only a few inches short.

"Drag it forward just a bit more," she said.

Grace and Franklin Howe came about from the hind legs, and dragged the robot forward a few inches. The wire came closer and closer to the port, until Stephanie jammed it into the port, yelling "Ok, I got it!"

They now waited a few seconds, no one saying anything. It was a very long 30 seconds. But Stephanie heard a click sound in the port, and just then the door mechanically lifted. All the way up into the ceiling until there were only a few inches of the door left hanging above them.

"It worked!" Stephanie cried. The others cheered as well. But there was another identical door just ten feet in front of the first one.

"This better be the last door," Eric said.

"Wait, how do we keep this door open while moving the thing?" Grace asked.

"I'll keep it plugged in as long as you can while you guys carry it forward," Stephanie replied. "Remember how there was a short delay?"

Grace and Franklin Howe got back in position, and together with Eric and Larry they hauled the robot forward another few feet. Stephanie carefully held onto the wire from the robot's head, ducked both of the right legs as they passed, until everyone but her had cleared the door. Stephanie then yanked the wire out of the port and ran past the open door. Running in these circumstances was essentially aggressively planting and lifting the magnet boots. There were about 30 seconds while the door was still up, and after those seconds it slammed back down into the floor. Stephanie had made it through still holding onto the wire. But the ends of the robot's two hind legs were caught in the door.

"Great, we can't move it now." Stephanie said. She stepped over to the front end of the robot and stretched the wire as far as it could go, but it was no use. She was still two feet short of the next port.

"We're stuck!" Stephanie cried.

None of them knew what to do. Larry cautiously placed his hands on the sharp metal blade at the end of the leg he was holding and began to pull. Eric noticed this and went to help.

Eric sidestepped over around the robot and grabbed the spine of the blade with his robotic hand. His metal fingers fiddled around a bit, lacking that spatial awareness that comes with a normal hand, but he found a good grip. Larry and Eric ripped the blade out of its socket, careful to keep it steady as it was yanked out. They came over to the two wiry legs caught in the door, and set the blade to one of the legs' joints, its thinnest part. They began to saw back and forth. At first there was just friction, but the joint eventually began to give way, until it came loose. They repeated this with the joint of the other leg, and the body of the robotic spider was free. They then got back in position and hauled the robot another few feet forward, until Stephanie could plug the wire into the port of this second door. They waited until Stephanie heard that same mechanical click, and the door flew open.

But before anyone could say anything, air rushed out from behind them. The opening where the door had been they could see the black vacuum of space. Five of them had both feet planted on the ground, the gust was shoving them forward and they could just barely keep themselves grounded. But Quint had been leaning against the wall with one foot loose. The rushing air quickly overpowered him and he flew outwards into space, tumbling as he did.

The blade they had used to cut the robots' legs also flew forward, barely missing Stephanie's head as it went past her. The heavy body of the spider robot grinded forward slowly, almost reaching the opening. As the last of the air rushed out, Eric's boots also came loose and he flew forward, hitting his helmet on the body of the robot. This stopped him enough that he was able to plant his feet back down. The gust ended, and they were left with three panting crew members in the back, Eric on the ground, Stephanie at the front who was almost crushed by the robot body. And Quint nowhere to be seen.

Stephanie, holding onto the wire in the wall as a meager last-ditch effort to keep herself from being sucked out, now cautiously turned around and peered through the opening of the door. Looking straight out one could only see the vacuum of space. But on closer look, Stephanie saw an entire unfinished portion of the Station just below them. There were loose cables and metal walkways branching out through the vacuum. As she peered to the left, this part was even more massive. There she saw several large rockets pointing out into space, docked on docking ports not unlike the one the Orca was currently parked on, except there was no wall the docking ports were built into. There were a series of metal pathways of a mesh material leading up to the docking ports, but in between and all around them was wide open space. There was a walkway running horizontal right outside the doorway she peered out of, and looking to the left and right there were door openings dozens of feet out on each side. Overall, the section was a massive gaping area with just a few pathways for anything to hold onto, like the thin intricate branches off the trunk of a tree, reaching out into the air. Everything was completely exposed.

And then of course there were spiders. She could see them from the distance. Spiders crawling everywhere, jittering about. Some were carrying things, plates of metal, beams, other parts. It was clear they were doing tasks. Amazingly, these robots could carry an object with one leg, and then move with the other three legs, almost as efficiently as they could move with all four. Most of what Stephanie could see were spiders, but there were some, bigger, different robots that she couldn't make out. Not just gorillas, but possibly other stranger things too.

On one of the pathways leading to a docking port she spotted a white, human-shaped figure laying on its back. It was Quint. Just after she spotted him, she heard his voice in her earpiece, and the others did too.

"Guys, guys, can you hear me? I'm still alive." Quint said, breathing heavily.

"We can hear you, Quint! I can see you. How are you alive?" Stephanie said.

"I got sucked out so fast, I tried to just plant my magnet boots on anything I could, and I happened to land on this walkway here," Quint said. "I'm fine now but I need you guys to come help quick."

As the others were still recovering from the incident, Stephanie raced out through the doorway to go help Quint. Franklin Howe followed her, ducking under a front leg of the robot they had been hauling around and going out the doorway as well.

"You heard the man, let's go." Franklin Howe said.

Larry was about to follow suit when Grace spoke up.

"Wait, Larry! Eric needs help, stay with us," she said.

Larry looked over to Eric, who was lying face first with his helmet leaned against the back of the robots' body, his magnet boots slightly peeled forward, just barely sticking to the ground. Grace headed over to go help him. Larry decided to stay put. Should any robots come through the now open doorway they had in front of them, the Doctor and Eric wouldn't be left defenseless.

Eric groaned as Grace came over to him. She placed both hands on his helmet and gently lifted it, inspecting it.

"There's a small crack in your helmet," Grace said.

"I'm aware," Eric replied. "Looks stable for now, but I can't take a hit like that again."

"Definitely," Grace said. "How are you feeling?"

"My head is rushing," Eric said. "My vision's blurry, and my ears are ringing."

"Sounds like you have a concussion," Grace said. "I can give you something to take the edge off."

"No no," Eric said, slowly getting back to his feet. "I have to stay alert in a place like this. I can manage."

"Well here," Grace said, reaching in her tools and pulling out a small syringe. Larry noticed it was the same one she had given him for sleeping earlier. "If you change your mind, you'll have something. One spritz only."

Larry glanced at them occasionally, keeping his guard up. But more so he watched Stephanie and Franklin Howe bounding ahead, out into that massive open area, until they were out of his field of view.

• - -

As Eric's disorientation cleared a few minutes later, they decided to rejoin the others as quickly as possible. One by one, Larry, Eric, and Grace sidestepped around the large robot carcass once again, lifting the joint of its front leg up out of the way and making it to the open doorway. Larry peered out with his head and gun first, looking left and right, before going through.

What he noticed as he walked out was immediately troubling. He spotted Stephanie, Quint, and Franklin Howe as three figures making their way across a long mesh walkway like a boardwalk, heading back to land. And some of the robots that were farther out still hadn't noticed them. But a sizable group of the spiders, who had once been busy bustling about with tasks, were now mostly stationary. Facing right at those three crew members, looking down from ledges above the walkways, or looking across from other walkways. Just about all angled right at those three people, like a crowd of eager spectators at a stadium.

"Stephanie, can you hear me?" Larry said, using his earpiece. "There are about a dozen robots ready to pounce on you guys at any moment."

There was brief radio chatter. "We know," Stephanie

replied. "Quint's afraid to shoot because he doesn't wanna set them off."

Eric and Grace stumbled out of the airlock next to Larry, and they both took in the situation with foreboding reactions. Eric was still clutching his helmet.

"What do you suppose we do?" Grace said. "We only have one gun. Go in after them?"

Both of them turned to Larry, who took his time to think but stayed vigilant. He took a more detailed account of the grim situation. At this point, Stephanie's group was halfway across the boardwalk, which led to a ramp, and the ramp led straight up to a horizontal pathway spanning the width of the entire area. There was a door all the way left and a door on the right. The airlock where Larry's group stood was closer to the door on the right. Larry angled his head to inspect this door. It had a port, just like the one for which they had needed to use a robot to open the airlock. Of course. Nine of the dozen robots were on the right side of the area closer to Larry's group, three on the left side closer to Stephanie's group.

"We're staying put for now, but you need to create some sort of diversion Larry!" Stephanie said.

"Yes. That's what I'm thinking," Larry said. He turned to Eric and Grace. "We're going to need to take the brunt of it. I bet we can lure those nine of them over to us."

"You're insane," Eric said. "We'll get overrun."

"I know, I'm thinking," Larry said. The robots were lined up in a ring around Stephanie's group, barely even twitching. They looked frozen in place, ready to pounce the moment Stephanie's group came within range. A few of the robots began to wander forward a bit, eagerly hugging the edge of the ledges they stood on. Larry looked back at the door to the right of the airlock. "See that door, guys? Looks about 20 feet away. That's our exit." Larry motioned to the robot carcass sitting right behind them. "That's how we'll open the door. We need to drag that thing over there without making too much noise."

"Larry, last time it took five of us to carry that thing," Eric said.

"Hmm..."

Both men were stumped, but there was little time for thought. Eric gave a heavy sigh, as Larry wracked his brain. All the while Stephanie, Quint, and Franklin Howe's precarious position was not getting any better. Until Grace spoke up.

"Saw off the legs!" She said. "We already cut two of the legs off that thing with its own blade to get it loose from the door."

Neither Larry nor Eric even spoke a reply to this. The three paced back inside the airlock as quickly as their magnet boots could take them. But aside from the robot body, the room was empty.

"No no no! The blade's gone!" Grace said.

"It's got one more," Eric said. The second blade on the other front leg was still intact, and Eric was already yanking on the spine of the blade with both hands. Larry joined, and they ripped it out of its socket just as they had done before. They went around to the joints of both fully remaining limbs and sawed through as quickly as they could. Filings were flinging off the metal joints as they worked. Each time a leg came loose, its detached part floated gently away due to their weightless environment.

When they finished, what was left was the body of the robot, a small shell just a few feet long. And four stumps for legs that were vastly reduced. They got in position to lift it at once, Larry taking the front, Eric pulling from the back, and

Grace taking the left. It was loose in Larry's grip, and tilted heavily to the right, but they were able to lift it.

"Stephanie, we have a plan," Larry said. "Just don't move, and keep their attention."

"Okay, hurry!" Stephanie replied.

Larry's group squeezed through the door of the airlock, Larry backing all the way out. Larry remembered what had happened when Stephanie removed a wire from a door, how it came crashing down. So he held the wire of the robot firmly in its socket, stretching it until Eric was clear, and then yanked it out. Larry then quickly backed out more, until he planted his right foot back and barely found any ledge to put it on. 30 seconds later, the airlock door came crashing down, inches from Eric's back.

"Watch it Larry!" Eric said. "You're right at the edge."

"It's alright, I'm good. Move around a bit. Slowly turn us." Larry said.

And that's what they did. They inched around until they had turned a full 90 degrees. They now started to head for the right door, Grace sidestepping, Eric marching forward, Larry backing up as quickly as he could. They hugged the wall as they did this, feeling completely exposed. At any moment if just one of the spiders decided to turn and attack them, they were entirely vulnerable. Eric stared out at the looming threat.

"Eric," Larry said. "I need you to look where I'm walking."

"Right," Eric said.

"Besides. If they spot us, we're dead anyway," Larry said.

"You're not wrong."

They were getting closer to some of the spiders now. Larry could see them out of the corner of his eye, on a ledge jutting out into space. But they all faced away, toward Stephanie's group. Despite his response to Eric before, Larry maintained his attention on these robots from the corner of his eye. If any of them moved or turned at all, he would know. They had now made it far enough to have a chance.

A moment later they finally arrived at the door. Eric stopped just before Larry was about to back into the wall. They laid the now mutilated robot carcass on the floor, panting.

"We made it," Grace said, exasperated.

Larry had already spotted just one of the spiders, the closest to them, shifting its attention. He nodded to his two crewmates. "Time to go." He plugged the same cable into this new port, hoping the thing still had juice left, at least this one last time. Sure enough, the door to this new airlock flung open. Eric and Grace lit up. Larry did as well, giving a sigh of relief. Until they were immediately greeted with a gust of air rushing out of the room. They were able to keep steady, and luckily no objects flew out at them from the new airlock. But they were starting to draw attention fast.

"Quickly, we need to keep this door open from the other side," Larry said. Larry switched positions with Eric at the rear, and they carried in the robot carcass just a few more feet, squeezing through the entrance to the airlock. He then grabbed the wire out of the wall, only to plug it in on another port for the same door, on the inside. Eric and Grace backed into the airlock and then both settled on the ground, exhausted. Larry still had one more job to do. He ran back outside the open door.

"Stephanie, time to go now!" Larry said.

There was a slight delay, and then a response. "Ok, we're on the move." And Larry saw the three figures, now very much in the distance, making their way across once again. He would have to keep the attention of all his nearby robots long enough that Quint and Franklin Howe could face their three spiders, hopefully getting one close enough to open their own exit door. He had to create a distraction for as long as absolutely possible.

The spider that had spotted Larry's group just a few moments ago was now racing towards Larry. Larry aimed straight down his line of sight, firing several shots, and ripping into it. This spider was stubborn, pushing through the bullets, but it collapsed several feet in front of Larry. The other eight robots turned and began to charge at Larry. There was now a stampede headed right for him.

Too many to aim at just one, Larry fired wildly into the crowd of spiders as they came at him. They moved in a crowd each diagonal from the other, like a jagged line, filling the narrow width of their platform optimally. He held his breath as they closed in, 30 feet, 20 feet. He checked to his left to see if Stephanie's group was making any progress. For a moment the three white figures were nowhere to be found. Then he glanced over and saw them at the ramp, pressing forward one magnetic step after another, two of the figures with their guns out shooting. It was as good as they could manage. Larry held until the robot leading the charge was stepping over the body of its friend, who Larry had just shot to pieces.

At this point Larry was just about to sprint into the airlock to his right, before remembering a crucial detail. He hastily fired three shots into the outside port of the door. Bits of debris came flying at his helmet. Now that the port seemed reasonably damaged, Larry quickly rejoined Eric and Grace in the airlock, stepping over a stump of the robot carcass. He then ripped the wire out of the port.

30 seconds later, the door slammed shut. Another 30

seconds from that, they heard aggressive banging and scraping on the door from outside. He also heard the sound of something being jammed right next to that. Larry went and sat on the ground with Eric and Grace, catching his breath.

"I really hope that holds," Larry said.

"Agreed," Eric and Grace both replied.

11

They were sat up against the wall, listening to the soothing sounds of banging and scraping for the better part of ten minutes. At this point, the sounds started to subside, and it seemed as though the robots were finally giving up, maybe deciding that the chase wasn't worth their effort.

"I'm gonna try again, hold on," Larry said. "Stephanie! Can you hear me! Did your group make it?"

Silence. Larry had tried this three times in the past few minutes, he could only hope they had been too busy at their end to reply. Were there no replies after a few more times, he was ready to move on. But just then, he heard a response. A distorted response filled with chatter, but a response.

"Hello, Larry?" Stephanie said. "We made it. We're on the other side of a door right now."

"Stephanie. Good to hear your voice," Larry said. "We're talking out whether we're gonna move forward or wait this out."

But the sound was hard to hear. There was static in Larry's earpiece that was hurting his ear. Nothing he wasn't used to, but it was still hard to bear.

"Larry, I'm having trouble.... I think we're breaking up. Look, Howe and I agree you guys should move forward, we'll contact you later."

"Alright, we'll see what we can find," Larry said. He turned to Eric and Grace. Eric had a grim look on his face. He had a hand on his helmet, still wincing slightly from pain, but it looked milder. Grace was solemn and said nothing.

"So, if I heard some of that right. She wants us to press forward?" Eric said.

"That's right," Larry said. "Nowhere left to go but forward. Hopefully we can find a way to meet up with them soon."

"Hopefully," Eric said. He perked up. "Well, time to get moving I suppose."

The three of them dragged the robot carcass once again, using its wire to open the other airlock door. The door flew open, and they saw another tunnel resembling those they had just left recently behind.

"Excellent," Eric said. "But suppose we come across more doors."

"We could carry the robot here for more of the way. I'm a bit sore myself but I could manage." Grace said.

"I'd rather not be encumbered. Let's just go on ahead without it. If we need it we'll go back," Larry said.

"And if it decides to finally die before that time comes?" Eric said. "Run out of battery or whatever the hell it runs on?"

"Well," Larry said, taking a deep breath. "That's the risk we signed up for, isn't it?"

"Oh great, we have a Franklin Howe stand-in," Eric muttered. Though he smiled as he said it.

The three of them, this new half-crew, pressed on through the tunnels, leaving the robot carcass behind.

● -   -

This time the tunnels were more refined than the previous ones. The walls were smoother and less jarring. It felt more complete than anywhere else they'd been on the Station so far. The same maddening red light flooded the room, as well as a constant low buzzing.

Larry, Eric, and Grace trudged on ahead through these tunnels. Eventually, they saw an opening in the distance to another room.

"You guys all see that?" Larry said.

Looking ahead, it was another computer room like the one before, with two rows of prism-computers visible so far. From their narrow viewpoint, they could see that this computer room was bigger than the last. There was also much more movement in this room. Larry counted two spiders, as they quickly sped in and out of view. And one bigger, familiar lumbering pair of legs, its shoulders topped with pointer devices; a gorilla. The crew of three stopped in their tracks.

"Alright Larry, you ready for some more shooting?" Eric said.

"No," Larry replied. "I don't like the way our view is restricted. The three I've spotted are already hard enough to handle. There could be more. And they're all way too close."

"So what do we do? Try and sneak past?"

"That's what I was thinking."

The three of them edged forward carefully, until they were just several feet from the entrance. A spider passed into view again, not noticing them. The lack of peripheral vision was seriously helping them out.

"Can they hear our magnet boots?" Eric asked.

"No clue. But I feel like they'd be too cumbersome anyway. Let's try floating."

"Agreed."

Larry prepared himself a brief second, and then leapt forward, pulling both feet up as he jumped. Immediately he felt an almost claustrophobic feeling from the weightlessness, like he was *too* free. Like being yanked forward while tied to a car. The force of his jump propelled him forward into the room, and he landed grabbing the corner of the prism, just as he'd aimed for. He quickly used his arms and shuffled across to the middle of the prism, to make sure no robots could spot him. He had to be careful to keep his magnet boots pointed away from anything, both the ground and the prism, so they didn't loudly stick to anything. So he kept the bottoms of his feet pointed up.

There were three more rows of prism-computers to the right of him, all just a few feet apart from one another. Using his arms to pull himself, he moved over to the second, and then third, and then fourth row. As he got to the third row, Eric landed carefully on the first prism, hugging it with his left arm, before laying his robotic hand gently on the prism, and then squeezing. Larry couldn't help but admire the way Eric had gotten better at adapting to his robotic arm. Eric then moved over to the right just as Larry had.

Grace was far less coordinated, basically crashing into the prism as she landed, making a small thud sound. Larry and Eric cringed, and they all waited a second to make sure the robots hadn't heard them. They still heard the same busy metal legs pounding the ground just as vigorously, so they assumed they were okay. Grace navigated her way to the second row of prisms, Eric was on the third, and Larry was on the fourth.

Larry peeked out to his right. There was about a foot and a half between that fourth row and the wall. It was a narrow fit, but doable. The rows themselves were quite long, about a dozen prisms or so. The robots had a lot of processing power. 'A lot' being a massive understatement. The space Larry had looked at was clear of any robots.

Larry looked to his crewmates, Eric poised to get going, Grace clinging onto her prism and shaking a bit. He gave them a thumbs up and started to gracefully pull himself around the prism he was on, and down each prism in his row going forward. Eric and Grace followed over to the fourth row, and in time each of them was making their way across the room.

As they crossed, Larry couldn't see much with such an obstructed view. But what he did see were glimpses of a few of the spiders moving about, and as he got to the middle, glimpses of something against the wall at the far side of them. A series of parts, plates and wires, something under construction, pinned to the wall. It was big, going as high as the ceiling, which was at least ten feet high, if not more. Larry couldn't catch much of it, and most of it looked to be incomplete anyway, but he noticed its head. It was wide, and flat. Like that of a Hammerhead shark. He supposed that is what he would be calling this thing, if he were ever unfortunate enough to run into it. He saw as Eric passed by the same view as he had, how Eric was taken aback.

Larry reached the end and turned the corner. He then pulled himself over, back to the original row he started on. He could now see the exit leading to more tunnels, it was right behind him and to the side a bit. He waited until Eric and Grace came around the corner and caught up with him.

"What are you waiting for?" Eric whispered. "Peak your head around and let's go!"

"What if I get spotted?" Larry shot back. He thought for a bit. "Does anyone have anything reflective? So I can use it to peek. Grace, somewhere in your toolkit?"

They both looked at Grace, who shook her head. "Nothing."

"What about your visor?" Eric asked. They were all still wearing their tinted visors that Stephanie had handed out in the beginning. It made it a little harder to see things, but it would hopefully protect them from getting blinded.

"I'm not taking off my helmet with this air," Larry replied. "It's way too thin."

"Fair," Eric said. "Not my best idea I've had."

"Whatever, I'm going for it," Larry said.

Larry quickly jutted his head out. He looked for just a moment, and saw a handful of spiders and a gorilla, all preoccupied with tasks. Now was his chance. Without missing a beat, he pushed himself off the prism and flew to the exit, to the next tunnel system. He came at it at a good angle, only bumping into the wall after flying forward for at least ten feet. Larry then thrust his feet down and the magnet boots re-engaged. He stomped forward several more feet to make sure he was clear. He then stopped in place and turned around.

Eric came next, flying about the same ten feet as he did before hitting the wall. Grace came last, only making it maybe six feet. As she bumped into the wall, her magnet boots re-engaged, and she was pulled harshly to the ground. Her feet slammed, and she looked up at them and froze. Everything was silent for a moment, Grace caught her breath, but the bustling of the robots in the background continued. They were safe for now.

"Come on let's go!" Eric mouthed at her.

Grace raised her foot and cautiously planted it forward on the ground, doing this with each step, slowly making her way. Larry had a feeling she was sweating inside her suit. This procedure kept on for another 30 seconds, before Grace finally reached them. Then they all went forward together, getting out of there as quickly as they could. After five minutes of furious fast-walking, they stopped and relaxed for a bit. Grace gave a sigh of relief.

"Good lord, that was terrifying," she said.

"Hey, but we made it." Eric said. "That's how we should do things from now on. Sneaky, and deliberate."

"Agreed," Larry said. "Way better than guns blazing."

"All I know is, we need to get out of this place," Grace said.

And they pressed on, another round of tunnels.

• -   -

After several minutes they reached the next room. Peering through the door Larry could already tell two things. That this room was bigger than the last, and that there was no doorway directly across from it, unlike any other room they'd been to so far. Maybe this was the last one of this section.

Upon entering, the room was at least 20 feet wide, had a high ceiling, and there were no exits straight ahead. As Larry looked to his left, there were two massive cylinder shaped tubes, each at least six feet in diameter. They were pointed directly into the wall, taking up a good portion of the entire room. They were made of aluminum. They each had a small hole at the center of the plate closest to Larry and his crewmates, and these two holes were crowded with several other strange little instruments that were set up. And with wires leading outward going into the wall right next to the tunnel they had come from. The cylinder on the right was slightly bigger than the one on the left.

"Bizarre," Eric said. "These look like telescopes."

He moved in towards the right telescope, bending over to peer into its hole. There was a thick wire hanging over in his way, which he grabbed with his robotic arm and ripped out, tossing it to the side. As he peered in, the hole was fairly small, but he could still make things out.

"Definitely a telescope," Eric said. "Ugh, the image is all red-shifted. Of course. But I can still make something out... it's looking at... the Sun!"

"The Sun?" Larry said.

"The Sun," Eric repeated.

"Well don't stare at it too long Eric, seriously. You'll hurt your vision." Grace said.

"Yep, I'm done," Eric said, retreating from the telescope. Larry, Eric, and Grace were now all standing around it.

"Guys, this is bizarre," Eric said. "First of all, why would the Robots need a telescope? Secondly, why are they looking at the Sun, of all places?"

"Well, I mean, with these little instruments they have set up here, it looks like they're gathering some kind of data into their computers," Larry said.

"Right," Eric replied. "But why? Why are they all of a sudden into astronomy? That doesn't sound like a very survival efficient area of study at all. Next thing you'll tell me they paint paintings,"

"Even robots need to find themselves," Grace laughed.

Larry shrugged. "Maybe they've got their eyes on some resources they want to harvest."

"From the Sun? Instead of a planet? No, I don't think so," Eric said. Everyone was silent, thinking. Eric pondered for a long while. Before he spoke again in a more alarming tone.

"So the Robots have got several rockets, missiles maybe. A space station. They could have hundreds, maybe even thousands of actual robot units, it looks like. A metric ton of processing power. All for a little tiny human colony."

"It's a bit overkill," Larry said.

"More than a bit. All this stuff is way too excessive for pure survival. Personally, I think they're gearing up for a war."

• -   -

Larry raised an eyebrow. Grace's whole demeanor changed. "That's... a troubling thought," Grace said.

"Hold on, a war with what?" Larry said. "Humanity? Even with all this fancy stuff, there's no way they've cracked near-light travel."

"Who's to say?" Eric said.

"Well it seems highly unlikely. And very unworth their time and resources," Larry said.

"True," Eric said. "The other possibility is that there's something else out there. Something at or near this system, that the Robots perceive as a threat."

"Well it's not like there are any other people out here in this system," Larry said. "Even if there were say some....rogue colony, some private company somehow organized that massive ordeal without the government, I doubt they could go ahead and just populate it under the radar."

"Correct," Eric said. "Meaning the only possibility, if there aren't other people in this system, and the Robots aren't headed for Humanity back at Home System, is something else. They're gearing up for something else entirely."

Now there was silence again. Complete silence from the three of them. Grace muttered a simple "wow," and that was all. Eric took one more quick look into the telescope, this time with his left eye. But there was nothing more to see. Just a massive, red-shifted close up of the Sun, and the space around it. Nothing more to see.

"Alright, onto the next shocking discovery," Eric said. He walked over to the second, smaller telescope on their left. He again pushed and pulled some wires out of his way so he could get a good look. He peered in.

"This one is.... a planet. Looks like Gamma-2." Eric said.

As ESSO[Eh-So]-3 was the third colony of its kind in the E.S.S.O. program (ExtraSolar-Settlement-Operation), the other planets in its system had been renamed using Gamma designations. Planets in ESSO-1's system had Alpha designations, and those in ESSO-2's system had Beta designations. ESSO-3's neighboring planets were referred to as Gamma, followed by the number indicating its order in terms of distance from the Sun. Gamma 1-7 in the system total, with ESSO-3 also going by Gamma-3.

"So for this one, I bet your first theory might be right, Larry. Maybe they want to, or already are, using Gamma-2 for resources. That would explain them monitoring it from space."

"Fair enough," Larry said.

"Well," Eric said, taking a deep breath. "Who knows how big or widespread these robots are. They're like a virus honestly, a disease. But I know where our next stop should be for answers. Gamma-2."

"Agreed," Larry said. "If there's anything else out there, we need to find out. Not just for us, but for Humanity."

The three of them agreed to this plan. They decided they were definitely ready to move on now, and take steps to leave this nightmarish Station behind. They located the next tunnels, on the far side of the room, but this time instead of heading straight, they headed back and to the left. In the direction of Stephanie's crew's section, it looked like. Which was perfect by them. The crew of three headed down this new branch of tunnels.

A little after they had begun making their way down the new tunnels, Larry heard static in his earpiece. Which eventually turned into Stephanie's voice.

"Larry, Larry you there?" she said.

"Hey Stephanie, I'm here," Larry replied.

"Your crew all in one piece?"

"Yes, thankfully."

"Well we're not. Franklin Howe got killed in an attack. It's just me and Quint now."

Eric was close enough to Larry that he heard this line, which instantly caught his attention. He muttered "Jesus."

"...Okay, all the more reason for us to meet back up," Larry said. "We found a system of tunnels headed back in your direction, we need you guys to stay put, we'll come find you."

"Alright, we'll do that."

The transmission ended.

"I definitely heard that right," Eric said. "Howe is dead."

"Howe is dead?" Grace said.

"Howe is dead," Larry said, cementing it.

There was little reaction to this statement. Whatever the consequences of it would be, they would handle it when they got back. Back to the ground, back to what was man-made.

12

The tunnels branching off to Stephanie and Quint's direction lasted 20 or so minutes, and they were mostly a straight march through. Larry, Eric, and Grace carried on ahead until they finally emerged at the intersection, a tunnel branching off left and right from where they were. They had presumably at this point reached Stephanie and Quint's section, but given the maze of tunnels they had traversed through for the majority of their time on the Station, it was difficult to know for sure. Nevertheless, they decided to head to the right, figuring Stephanie and Quint would have made it pretty far at this point.

They trudged on ahead in this direction briefly. Then they saw Stephanie and Quint emerge from a turn no more than ten feet ahead of them. The two of them stopped in their tracks. So did Larry's group for a brief moment, before Grace stepped forward warmly.

"Stephanie, Quint, good to see you two in one piece!" Grace said.

"Ah! Glad you guys made it," Stephanie replied.

"Back together again," Quint said.

Larry and Eric looked at each other, and then back at Stephanie and Quint. Larry spoke up. "Thought we agreed you two would stay in place. You were clearly on the move just now."

Stephanie scowled. "We figured we'd head back and meet you along the way. We'd like to get back to the ship as soon as possible."

"Couldn't agree more," Grace said.

Eric's face lightened. "Ah yes, we've got a lot to tell you two, from what we've discovered."

"Great!" Stephanie said. "We can discuss it back home. Let's get moving."

The five of them turned and head back the way Larry's trio had come. They passed the entry the trio had come from pretty quickly. Stephanie and Quint lead the way down what was to them familiar territory. The five of them all agreed on the sheer relief they felt, not having to worry about any surprise robots on this path.

"I don't know about you guys, they've been relentless for us," Quint said.

They came to another computer room, the fourth one Larry had seen at this point. This one was larger than the last, five rows of prisms on each side. The red lights were especially bright here. They were about to pace through this room just like the last, when a couple of them noticed something in the back corner of the room. An environment suit, slightly scrunched, lying facedown on the ground. Except at closer look it was actually a body.

"Jesus," Eric said. "That's him, isn't it. Franklin Howe."

"It was brutal," Stephanie said.

Grace hesitated, then approached the body. She gently rolled it over so it was face up, sticking the magnet boots still on its feet firmly to the ground as she did so.

"What are you doing?" Stephanie said. "I thought we were getting going."

"How'd he die?" Grace asked.

"Robot attack. We were overwhelmed," Stephanie said. "It was a blur."

"I'm going to run an autopsy. We're here to learn about the Robots, finding out how exactly they killed him would help." Grace said. "We haven't gotten this opportunity before."

"This is unnecessary, Doctor. Let's just get out of here." Quint said.

"I'm just as eager to leave as you are, Quint. If not more. But this is important,"

"Fine," Quint said. "Make it quick."

• -   -

Grace worked quickly using her tools. She had taken the helmet off the body and pulled the environment suit down to its legs, exposing the body to the thin but still present air around them. From the get-go it was clear Howe had not died from a slash wound. The other four hovered around, no one saying much.

"This is....strange," Grace muttered. She spoke up, "It looks like two things. I can't be exactly sure with these on-the-go tools but.... blunt trauma in the head, and heavy metal poisoning."

"Heavy metal poisoning?" Larry asked.

"Yep. There are welts all over his skin. And lesions. He must've been exposed at least 30 minutes before death. Did you notice anything strange, Stephanie and Quint?"

"Yeah, now that you mention it," Quint said. "He was weak, feverish. Something seemed wrong before the robots killed him in the fight."

"The poison might not have fully progressed," Grace said.

"They use poison now. That's terrifying. But it makes sense," Stephanie said. "They must be starting to feel threatened by us now."

"They could have harvested it from the planet, honestly," Grace said. "Metals like Arsenic and Cadmium are pretty abundant down there. They're even in the water, they get filtered out as waste by our Water Treatment Plant, matter of fact."

"We had all better stay vigilant," Stephanie said.

Grace began to pack up her tools. "Alright, that's all we needed to know. Glad I did that, it was useful insight. Now I agree with Stephanie and Quint, time to get out of here."

Larry had wandered around the room a bit. He was standing right by a row of computers to the left, closer to the exit leading back to the ship than the others. He looked over at Stephanie's tool kit. It hung from her hip, fitting neatly onto her environment suit. He also noticed on her other hip, tucked away, a gun. Franklin Howe's revolver.

Grace had packed up her tools and they were all about to get going.

"Stop." Larry said firmly. Everyone looked at him. "Stephanie, may I see your toolkit?"

Stephanie frowned. "Why."

"I need to see it," Larry said. She did not respond. Larry hesitated, before proceeding. "I have reason to believe you might've poisoned Franklin Howe."

They all looked at him like he was off.

"What gave you that idea?" Stephanie said.

"I just need to see your toolkit. If you have nothing to hide, show me, and then we can be on our way."

"This is absurd," Stephanie said. "I'm not doing that."

Eric approached him with a worried expression. "What are you talking about Larry?"

"I think you may be getting a little paranoid there Laurence..." Quint said.

Larry hesitated again. He then drew his gun on Stephanie. She flinched. Everyone took a step back. "Toolkit. Now." Larry said.

"What the hell are you doing?" Stephanie shouted.

Quint put his hands up, and attempted to de-escalate. "Look buddy, this is not worth it. You might be getting a little paranoid. Just put the gun down. Let's just go back,"

As Quint quickly realized Larry wasn't backing down, Quint's hand drifted to his own holster. Larry started to back up slowly, keeping his gun trained mostly on Quint now. Larry was now standing several feet back from them, right next to a prism-computer. Stephanie then threw her hands up in an exasperated motion.

"Alright Larry, you psychopath," Stephanie said, "I'll show you what's in my toolkit."

She put a hand on it and slowly set it down on the ground. It drifted upwards a bit from the weightlessness. "Come look."

Larry, now with one foot behind the prism, shook his head. "Grace, take a look in the toolkit," he said, his gun still trained.

"....Alright," Grace said. She made her way to the toolkit, knelt beside Stephanie, and grabbed it. She then opened it gently. Larry watched as this happened, there were several things strapped down inside the compact case, from simple tools like wrenches, to gadgets and devices. Several things floated out loose and he couldn't make out each individual one. He did immediately spot one thing though that was not like the others; a sealed vial.

Larry had only been distracted for a moment, but that was enough. Quint drew his gun to fire at Larry in one motion. Larry had just enough time to duck his head under the prism-computer, narrowly avoiding the shot. Moving on instinct, he grabbed his exposed foot while moving it and yanked himself fully behind cover, as Quint fired a second shot at where the foot had been within seconds. Larry was pelted at a few more times.

Larry could hardly see, but peeking out to his right from the corner of his eye, a disoriented Grace tried to get back up to her feet, before a revolver was put right at her head. Larry looked away as her helmet was shot cleanly through, and her body collapsed to the floor.

Larry then whipped his head around to the left. He could see Eric just barely make his way over to cover, in another row of prism-computers, before shots started getting fired his way. Larry stuck his gun hand just slightly over his prism and fired a few shots blindly. He saw as feet quickly shuffled back, until Quint and Stephanie were out of view, as they got to cover themselves. It was now four crewmates lined up in two rows of prism-computers, Quint with Larry, Stephanie with Eric, three of them armed and ready to rip each other to shreds.

Larry looked over to Eric, and they used earpieces to talk.

"This is insane!" Eric cried.

"We need a plan," Larry said.

"I can't think!"

The shots had ceased at this point, and there was dead silence. Larry quickly gathered himself, and peaked his head out. Before he even made it, as the tip of his helmet emerged from cover, shots were fired at him from both sides. He ducked back down instantly. Stephanie and Quint had the edge.

Larry started to raise his hand, thinking to shoot over the cover blindly again, but he couldn't bring himself to do it. He was shaking at this point. Only a few inches of cover above his head were keeping him from being completely sprayed down. He had no idea if Stephanie and/or Quint were still trained on him. Stephanie only had six shots before she had to reload. But Quint's weapon was just like Larry's, it had a full magazine.

"Larry, they can't leave without the Orca!" Eric said. "And the exit is behind us. I'm going for it!"

"Wait-" Larry started, but Eric was already going. He had gone from sitting up against the prism-computer, to awkwardly crawling down his vertical row, with his feet flat to plant his magnet boots. His head was as close to the ground as possible, of course.

Larry waited anxiously as Eric made his way down the row towards the exit, knowing what he'd have to do once Eric got there, and was ready to make a run for it. Luckily for them, the tunnel leading back towards the ship from this computer room made a sharp turn, so if Eric was quick, he wouldn't be exposed for too long. As Eric arrived at the last prism in his row, Larry counted to three.

"Go!" Larry shouted to Eric. As he said this, Larry sprung up out of his cover. First sticking his arm up and firing rapidly, left to right in a sweep, and then poking his head up to look around. To Larry's amazement, both Stephanie and Quint were nowhere to be seen. Larry didn't dare look back at Eric, he kept his eyes set on a spot he imagined directly between the two shooters. Sure enough, Quint peaked out of cover and started firing again. Larry ducked back down, he could only pray his distraction was long enough.

His prayer was answered. He heard Eric's heavy breathing, and Eric said "I made it. I made it."

"Good," Larry breathed. "You're out of harm's way. Now I just gotta worry about me."

Larry was sitting, his back leaning against the prism-computer, when something whirred through next to his right shoulder. Larry looked over and saw a bullet hole right at the spot. In a brief, terrifying moment, Larry laid himself on his side, so hard he banged his helmet. As he did, several more bullets flew through the prism-computer where his head, neck, each shoulder, and chest had been a split second ago. His cover was not safe.

As the bullets stopped, Larry waited for a few more seconds, until there was no more shooting. Larry took the risk, stood halfway up on his legs, and ran as fast as he could out of harm's way. He ran all the way to the edge of the rows coming up on the wall. More bullets came through Larry's former cover, absolutely pelting it. Larry watched briefly, but before the bullets stopped coming through, his mind shouted at him. He knew what he had to do. The risk he had to take, if he ever wanted to get out of this. He was pinned down, it was a two-on-one, for just a moment Quint didn't know where he was, and there was only one way to use this opportunity.

Larry peaked aggressively, standing up fully with both hands on his gun, pointing it outward. And there it was, a full view of the room. Stephanie on the left side, he could see part of her crouched behind her prism-computer. Quint on the right side, also behind cover, firing blindly into the prism in front of him, down the row into the spot where Larry once was. For once Larry saw from Quint's face, Quint looked just as terrified as anyone. But Quint had no idea what was coming next. Larry shot Quint from 45 degrees, several shots into his body, and Quint collapsed on the ground, unable to retaliate.

Stephanie glanced around frenetically, until she saw Larry with his gun aimed right at her. Before he could shoot she whipped around to the other side of the prism, out of Larry's view. Larry shot through the prism, a trick he had just learned from Quint, as Stephanie crawled frantically out of the way. Stephanie shot back at Larry with her revolver as she did this, and Larry was forced to duck back into cover.

Stephanie made her way down her row of prisms as quickly as she could. She and Larry exchanged shots, but Larry was unable to land one on her. As Stephanie came to the end of the row, she bravely fired two shots at Larry, and leapt forward into the same exit Eric had gone into. Larry caught a glimpse of her just as she made her way in.

"Eric," Larry said. "Stephanie is coming down your tunnel. Get out of there."

"Got it," Eric said.

Larry followed in hot pursuit. He made his way to the entrance of the tunnels. He made the first turn down the narrow, gray, metal walls of the tunnel. As he did, he spotted Stephanie making another turn, ten feet in front of him. He fired at her, but missed, as he was just barely too slow. Stephanie stuck an arm out and fired a shot back at him. Larry was forced to retreat.

"Lead her all the way to the airlock, if you can Larry!" Eric said.

Larry obliged. What happened next was perhaps the worst thing Larry experienced in this fight. He chased Stephanie down this series of tunnels, which were especially windy, and at every corner or turn he had to peak out quickly, to make sure she wasn't staring back at him, ready to blow his head off. Lucky for him she was continuously on the move, and he usually caught her from the back just making a turn. But usually she fired a shot back, and this combined with her head start was enough to keep Larry from shooting her. They kept up this adrenaline-fueled dance as Larry pursued her.

At one point Stephanie fired two shots back down the tunnel before Larry even made it to his turn. She then fired another shot intermittently every few seconds. Larry presumed she reached the end of the tunnels. "She's at the airlock, I'm sure of it," he told Eric.

Larry counted the shots. She must have reloaded on the way, which impressed him given she was using such an old-fashioned weapon. When he counted five shots, he knew she must be on her last one.

Larry heard a faint mechanical click. Not the gun, but the familiar sound for a door on this Station. He was about to peek out, waiting for Stephanie to fire her last shot before he did it. But she never did. She was too clever for that. Just as Larry decided to himself to peek out anyway, a shot was fired, before he heard the slamming of the metal door. Larry hurried out, gun raised, but all he saw was a smooth, solid door between the thin tunnel walls, in a room flooded with red light. He didn't know how Stephanie got through so quickly. He walked forward to the door, with an empty port right next to it. He lowered his gun and simply waited.

• - -

The first thing he heard in his earpiece was a large slam against a wall. He heard struggling from Stephanie's voice, and Eric grunting. He could hear Stephanie screaming and thrashing, through static interference. He almost had to cover his ears, it was such a harsh sound.

"Larry! I got her pinned to the wall!" Eric said. "She's trying to break free."

"I'm trapped behind the door, I can't help you," Larry replied. Then a sudden, apparent thought came into his mind. "Eric, don't kill her! You can't kill her!"

The struggling got more violent. "What? I... I can't hold her for long!" Eric said.

Larry spat out the next words as quickly as he could. "We need the Chief Engineer. She thought the idea... how to open these doors in the first place! She's valuable. Keep her alive."

Eric grunted again. "Okay, okay! But how?"

There was no time to think. Larry blurted again. "The sleep medicine! The pain med the Doctor gave you. Knock her out."

There was shuffling, which created a lot more static in his ear. Followed by another slamming sound. Larry could hardly tell what was going on, whether Stephanie was getting the upper hand. Then Eric spoke again.

"How many spritz-"

"Three!" Larry interrupted. "Three!"

A brief delay, and then he could hear Stephanie shriek. "I got her!" Eric shouted. "I got her. I'm holding her steady."

• - -

They waited a few minutes, as the situation calmed down. Larry heard fewer and fewer noises from his earpiece, until all was quiet. All the while Larry stood in place behind the big empty door, basically a wall in front of him, waiting patiently.

"Okay, she's out cold," Eric said. "Hold on, I'm going to get the door."

Larry waited another minute or two, before the big gray wall in front of him opened up. Now, standing right in front of his face was Eric, grinning, holding just the small body of a spider in his arms, with none of its legs attached. The wire coming out of the thing's head was connected to the door's port.

"No time to waste Larry, let's get moving," Eric said. Larry nodded and stepped forward into the airlock. They repeated the usual procedure, closing one door and opening the next. The air came rushing out of the room, as Larry and Eric stood steady, their boots planted firmly on the ground. And they were now looking once again at the unfinished, massive open area with the rockets and the docking ports. This time from where Quint, Stephanie, and Franklin Howe had made their close escape, as Larry, Eric, and Grace had run the opposite way. No more than an hour ago, but it felt like a year.

Eric cradled the robot body in his arms. "Thank God Stephanie and Quint were clever enough to chop this little robot head down to size. It's like a portable door opener!" Eric went on. "And Howe was there too, I guess. Maybe it was his idea, who knows. Before they iced him, apparently. Haha."

This was the conversation Eric made as he and Larry marched out the airlock, back to familiar territory. There were still several robots they could see roaming this part of the Station, but none too close to have to worry about, hopefully. Larry looked to his right and saw Stephanie's body laid down in the corner of the room, her helmet cracked but intact. A syringe floated in the air around ten feet to the left of her. And right near that syringe, Franklin Howe's revolver.

"The last survivors of the crew!" Eric laughed hysterically. "Alright, let's do this."

They walked over to Stephanie, and Eric handed Larry the robot body. He then hoisted Stephanie up on his shoulder. They walked over to the original entranceway, the one that would lead them back to the Orca. On the way, Eric reached up and grabbed the revolver with his opposite hand.

"Nope," Larry said. "Hold her with two hands, Eric. We can't let her drop. I'll hold the gun."

"Fine." Eric said. "But you're giving that back to me later. That's my gun now."

"Fine." Larry said. Eric handed him the gun. Larry held it in one hand and cradled the robot body in his arm. Since it was an awkward way of holding things, Larry switched on the gun's safety. Which he had to fiddle around a bit to find.

Together, Larry and Eric made their way to the original entranceway, opened that door, came out the other side of the airlock, and kept going. They came back through the original round of tunnels, through the original computer room they had first found, all the way back to the ship. Stephanie's tracking device, along with the rest of her tools, had been left behind during the fight. But they had found their way back without needing a tracker, and tools could be replaced.

They reached the circular opening back to the ship, both men taking deep sighs of relief. Larry carrying two guns and a disfigured robotic spider body, Eric carrying one Chief Engineer, they stepped through the only door that didn't require one of those irritating ports, and together they boarded the Orca.

13

L arry and Eric entered the Cargo Hold, gently pushing some floating crates out of their way. With no one but them, the ship felt a bit bigger, eerie, and empty. Eric stopped at one of the cryo-stasis chambers up against the wall of the Cargo Hold.

"Let's freeze her, so she doesn't wake up on us at the wrong time," Eric said.

"Good thinking. Be gentle," Larry replied.

Eric pulled a lever on the side of the cryo-stasis chamber, and the glass lid popped open. He took off Stephanie's environment suit, and carefully laid her in the contraption, strapping her in, and then shutting the lid on her. He pressed the Freeze button, gasses came down, and Stephanie's face disappeared as the glass fogged up.

"That's it," Eric said. "Taken care of."

Larry and Eric walked over to the front of the ship and sat

down in the two chairs by the controls. Out of their front view, hardly anything besides the blackness of space.

"Now we just have to fly home," Larry said. "With no pilot."

Eric cursed under his breath, "We were so close, Larry. So close to making it out."

"Hey, we're not done yet. Let's at least try, right?"

"Sure. Where in the world do we start?" Eric said, gesturing at the array of buttons, levers, and handles in front of them.

"Well, I watched Quint when we were coming here, actually. I was mostly just curious. I remember he used this lever for the docking clamps…"

Larry pulled the lever. There was a bit of resistance, but he brought it back all the way. He heard several small clicks from behind them, and soon they could feel themselves floating, ever so slightly, forward.

"It worked," Larry said.

"Good job," Eric lit up. "Actually, I remember I read about earlier predecessors to the Orca models as a kid."

"Really?"

"Yeah! I wanted to be a pilot for a little while. Before I got more into science. It's all coming back." Eric pointed to a lever and a handle. "This model is vertical land and take off. So Quint lowered the engines when he docked. Use this one, I think, to raise the engines, and then *lightly* pull this lever for throttle. It's sensitive."

"Alright, I'll give it a shot."

Larry pulled the handle hard, and they could see a burst of white gas through the front window. It jolted the ship backward a bit, and Larry cringed as they bumped into the docking port behind them, and the ship shook. They bounced off and floated forward a bit.

"My bad, wrong one." Eric said. "This handle, I'm sure of it."

"Are you actually sure?"

"Yes."

Larry pulled the corresponding handle, and they heard two pairs of large heavy mechanical cranking noises. Then shudders, as they heard the engines locking into place. Larry then lightly pulled the lever Eric had gestured at, and they could hear the engines purring. The purring turned into a roar, as they were throttled forward. They kept going for a good 30 seconds, until they were somewhat clear of the Station. Then Larry released and they drifted.

"There we go," Larry said.

"Haha! I told you." Eric said.

"Ok, next we need to rotate the ship. Turn it all the way around." Larry said.

"Okay, okay. We need to use the ship's RCS. It has a bunch of little thrusters on the side that can turn us around. Try... that one."

"No no, I think I remember Quint using this one, right next to it. Back when we were docking."

"Hey man, you're remembering from a few hours ago, I'm remembering from 20 years ago. I guess technically 30 years, given the cryo-sleep journey we took to get to ESSO-3 in the first place. Anyway, do what you think."

Larry used the control he was thinking of, and sure enough, the ship slowly and heavily yawed, until they had rotated a full 180 degrees. They were now looking right at the foreboding Station, dead ahead in front of them.

"Now we're cooking," Eric said. "Turn on the display. Quint already set a course, we just have to set it back."

"Alright," Larry said, pushing a button next to the screen.

Sure enough, the screen came on. With a dim red line pointing in the direction for them to head.

"Just follow that course back, and we should be right above the Colony," Eric said. "Easy."

"And how are we gonna land once we're there? That's the hard part."

"One thing at a time," Eric said. "Worry about that when we get there. For now let's just follow the course, don't you think?"

"Fair enough," Larry said. He rotated the ship around a little more, activating the throttle, and they rocketed forward, clearing the Station in no time. For the next chunk of time they pushed on ahead, following the course set for them with little trouble.

• - -

"You know what's funny, Larry?" Eric said, as the Orca pushed ahead, dark blue light of the massive ESSO-3 pouring in from the side of their window.

"What?"

"Not a single one of us, from Franklin Howe's hand-picked crew, died by a robot. I almost did, personally, a spider was standing right over me at one point. But in the end, we all killed each other."

Larry gave a wry smile. He had noticed this too. "True."

"I mean, Stephanie killed Grace, the poor woman. You killed Quint. And Howe, well, apparently her and Quint poisoned him at some point, and took care of him. Makes sense, Stephanie would've taken his place, as Second in Command. By the way, how'd you deduce that Larry?"

"Well, it really was just a hunch. It was already suspicious the way in which the two of them were rushing to leave the Station. Then when Grace said Howe died of heavy metal poisoning, and blunt impact, it just made no sense. Blunt trauma, sure, I guess, even though robots use sharp weapons. But why the hell would they carry poison? It's not useful or efficient at all, besides just for killing humans. If they wanted to kill humans all the time they'd use guns."

"True, true."

"And I also was wandering one night back on the Colony, and came upon a person collecting from the waste disposal at the Water Treatment Plant. I'm now 99% sure that was her."

"Ah yes. It all makes sense now," Eric said. He grinned. "Also, that's the most I've ever heard you say about any topic."

"Wanted to get it off my chest, I guess."

Eric fiddled with his robotic arm, looking out into the distance. They could see the horizon of the massive planet beside them, getting ever closer. They were getting close to the waypoint. Larry had needed to make a few turns and maneuvers with the RCS, but luckily for them the course was forgiving.

Eric chuckled to himself. "The humans all killed themselves. Didn't even need the Robots. What would that say about us as a species?"

Larry shrugged.

"Sounds like a question my wife would ask," Eric muttered.

"You have a wife?" Larry asked.

"Had, actually. We got divorced right before my trip here. You know, 10 years to this system, there, and back. Plus a couple years actually working at the Colony. That's around 23 years total. No sane person would expect someone to wait on them for that long."

"Silly question, but, were you.... happy?" Larry asked.

"Yes. I loved her."

"Then why'd you come here?"

"How could I not," Eric said. "I could live back home, have a nice career, family, that stuff. Hell, I was almost rich enough to get a nice little cottage, move to Earth. How about that?"

"But you didn't."

"I couldn't. The opportunity to go out there, into the universe. On the cutting edge of science. Push humanity forward. I couldn't pass up that chance. Who knew I'd get stuck working for guys like Howe...."

"Well, Howe's not in charge anymore."

"Yup."

Eric looked at Larry inquisitively. Larry was simply looking straight ahead, making his little adjustments, navigating. Just slightly disengaged, as Eric had noticed with Larry a number of times.

"Why are you here, Larry? What brought you to ESSO-3?"

Larry took a deep breath. He did not answer immediately.

"Did you have someone back home? Like a girlfriend, or something?"

"Nope."

"Family who'd miss you?"

"Nope." At this second 'nope,' Eric recoiled a bit. Something that came off to Larry as genuine surprise.

"So that's it then. You came because you had nothing to lose. No one to leave behind." Eric said.

"Well, sometimes I wonder why I'm even here," Larry said. "Not 'here,' as in the place where I'm at, in this case ESSO-3. But why am I *here*, at all? And when I'm out at the edge of

Humanity's reach, doing physical work, bare survival, getting through the days, I don't have to think about it."

Larry looked over at Eric, who nodded.

• - -

"Alright, We're coming up at the spot," Larry said. Larry pushed the ship forward for a few more seconds, and then the dim red line on the screen in front of him disappeared. Larry cut the engines.

"That's it. We're here," Eric said. "Now to land."

"Now to land," Larry said.

"Alright... bring around the engines first."

Larry used the handle from before, and the engines slowly cranked even further up. They rotated until they were completely vertical again, pointed straight up.

"Point them a bit further, at an angle," Eric said. Larry complied. They then took off, rocketing into the atmosphere of ESSO-3, with such powerful engines they were slamming right through the air. The view around them went from black, to a light purple, to a deep saturated blue. Pretty soon that blue air around them was turning a bright fiery red.

"Careful! We're burning up!" Eric reached out and slammed on the rotation controls. Pitching and rolling the ship up and to the right. Larry eased up on the throttle as well, and the air around the ship cooled down slightly. But it was still very hot, as the atmosphere got thicker with their descent.

The screen which had originally shown their course now switched on automatically, with big yellow warning lights, and a gauge showing their velocity. They had no idea how high up they were. With nothing else to do, Larry continued slamming through the atmosphere. The ship, tough as it was, was taking a beating. Yellow warning lights turned to red, as they finally began to see the ground. The dark, rocky gray surface entered their vision, with a couple of mountains in the distance.

"The engines, you have to rotate the engines!" Eric yelled.

Larry frantically pulled on the handle, rotating the engines around. They were jerked forward a bit before Larry realized his mistake, and cut the engines' power, before continuing to rotate them around. They were freefalling. Larry's heart felt like it was pulled up to his throat. They could hear parts of the ship starting to buckle, as they hurtled towards the ground.

"Larry!"

Larry felt the shudder of the engines snapping into place. He then had to rotate them again, another 45 degrees. He did not have enough time to wait for that. As soon as the engines cleared another 10 degrees or so, he threw them into full throttle, and they rocketed forward and upward at the same time. This shot them quite a bit forward, but also helped them slow down somewhat, until the red warning lights turned back into yellow. Larry cut the engines and made the rest of the rotation, as the yellow lights returned to red. They were only a few thousand feet from the ground.

But the engines snapped into place, vertical once again, and Larry re-engaged them. Their freefall rapidly eased as their velocity dropped, and within 30 seconds they were falling gently, several hundred feet from the ground. Just as their velocity was nearing zero, Larry cut the engines, allowing them to fall another hundred feet, before re-engaging them ever slightly. He continued this little ritual, cutting the engines, dropping, and re-engaging them, until they were practically right on top of the ground.

"Landing gear?" Larry asked.

Eric flipped a few levers, causing some white gas to fly out and lights to turn on and off, but he found the landing gear. He held that lever down as he heard the slow mechanical whirr of legs coming out. As the legs snapped into place, and they were just over a dozen feet from the ground, so little distance that Larry could hardly tell, Larry allowed the ship to drop fully. The ship shook violently as it collided with the ground, but it was stable. They had landed.

• -   -

They got out of their seats and looked around. Eric shoved off his magnet boots before he stood, stumbling a bit. Larry did the same. The first thing Eric did was to go over to the Cargo Hold and check Stephanie's stasis chamber. Still intact, no cracks in the glass. She was still frozen. Larry peered through the front window from different angles, but he saw nothing but open land, and looming mountains in the distance.

"Can't see anything," Larry said.

"Even with your crazy steering," Eric said from across the room. "We couldn't have landed too far from the site. It's a vertical landing ship."

Larry got out of the Orca, walking down a ramp from the door, a dusty wind slapping his face the moment he did. As he stepped down on the ground and looked around, his legs happy to be back to relatively normal gravity, he gave a sigh of relief. Beyond the ship, way out in the distance, he could see the Shipyard out on the horizon. They had made it off the Station, they had made it to the ground in one piece, and now, they could return to the Colony. The sole survivors of the Six-Person Crew.

PART II

14

Franklin Howe's Office without the Boss himself behind the big desk was an uncanny sight. Even more uncanny, Eric sitting there comfortably in his place, managing the same digital messages and reports between branches of the Colony as Howe once had. When Larry entered the room, there were crates spread out for people to sit, just like in the Infirmary meeting before. Larry dutifully took his seat, looking around. Besides Eric there were three others present. Ken, closest to Eric. David, the engineer who had been with the crew Larry and Stephanie rescued during their nighttime mission. That seemed like ages ago now. David sat up straight, greeting Larry as he came in. And lastly there was a woman Larry didn't know, leaning against the wall, who looked dignified.

It had been two days since Larry and Eric touched back down on ESSO-3, with Stephanie frozen in cryo-stasis in the back of their ship. Since then a lot of changes had begun. As they returned to the Colony they were greeted by a host of engineers and medics available, shocked to find only the two of them, Larry and Eric, neither of whom was Franklin Howe. Eric took the opportunity to have everyone gather their senior officers, organizing a meeting. A meeting where he explained the situation, and more importantly declared himself leader. As was pointed out, technically, given the Chain of Command, Stephanie should be in charge. But after hearing of her actions on the Station, in detail, no one hesitated to allow Eric to take the position instead.

Larry hadn't worked a moment in the caves or on the driving job since they returned. Those jobs were redelegated. Larry, Ken, and a few other names were declared "advisors" for the time being. Eric oversaw plenty of scheduling changes, and this so far was only basic logistics, not even any of Eric's own vision. Part of which Eric had espoused plenty to Larry over the two days. This private Colony was under new administration, and there was no doubt in anyone's mind, change was going to be made. This all brought Larry now to this meeting, called by Eric, to discuss their disturbing finds onboard the Station.

Larry approached the woman he didn't know and extended his hand out.

"Hey, I'm Larry."

"Monica. Pilot," she replied plainly.

Just as this happened Eric spoke up. "Good, good, most of you are here. Why don't you take a seat Larry, let's get started. The others will join us pretty soon."

Larry took his seat, and the four of them, himself, Ken, David and Monica, turned their attention to Eric. Eric sat back in his chair and cleared his throat.

"Alright, so all of you have heard of the Station Mission,

which Howe drafted a collection of us senior officers to go on. To explore the troubling find of a complex, functional space station looming right above our noses, all autonomously built. Six embarked on that mission, only three of us returned, including me and Larry."

Their eyes briefly turned to Larry, who nodded.

"You're probably wondering over there, engineer," Eric continued. "What's your name, Darren? David, right. You're probably wondering why your chief officer is being held in the Infirmary 24/7."

"Yes, I was in fact wondering that," David said.

"Well, me and Larry decided not to inform all your fellow colonists just yet of why she's being held there. They probably assume she's injured, or sick. Aside from minor bruises she has no injuries. She is sick though, alright, sick in the head."

"Halfway through the mission, while we'd been separated as a crew, she decided to murder Howe. Poisoned him, in fact, before finishing him off. She and her lackey, Quint, tried to cover it up. But me and Larry saw right through it. They then tried to escape, murdering Grace Sullivan in the process. Me and Larry had to work together and stop her."

"So how is she still *alive*, then, if you stopped her?" Monica asked, raising an eyebrow.

"You can thank Larry for that," Eric said.

The eyes on Larry, the unwanted attention, was palpable. But if it had any effect on him, it did not show. Larry kept a neutral face, listening intently, nodding at the parts of the story that were accurate, smirking at the little embellishments Eric threw in.

"No no, I mean that in a good way. I now agree with Larry. As horrible of a person she is, Stephanie's highly intelligent.

She's gonna help us. Her improvisation on the Station got us out of a major jam early on. That brings me to the real reason you all are here. On the Station, we discovered two large telescopes in use, built by the Robots. One monitoring the Sun, the other monitoring Gamma-2, the planet."

"We now have reason to believe three things. One, that the Robots are much more numerous, more organized, and more widespread than we ever thought. Two, that they have some sort of investment, more than likely a presence, on Gamma-2. Three, that they're preparing themselves against something, something in all honesty, that is probably not us."

At this last sentiment, David, Ken, and Monica all reacted, David with his eyes widened. Even hearing the news again himself, Larry processed it.

"We'll have a pilot fly by the planet tomorrow morning, just to confirm things. Probably you, Monica. But most of all we're going to put together a crew. If you all choose to accept. And venture down to Gamma-2 ourselves, and get answers."

"Howe should've picked me in the first place, instead of that rat Quint. I'd have done a better piloting job anyway," Monica said.

"I know you would have." Eric said. "So what if Quint was supposedly the 'efficient' choice on paper? More important to bring people you can trust, as was clearly shown."

After Eric said this, the airlock to the room opened. In came three people, taking off their environment suits. Except two of them actively did this, while the one in the middle just stood with their head down, hunched over at an unnatural angle. Larry realized this is because the person was handcuffed, waiting for the other two to carefully help them out. It was Stephanie.

Stephanie's environment suit had to be slowly brought down, one sleeve at a time, but they managed to get it off. As the three entered the room, it was two field medics who had accompanied Stephanie. The medics took their seats right away. Stephanie slowly crossed the room to her seat, her head down, dragging her feet. Monica glared at her the whole way. David looked pale. As Stephanie sat down, her hair covering her face, Larry just barely caught her eye. Nothing but a cold, empty expression on Stephanie's face. Eric addressed the two field medics.

"Ah, Devin, Jose, good timing. I was just about to go through the mission roles. Howe made two big mistakes when deciding his crew, mistakes I won't repeat. One, you need backup roles, in case someone unfortunately gets incapacitated; or killed. And two, trust, of course. Aside from *her*, this will be a crew of people who trust each other."

Stephanie did not reply, or even react, as Eric took that explicit verbal jab at her.

"Alright, let's run it down. I'll lead the mission, and act as Science Officer, help interpret what we find. Devin, Jose, both you medics are coming along. Stephanie is the Chief Engineer, with David as backup. She obviously will not be left alone and will be searched periodically."

"Larry, Monica, you know your roles. I want you guys to actually be each other's backups too. Monica, teach Larry how to pilot, and in turn Larry will train Monica to shoot well. Lastly, I need Ken to hang back here on ESSO-3, as Mission Control. I trust you to run things while we're gone, this mission may take significantly longer than the Station did. Also, in the event we need to coordinate some kind of rescue, we'll all feel good knowing you're here Ken."

"Sounds like a plan Eric," Ken said. "Anyone object?"

David shrugged. Monica shook her head. Larry shook his head as well.

"Now," Eric said. "Let's go over equipment. Obviously we'll know more once Monica runs her reconnaissance, but we'll start with the basics. Weapons!" Eric dug into the drawers of Franklin Howe's former desk. "Apparently," Eric said, rifling through drawers, "Howe was quite the 20th century weapons collector. Apparently before his leadership, this used to be allowed...."

Eric first pulled out the revolver Howe had taken to the Station, and set it down flat on the desk. Next, Eric reached under with both hands and pulled out a long, heavy, black gun. A shotgun, something that had gone out of fashion in the 21st century. He set that one on the desk. Lastly, he pulled out a huge knife, one with an ornament wooden handle, setting it down.

"Howe you strange, strange man." Eric muttered. "Alright, the revolver goes to Monica. Again, Larry will train her to use it well."

Monica strutted over and grabbed her new weapon. As she returned to her place she inspected it, spinning the cylinder. She held it out and pointed it at Stephanie, which got Stephanie to finally raise her head slightly.

"Hey, let's not point that thing at people," Larry said firmly.

"It's not even loaded." Monica said.

"Anyway," Eric said. "The shotgun is mine. My right arm is not touch sensitive enough to safely be a trigger finger, I know that. So I'll use it lefty, and I might saw-off the barrel to make it easier."

"Why not just give it to David, who's got two fully effective hands?" Larry asked.

"David might have his hands full monitoring Stephanie....should the medics be occupied. It's also a volatile weapon, and I'll be out front, so that is what's safest."

"I don't understand your reasoning," Larry said sharply. Ken and Monica looked over at him, staring him down a bit. "But go on."

"Ok...noted," Eric said. "David can take this knife, if he wants it."

"What good is a knife?" David asked. "A little primitive, isn't it?"

"Maybe for utility. You never know."

David stood up and strolled over to the desk, grabbing his new combat knife. He held it up to the light, shrugging, and returned to his seat. He would later hook it to the belt of his environment suit.

Eric clapped his hands. "Good. Too bad Howe had the real guns made hand weight sensitive, only Larry gets a modern gun. What a silly idea. I'd rather take someone I trust on a mission than some random security guard. Anyway, let's move on to the other equipment. Ideas? I was thinking, since this is a longer mission, we could use rations. That tracking device Stephanie showed, that blinks faster when you get closer to the receiver back on board the ship, that sounds essential. And I was also thinking of flares, in case we get separated."

Eric received nods all around for these ideas. No one had much to argue so far. Larry perked up.

"Hey, what about a buggy? If we could load one into the ship, I could drive us around, cut down on time," Larry said.

"Good thinking Larry," Eric replied. "Any other ideas?

Stephanie, this is why we even brought you back with us, remember? Would've left you to die on that Station otherwise. So you might wanna get thinking-"

Stephanie sat straight up and looked Eric in the eye. The motion startled David, as well as Jose, the medic right next to her. She brushed her hair out of her face. Stephanie beamed at Eric, speaking in an artificially whimsical tone.

"Yes, yes, let me think. Hmmmm. How about explosives? You know, demolition. Maybe if we can blow down a few walls, at whatever encampments we come across on the planet, we won't have to rely on utilizing robots to open all the doors."

Larry gave his usual nod of approval.

Stephanie smirked. "That's not even an engineering thing. You should know that, as a scientist, Eric. Don't we have compounds on ESSO-3 we can use?"

"Probably Nitroglycerin...." Ken muttered.

"Here we go. Now she's self-important." Eric said.

Stephanie rolled her eyes.

"Stephanie, keep going. What do you think the engineers could pull off?" Larry said.

"Well, weaponizing the ship." Stephanie said. "If the Robots have rockets, they might have missiles too. Let's make sure the ship can shoot."

"Sounds expensive..." David started.

"That's what you said about the visors, idiot. So we only made a few prototypes instead of mass producing. We'll do the same with this, we'll only weaponize one ship, bare bones. God, he's dumber than you Eric."

David shrunk back in his seat, still holding the big knife in his lap, which now looked oversized and cartoonish on him.

Eric also scoffed, though other than that he ignored the jab at him.

"Ah yes, visors," Eric said, without sarcasm. "In case we run into any more of those cheap light weapons. The robots never had a Geneva Convention, I guess. We recovered three visors, we just need four more made."

"I'd take that weasel any day over a murderer," Monica said.

"Oh, is that your thing, you call people animal names?" Stephanie laughed. "Quint was a rat, David's a weasel. Then you'd be a bitch."

Monica gave a fierce grimace. Eric shook his head. "Nobody in this room is going to back you up Stephanie, so you may as well cut the insults." Eric said.

"He seems to be on my side," Stephanie said, still beaming, gesturing at Larry.

"I'm not on *anyone's* side, I'm just being rational," Larry said. "Let's get back on topic."

Eric sighed. "Exactly. Larry proved himself back on the Station. Now, let's summarize. Survival gear, weapons. Explosives, me, Ken, and the other scientists will get on that. Engineers, weaponize one of the ships. More visors. And Monica and Larry will do their training. Am I missing anything?"

"The buggy," Larry replied.

"Ah, yes. We'll commandeer one of the buggies. Loading it onto the ship shouldn't be hard, that's how they were brought here in the first place. All of this will require a lot of scheduling adjustments and management to keep the Colony running smoothly. Jobs will have to be shifted around a lot. That's my task. All in all, let's aim to be ready for the mission in two weeks. Whatever is over there at the Sun, whatever interests the

Robots have, we don't want to wait around for things to change."

"Sounds like it's time to get started." Ken said.

"Agreed," Larry said.

"Excellent. Then in that case, you are all dismissed," Eric said.

With that, the six members of this new crew besides Eric stood one by one, and shuffled their way out of the room. First went the medics escorting Stephanie, which took a few minutes. Then David, then Ken. Lastly, Larry headed out, but he noticed Monica staying behind. Even as Larry finished putting on his suit, Monica still hadn't budged. So as Larry went outside, his eyes adjusting to the midday sun as he stepped out, he turned and walked around the corner of the office. He kept going straight ahead until he was almost at the end of the building, where he stopped and listened.

Though the walls were rather thin, he could still just barely hear Monica talking to Eric. He put his helmet up against the wall, focusing, he made out the words. It also helped that Monica was particularly loud.

• - -

"I can't believe you're going to let that sociopath onto the mission, Eric!" Monica said.

"I know, I know, I don't like it either. But like I said, she's going to be monitored constantly, and when we're down there it'll be in her interest to cooperate anyway."

"I knew she was bad news even when I first met her, months ago. And if she's so crafty like you say, she'll find a way to turn on us."

"That's not gonna happen. Me and Larry kept her in check last time."

"Oh don't get me started about Larry," Monica said. "Just met him, and he already seems questionable too."

"Hey, he was always a bit of a brown noser for Howe. I never liked that. But he's honest. He's at least got half my trust. We can use him Monica."

Monica didn't say anything. Eric added, "and he's highly capable."

"That seems to be the only thing he's got going for him," Monica said. "Whether or not it's true, well I guess I'll see for myself."

There was a pause. Larry stood there, wondering whether they had stopped talking completely, or just lowered their voices. It was a solid minute before Larry heard talking once again.

"You takin' him out on your little flyby mission tomorrow?" Eric said. "Maybe have him pilot a bit of the way? He did a really rough landing job when we returned from the Station, but he's probably got potential."

"Sure, I'll bring him along," Monica said.

"Alright."

"Okay. Bye Eric."

Larry began to hear her footsteps heading to the door, so he figured it was time for him to leave.

Larry returned to his quarters, where he would await further instruction from Eric. Work would not wait until his flying mission with Monica the next morning, where he'd pretend to act surprised hearing he was going to be included. His two day reprieve was definitely over. As it was on ESSO-3, work would start as soon as possible.

15

At the break of dawn, Larry drove a buggy hurtling over gray rock, its thick tires largely ignoring the big cracks in the ground. The sky was a strong purple in between the blue of day and black of night, with warm orange light spilling over from the horizon. Larry drove with Monica seated to his right, as they headed for the Shipyard. Her arms were folded and she looked off into the distance. For once, no one tried to make conversation, which Larry appreciated. They had only one brief interaction.

"I'll let you fly, but you'd better listen to every word I say. And go slow," Monica said.

"Of course."

They pulled into the vehicle lot, the very one Larry had just taken Howe's Crew of Six to a few days ago. A crew of people he knew, three of whom were no longer alive. It was chilling, as he noticed the empty spot where their Orca had been. Of course it was just at the main Colony for minor repairs, but the emptiness in place of its giant presence was eerie.

There were other ships, still Orcas but some of different makes and models. Monica eyed the smallest ship, which had the most pointed nose and slightly thinner engines, and as she got out of the buggy she walked over to that one. Larry followed her, and together they boarded it.

The ship's interior was identical to the previous Orca, with a longer tubular middle with a row of seats and straps, a board of controls with two seats plus a large window at the front, and an accompanying Cargo Hold in the back. Even this smaller ship could hold a couple dozen if it wanted to, so just him and Monica being in it alone was another strange feeling for Larry. This time, not planning on exiting the vehicle until they were back on ESSO-3, Larry and Monica took off their environment suits. Wearing their all black indoor outfits, Larry took the pilot's seat and Monica the copilot seat, and they were ready for takeoff.

"Alright, let's go," Larry said.

"Not yet. First check utilities." Monica replied. "Check your monitor, your slats, RCS. Come on, we aren't cowboys, there are procedures to this stuff."

Larry watched intently as Monica walked him through the controls for this process. Monica did this abrasively, almost not even looking as she did. It made the control board feel smaller, seeing more of the various knobs and levers Larry hadn't touched last flight being put to use. Monica sat back in her chair when she finished.

"Alright. Take us up. Go."

Larry gently pulled the throttle. He heard the whir of the engines as they revved up, quickly turning to a roar, and they were off. They ascended rapidly. They reached the tops of mountains in the distance, before these mountains began shrinking, and they reached cloud height. The ship began shaking.

"Angle the engines a bit. This is too rough!" Monica said. She reached out a hand to grab the rotation control, but Larry's hand beat her to it. As Larry pitched the engines slightly, she withdrew.

"I can follow your instructions, Monica. Please don't grab the controls while we're moving."

Monica said nothing. The ship kept going, now at a steady pace, as the strong purple dawn sky thinned to a light purple, and eventually became the black of space. Several seconds after Monica mentioned they were almost at orbital height, Larry cut the engines, just as he'd seen Quint do. The ship was suspended.

"Alright. Not bad. Not great, but not bad. I'll walk you through breaking orbit, and we'll be on our way to Gamma-2."

"Sounds like a plan. Just tell me what to do and I'll do it."

"Lucky for us, Gamma-2's very close for a planet. Only an hour and a half at top speed, I'd estimate."

Monica walked Larry through that part as well, until they were hurtling through space away from ESSO-3, on the path to Gamma-2. This part was simpler than takeoff, and Monica showed a lot less stress. Larry was the same either way, doing as he was told. With Monica the process was simple, less guesstimating as he and Eric had done on their return from the Station, and flying started to seem far less intimidating. Larry smiled. After a couple weeks of training, flying was one skill he should definitely have down.

ESSO-3's fading blue atmosphere drifted into the corner of

his eye as the ship passed the planet. Larry caught a tiny glimpse of the Station in the corner of his eye, hanging ominously in the distance. But this was only for a second, soon enough they were on their way, and ESSO-3 was behind them. They would soon see a tiny ball in the distance where they were heading, but not for a while. They carried on with little conversation for the next hour and change. The space around them was still. For a while, everything was quiet and peaceful.

• - -

"Looks like we're closing in. Gonna keep my eyes peeled," Larry said.

Monica had drifted, Larry was fairly sure she'd fallen asleep. She came to now as he said this. There was still the blackness of space around them, and the giant Sun looming in the distance, but dead ahead of them, taking at least a fifth of their view, there it was. Gamma-2. A massive, maroon sphere, with a haunting thin red glow around it. The surface almost looked smooth and glassy because of the deep saturated colors. But as they closed in, craters were visible all over its surface; they were just hard to see.

Gamma-2 was significantly smaller than ESSO-3. Just over a third, maybe 40% of the size. It hardly had an atmosphere. It had no polar caps, continents, or regions. None of ESSO-3's glaciers, clouds, or other intricate features. And definitely nothing as rich as an ocean. There was no water to be seen on this planet. All it had was a maroon rocky surface and craters. It looked the same from head to toe.

"No stations in orbit, that's a good sign, right?" Larry said.

"Well, I think so." Monica said. "Actually, with such a thin atmosphere, wouldn't they have no need for stations?"

"You're right. They could just do things on the planet, land and leave with no special equipment."

"Hell, you could enter orbit from this planet just by jumping too hard."

Larry gave a slight chuckle at this. As the ship further approached the planet however, they were both taken aback. With little to no atmosphere, one could get a clear view of just about everything on the surface from space. The view they got was nightmarish, to say the least. Structures, ranging across the entire surface. They were thin and very spread out, but they were there. Little buildings and landmarks scattered about. They looked like dots, one had to squint to see them. Woven in with the spots of craters on the surface like a strange, metal and rock tapestry. Or like little tumors coming out of the planet. In the far right corner of Larry and Monica's view was a single large cluster of structures, it looked almost like a city. Larry and Monica both spotted it.

"I think that's it. That's where we go to find answers," Larry said. Knowing she knew exactly what he was referring to. "If they have some sort of operations, that's the spot. The second being the Station, it's their biggest thing we've seen."

"Larry, this is insane. You realize how insane this all is."

"That they've built all this? That they're inhabiting a small planet? That they may not even be the biggest threat in this system? Yeah, I realize. And here we thought the camp was a big deal."

Monica took a deep sigh. "Why did people ever play around with AI and robotics in the first place?"

"Who knows."

"God, let's get out of here."

Larry rotated the ship around, something he remembered how to do without guidance, set his sights for ESSO-3, and fired up the engines. They returned home, again with little conversation on the way. Though Larry did give a few more details about the Station mission, which Monica took in attentively. For all her callousness, any details regarding the robots and their accomplishments garnered Monica's full interest and respect. Monica admitted that in her time on ESSO-3, she'd only had one brief encounter with a robot, the rest of her knowledge came from what she'd heard from others. Larry said she was lucky, Monica retorted she was looking forward to finally getting in on the action. He agreed and said he couldn't blame her for that.

As they reached ESSO-3's orbit and began landing, the ease of the long flight ended and things got tense again. Monica began shouting orders at Larry during re-entry, with little patience or regard for any confusion on Larry's end. Larry followed directions as swiftly as he could without a word, as Monica yelled "More pitch! That's the wrong way!" and "Ease up, we'll burn!" Larry took them into the atmosphere, the sky regaining its color, and the noise of friction and blasting engines all around them. The screen at the control board flickered with yellow warning lights at a couple brief moments, but never red this time. At one of these instances Monica reached to grab the throttle, and Larry firmly gestured her hand away.

As they closed in on the ground, they were now making a smooth descent, and Monica no longer had anything to complain about. Larry re-engaged the engines to slow their fall, deployed the landing gear from memory, and as they got to mere feet from the ground, he inched them down until there was a loud thud. Larry fully disengaged the throttle.

"Wasn't too bad for the first time, was it?" Larry said. "I'll be ready as backup pilot by the end of it."

Monica said nothing. It was now around noon on ESSO-3. They had landed much closer to the Shipyard than Larry's last venture, and were within walking distance of their buggy. The pair disembarked and returned to their vehicle, Larry driving them back to the Colony. They would have plenty to report to Eric when they got back. Monica said she would take care of it, and would see Eric personally when they got back. Larry did not argue.

• -   -

On the outskirts of the Main Colony, Larry drove around a bit until he got to a strange arrangement of rocks. That was where he parked the buggy and started to get out.

"Aren't we gonna drop off the buggy so I can go to Eric's Office?" Monica asked.

"Yes. But let's do shooting practice first," Larry replied.

"Oh right. Of course."

He and Monica hopped out of the vehicle. Ahead of them were the structures of the Colony, the closest in front of them was the Water Treatment Plant. Off just to their left was the arrangement for shooting practice. It was very impromptu, several tall piles of rocks, spare crates, and other junk. They were at varying distances, up to dozens of feet away. At the top of each pile was a target. Objects of various sizes, from as large as a water canister, to a small upright glove. All in all, a makeshift Shooting Range.

"Not bad, right?" Larry said.

"Yeah."

"Some workers and I set it all up yesterday afternoon. The engineers also promised us moving targets. They definitely have their hands full right now, but we'll get them by the end of the week most likely."

Monica nodded eagerly. She took out her revolver.

"Yep," Larry said. "Let's get started."

For the next hour they trained. Despite Monica's gun being dated, most of the same principles applied. Larry trained her on grip, stance, drawing the gun at a moment's notice. He would demonstrate, and then mostly stay quiet as she practiced, giving her pointers after she finished the motion.

"And don't *ever* point it at people you don't intend to shoot." Larry said.

"Stephanie doesn't count," Monica said offhandedly.

Monica aimed and lined up her shots at the targets. There were a handful of them set up, all stationary. She was only able to hit one on her first go. She cursed quietly as she missed her sixth shot and had to stop to reload.

"Your gun is different from mine, it only has six rounds of course. You've gotta learn not to waste shots," Larry said. "When you're done, before shooting again, empty the cylinder and practice reloading three more times."

"Three more times?"

"Three more times."

"Ugh," Monica said. "Sure wish I had your gun."

"I do too. Wish you had one of my gun's model, that is. But you can't change reality."

As Monica finished reloading, she immediately dumped the six bullets out of the cylinder and went again. And again. And the last time, she almost jammed her finger as she shoved the full cylinder back in its place to resume shooting.

"Hey," Larry said. "Stop rushing. Do it slowly and properly for now, go quickly later."

Monica lined up and shot at a target mid-way down the range, hitting it dead on.

"Good," Larry said.

Monica got to the last target, the upright glove in the distance, firing four times at it. She missed all four times.

"That one is too far." Monica said. "How can anyone hit that? I guarantee you can't."

Larry raised an eyebrow.

"You heard me." Monica said.

Larry nudged her aside and took her place. He drew his gun and aimed it down the line with one efficient motion. He took a deep breath. "You're right, it's a tricky one." Just as he said this, he fired and missed the target.

Now Monica looked at him, confused and angry. She was about to say something but Larry went on.

"One miss is okay. We're human after all." Larry shot at the glove again. This time he hit it, dead center, knocking it off its pile. "Four misses, not so much. We'll keep practicing on that one, before we move on to the moving targets."

Larry then had to drive over and set the glove up once again, before having her practice on it more. The rest of the training went fairly smoothly. Monica eventually hit the glove, the targets were beaten up and would have to be replaced for next time, and overall progress was made.

"Good enough," Larry said. "Let's head in. You're gonna go report to Eric now, right?"

"Right," Monica said.

• -   -

Larry once again stood against the side wall of Eric's Office, eavesdropping. It was fairly easy this time, he offered to drive Monica the whole way there, before returning the buggy to its vehicle lot. The buggies were electric, they were not loud vehicles, and it took time for Monica to put back on her suit and exit the airlock. Driving off like it was nothing would be easy. He might have to leave a little early before the conversation completely ended, was all.

"Hey, how was it?" Eric said.

"Hey," Monica replied. "Not great."

"I'm sorry to hear that."

"Look, I hate to say it, but I can't work with him."

There was a pause. He could faintly hear Eric sigh.

"I say we find substitutes for both of them. *Him* and *her.* Replace them with people we know better. That's all," Monica continued.

"Larry's a great shooter, we've been over this. And he's not terrible, like her. And I already told you my reasons for both picks."

"I know, I respect your reasons. I'm just saying reconsider...."

"He's the one who found her out, back on the Station."

"Yeah but he's too quiet. I don't like quiet people. He's like a ticking time bomb. With a gun."

Eric sighed again. Monica raised her voice.

"How long have you known him? We've been friends for a long time Eric. Don't you trust my judgment?"

"All I'm saying is, I'll consider what you're saying," Eric replied. He then added in a lower voice, "was he good at piloting?"

"Terrible. Hopeless." Monica said.

"Alright, that's enough. Give me some time to think. The mission details aren't finalized yet."

"Alright. Thanks Eric."

With that, Larry decided not to overstay and get caught. He hopped into the buggy and drove off past Eric's Office. He would swing around and take the long way back to the vehicle lot, just in case. He would then carry on with his schedule for the day like it was nothing, and come back to his quarters late in the evening absolutely exhausted.

16

It was afternoon, Larry stood at the edge of Main Colony, close to the Water Treatment Plant, and not far from his Shooting Range. He was quite familiar with this spot at this point. He stood and watched, as out in front of him stood the Orca. The one they had taken on the Station mission, anyway. Five engineers were working in and outside of it, making repairs. Two of them crouched on the ground, their tools sprawled about, working on the landing gear. One was inside the ship, Larry could vaguely see this through the ship's front window, though it was at an angle. That engineer was doing inspections. At the back he saw the circular docking opening, fully open, with a large ramp set up leading to it. Behind the ramp a man was backing up a buggy, carefully lining it up to be straight, while another stood to the side giving him directions. Larry heard the driver's voice from the distance, it was David.

"How much more? A little to the right?" David yelled.

"No no," the other engineer yelled back, holding a thumbs up. "You're good. Back up straight."

David did as he was told. His hand on the shoulder of the seat to his right, looking back, he backed up steadily onto the ramp. The buggy's tires smoothly climbed at a near 45 degree angle, until its rear reached the circular opening. From there it slowly disappeared into the ship, with only a few inches to spare on each side. Larry watched this with a smile on his face; the precision was satisfying. Of course they would have to remove the buggy and load it back in later, when it was time to go. But it was good to know they had that part of the mission plan down.

It'd been a handful of days since Larry's first flight with Monica. Most people on the Colony were settled into their tasks, and the well-oiled machine was running smoothly again. Larry and Monica trained vigorously, and both were making progress. Larry now knew all the utilities before takeoff without second thought, and could plot a course in orbit with relative ease. Landing was still tricky for him, but he was getting much better, and consistently only got brief yellow warning lights. Monica still wasn't smooth with drawing and aiming in one motion, but her aim improved rapidly. She could hit the far targets in just two to three shots, and was ready for moving targets. It looked like by the end of the training period, she might not have the speed, but her aim would rival Larry's.

While the latter details were discussed at length in Monica's reports to Eric, the former not so much. According to Monica, Larry was a nervous wreck at the controls. And she was an ace with the gun. Larry filed a few of his own reports, trying to keep things more balanced and realistic. Though based on Monica and Eric's conversations, which Larry now routinely listened in on, it wasn't hopeful he was getting through, to say the least.

Looking to his right, a man was walking up to him, his environment suit gleaming white in the late sun, must have just been cleaned. It was Eric, of course. Holding that heavy black shotgun from Howe's collection with both hands. Though the gun's barrel was at least 6 inches shorter than it used to be. Larry and Eric were going to meet and do some shooting at the same time. This of course put Eric in a good mood right away. Not too much shooting, bullets weren't dirt cheap and they needed every single one. Then again, Howe had of course brought some along with his private collection.

"Hey man," Eric said.

"Hey."

"Good to see you. Let's get started."

They walked over to the Shooting Range. At this point, Larry had to set it back up on his own after each session. Just added another half an hour to his already lengthy workday.

Larry and Eric stood a good ten feet apart. Larry drew his gun as he'd done a hundred, if not a thousand times, trained on a target in one second. Larry looked over and Eric was still fiddling with his gun. After a while longer, Eric held the gun out with his left fingers wrapped around the trigger, his robotic hand clumsily holding the barrel, his head cocked to the side. Eric considered for a moment, and then decided to pump the gun with just his left hand, pulling the heavy thing down. Finally, he held it back out, ready to shoot. The whole process took him 30 seconds.

"Larry, don't ever let anyone tell you a robotic arm is an advantage. It's strong, sure. But it's a disability."

Larry nodded. Larry fired a shot, hitting a midrange target perfectly.

"Now that was a good shot," Eric said. Eric held out his gun at the close target right in front of him, no more than ten feet. He fired an explosive boom of a shot. The shotgun whipped back, almost flying out of his hands. His robotic fingers slipped, but he readjusted them in no time. Larry didn't even have to look to know there was a wide grin on Eric's face. "And that's why we bring this gun! Not a ton of range, sure. But if anything gets past you, nothing gets past me."

"You're right about that," Larry said.

Eric blew up another close range target, shouting "Boom!" and laughing to himself. He not only hit the target, but knocked over the pile it was standing on too. Larry shot one more target for good measure, as Eric was looking, and then spoke up.

"Hey Eric,"

"Yeah?"

"How are you doing?"

"Pretty swamped these days, to be honest. You?"

"Pilot training is going well."

"Oh yeah," Eric said. "Well that's good to hear." Eric fired one more thunderous shot, before giving Larry his full attention. "Why don't you tell me specifics."

"Takeoff is much better," Larry said immediately. "In orbit, I'm comfortable at the controls. Landing is getting there too."

"Right...." Eric replied.

"It's the tru- it's the most accurate rundown I can give you," Larry said.

"Of course. I believe you Larry. Don't worry." Eric gave an awkward chuckle. He cleared his throat. "And Monica's shooting?"

Larry thought before answering. "Good. Just like I said in my reports. Good, not great."

"Well that's good to hear," Eric repeated. "She's excited about her progress. We're actually friends, she and I go back a while."

"I'm aware."

"Right. Well listen. I know this whole process has been pretty difficult. And complicated. I mean we just got off a mission, you and I. Racing off again is.... pretty insane if you ask me."

"I'm prepared to do my job,"

"Of course. And I just wanted to say thank you for sticking with it. For training Monica, for helping out. You're doing a good job Larry. You deserve to be recognized."

"Thanks Eric."

Together, they fired a few more rounds, and then figured they were done for the day. Larry had some free time before his final assignment for the day, Eric had work to attend to. So Eric headed back to his office. Larry, knowing Monica's schedule at this point, knew exactly where he himself would be in half an hour.

• -   -

Monica had already entered Eric's Office, Larry saw her go in, but as Larry listened in, Eric was in the middle of talking to someone else first. A man with a gruff voice, a worker who Larry didn't know.

"It was a disgusting accident, to be honest," the worker said. "She lost three fingers off her good hand."

"I'm so sorry to hear that. The doctors are going with robotic prosthetics, I'm assuming?"

"Yeah."

"I wish her the best,"

"Look," the man said, his tone getting angrier. "Is this coming out of her salary? Cause she's had horrible luck, already had a surgery a month back. She doesn't deserve-"

"No no, I don't run things the way Howe did, man. She can work some overtime if she chooses."

"At this point it won't be enough...."

"Which is *why*," Eric said firmly, "I'm not deducting her pay. The resources she needs are resources going to a good worker. If that means we don't have the time or means to finish one of the fancy toys for my mission, so be it. If we all have to take some of the fall, so be it. Howe's way was not right."

"Thank you, Eric. I knew you'd come through."

Larry heard the footsteps of the worker walking out. He debated whether he should hide, or move to the back side of the building, but he hoped the worker would just walk straight out and not look back. Which, luckily for Larry, is what happened. Now the next conversation, the one Larry was here for, picked up.

"Being a leader is damn stressful, Monica." Eric said.

"You look like you slept all of an hour last night," Monica laughed.

"Tell me about it."

"You're honestly a hero for taking this all on Eric."

"Right you are."

There was a pause.

"Look, you really think you can hold your own as a shooter on this mission, without Larry?" Eric asked.

"Yes. Larry should be part of Ken's Mission Control team. He can come in if we need backup."

"You do realize we're still bringing Stephanie, right? Who is, no matter how you slice it, much worse."

"I can't talk you out of that one. Even though you hate her, funny enough. But at least she's not armed. If it's just you and me with guns, I'll feel safe, and I will come through."

"I have nothing against Larry," Eric reiterated. "But clearly you do. And I need you with me. So I thought of an idea."

"I'm listening."

"Some workers discovered another camp, not far from here. Camp of robots. It needs to be cleared out. You, me and Larry will go. There you can show me your skills."

The previous camp Larry had discovered, which practically set off the whole chain of events thereafter, had already been cleared out apparently. Not long after Larry and Eric got back from the Station, Eric sent an impromptu armed team, mostly from security, over to deal with it. Larry hadn't heard too much about the brief mission, but apparently it was a clean success, which was good. What he did know was he didn't hear ringing at night after that, which was nice. Not sharp, blatant ringing, anyway, but at night on ESSO-3, he always felt he heard something.

"Shouldn't it just be you and me?" Monica asked.

"If you can hold your own without Larry, then I'll see about your proposal. If you can't even do that, and he has to step in, this debate goes no further."

"Fine. I'll show you what I got," Monica said.

That was the whole conversation. Monica started heading for the door, and Larry knew it was his time to leave.

• -   -

It was evening now, after hours. Larry sat alone in his quarters, on his bed, head down, thinking. He inspected his gun, unloading it, dropping the magazine on the floor. He picked up the magazine and dug through its bullets. He took out and inspected one of the bullets. Its dull, brown and slightly green, worn copper jacket. Its pointed tip, which reminded him of the nose of the Orca. If fit between his thumb and pointer finger. Light as a feather. He flicked it in the air and caught it. It made a nice *ding* sound. That was when he got the idea.

He quickly placed the bullet back into the magazine, fumbling with it. He jammed the magazine back into his gun, laid the gun in its holster, stood up, and headed to his front door. The working shifts were over. Aside from night shifts, like security. He once had one of those jobs, in his first month and a half, a brutal placement for freshies. But other than night shift security guards, there was still one person he could go see. Just the one he had in mind, matter of fact. Larry gathered his environment suit and headed off.

• -   -

Back at the Infirmary. Larry entered, it looked basically the same, but a little more empty. The lights were dim. No doctors to be seen, save for one. Near the entrance, talking in the corner of the room to the single security guard present. Larry saw the holstered weapon at the man's hip. Other than those two, there were a few crates off to the side, and a row of empty cots. Empty except for one, over at the other end of the room. That's where Stephanie was lying down, innocuous, holding up a tablet and reading. No handcuffs or restraints on her, but she was clearly being supervised at all times, at least lightly.

As Larry began walking over to her, the security guard stopped and turned to him.

"You got business here? Why are you here after hours, man?" the guard asked.

Larry kept on, as if not giving it a second thought. "Eric sent me. I'm one of his advisors."

"Oh right. Go ahead then."

Larry marched over all the way to Stephanie at the back of the room. As he approached her, she kept reading, unphased.

"Hello Stephanie," Larry said.

Stephanie frowned. "What do you want?"

Larry looked back at the security guard and doctor. They were back to their conversation, paying no attention to him and Stephanie. Larry lowered his voice anyway. "I need your help."

Stephanie kept reading. "No shit. Why else would you come here? To chat?"

"No, I mean *I* need your help. Not for Eric, the mission, or anything else. In fact, I'm going behind Eric's back."

Now Stephanie lowered her tablet and looked at him. Though her face was unchanged. "I'm listening."

"You remember, from the meeting, I've been training Monica to shoot, and she's teaching me to pilot?"

"Yeah."

"Monica has been giving.... biased reports, to Eric. About me. She doesn't like me, and she wants to get me off the mission."

"Okay... have you tried just getting her to like you? I know this is a foreign word to you, but showing a little charisma?"

"I've been completely reasonable, Stephanie. I've been

patient with her. But she just has it out for me." Larry sighed. "She's been doing everything she can to swing Eric to her view. I've listened to their conversations. Eric's not totally convinced, but she's working on him."

"What do you want me to do about it?"

"Here's where you come in," Larry said. Larry explained to her what he had heard about the new camp, how Eric wanted himself, Monica and Larry to go there, and for Monica to show-case her shooting skills. That this test would influence whether Monica takes Larry's place on the mission.

"Wow. You're really on the hot seat," Stephanie said. "After all that work you did getting shot at by me and Quint. What a shame."

Larry ignored this comment. "Here's where you come in," Larry repeated. "I need to make sure Monica fails her test."

"By doing what?"

"By replacing her bullets with blank rounds."

Once she heard this, Stephanie gave a callous grin.

"I'll give you the rounds. Can you turn them into blanks?" Larry asked.

"Of course," Stephanie replied gleefully. "You think I don't know about guns? I can do it with my engineer's tools."

"During your shift tomorrow, right?"

"Of course. Easily." Stephanie said. "What's in it for me?"

Larry's face fell. He tried not to show it, but she definitely picked up on it.

"What's the matter? Got nothing to offer?"

"I saved your life. If not for me, Eric would've finished you off on the Station."

"And if not for you, everyone but Howe would've made it back, and I'd be running this Colony. Next."

"Well," Larry said, "It gives you a chance to get at Monica. Don't you hate her? Don't you find her... self-righteous?"

Stephanie laughed. "True." Stephanie then slowly shook her head and gave him a look, he couldn't tell if it was pity or patronizing. Probably the latter. "So your plan is to humiliate Monica? Make her think she's missing her shots, when it was actually rigged. Ooh, that's probably gonna destroy her confidence. Not to mention recklessly putting her in danger, to put on a show for Eric? It's more sadistic than anything I could've thought of, Larry."

"Oh please," Larry said. "I'm just doing what I have to do to prevent myself from getting kicked off the mission. And I'll be there at the camp, I won't let any harm come to her should a robot get too close. It's not sadistic."

"And why do you care so much about being on that big mission anyway, Larry?"

"My skills are essential," Larry said plainly.

"Yeah right."

"And I care about the outcome. I want to be there, it gives me purpose," Larry said.

"Sure, okay."

"And I'm tired of letting people push me around."

Stephanie beamed at him with satisfaction. "There you go! There you go. That's the real answer Larry."

"They're all real answers," Larry muttered, in a shakier voice than he intended.

"You know what? I'll help you set that bitch up. I won't even ask anything for it. I just want you to come back and tell me the look you saw on her face. Got it?"

"Sure. Whatever." Larry said. "How many rounds do you think is a good idea, in your opinion?"

"Six. No more," Stephanie said. "She's carrying the revolver, right? You'll have to load her cylinder with six blank rounds right before you guys go to the camp. There's no way she loads a blank round herself into the gun without noticing it's been tampered."

"True. That makes sense. I'll have to get a hold of her gun for a moment."

"Yeah, you'll have to pull that off," Stephanie said.

"Alright, sounds like a plan," Larry said. But as Stephanie went back to the callous grin, he knew she wasn't finished yet.

"So what's the difference between your plan, now, and me killing Howe? We're both just opportunists, after all," Stephanie said. "I'm just a little more opportunistic. I saw the opportunity right after Quint, Howe and I got separated, the resealable flap on his suit-"

Larry hesitated with what he was about to say next, he knew it wouldn't be wise to put his helper in a bad temper, but he couldn't resist. "I don't need to hear your bragging, Stephanie. How you killed Howe, I frankly don't care."

Stephanie glared at him. But that glare quickly turned to just a frown. And then an amused chuckle. "Fine. Just give me your rounds, come by sometime tomorrow, I'm usually right here even when I'm working. And I'll have your blanks ready."

"Thank you," Larry said. He glanced over again to see if the security guard and doctor were still occupied. They were. He took out his gun discreetly and ejected the magazine into his hand. He counted out six bullets and handed them to Stephanie. Then he took out two more and gave them to her as well. "A couple spares, just in case you need them."

"That's insulting Larry."

Larry put his gun away. He turned to leave.

"This is the second time I'm helping you. Remember when I wired your earpiece, cause you were hearing ringing? You owe me one and I should cash in...."

Larry said nothing, made his way to exit the Infirmary, and walked off.

17

The next morning, the previously empty Infirmary was now plenty occupied with workers. First, a security guard by the door, different from the one who was there the night before. Then the usual medical staff, who Larry didn't know all too well. Which was a good thing; there were all sorts of ways to wind up spending long hours in the Infirmary, none of which were pleasant. Anything mild was just dealt with easy pills or medicine. 30 seconds in and out. Spending longer time away from work could be achieved a couple ways. No one on ESSO-3 had pre-existing conditions, they would've never made it past the selection process if they had. But losing a limb, digits, or suffering even worse injuries, unfortunately wasn't too uncommon.

Another way was catching a nasty virus. ESSO-3 was barren but it had microbes. If one wasn't careful, didn't sanitize well, or one did everything right but was just unlucky, they could easily catch something. Something human immune systems were never built for. The most common was affectionately called "Alien Flu." Larry didn't know the exact symptoms, but he knew it led to patients aching, sweating, and becoming so weak they could hardly walk. Bed-ridden for a week and a half at least. Even worse, the pain. Pain so crippling, rumor had it one couldn't even talk straight, it was too hard to think.

So Larry walked past this group of medical workers he hardly knew without a second thought. The only one he had known was shot dead by the same person about to help him out. That was something to think about.

Past the medical staff, towards the back of the room, a group of three engineers who had migrated there were sitting on the floor. Their tools were laid out across the floor, two of them hunched over, each working with delicate tools on one of the special visors for the Mission. Visors that would hopefully save the crew from being permanently blinded by one of the gorilla-type robots, who couldn't care less about the unfairness of their weapons, and the lifelong curse they put upon the recipient.

A few feet past the engineers, in her comfortable spot at the back of the room, Stephanie sat on the floor leaning against one of the mesh cots. She had a wrench in hand, her full toolkit next to her, and she looked rather peaceful. She looked up as he approached.

"Ah, you're early, but I have it done anyway," Stephanie said. "Come look at this," she added in a low voice.

Larry went over to her and knelt down. Stephanie reached into her toolkit, hardly having to dig as everything was tightly organized, and grabbed something in her hand. She held out in her palm the eight rounds. They looked almost the same as before, still the worn brown-green copper jacket, but they had no pointed tip. All eight were empty, flat topped cases, filled with gunpowder but with no actual bullet at the top, nothing for the gunpowder to launch out. Larry took the rounds graciously, fitting them into his magazine, making a mental note.

"Don't be stupid enough to get caught," Stephanie said. "You gotta just slip them in her cylinder while she's distracted, no hesitation."

"Got it. Thanks." Larry said.

"Alright. We're done here. Get out of my hair," Stephanie said.

Larry gave no argument. The security guard glanced over, so Stephanie grabbed his hand and shook it, and they exchanged a few quick fake pleasantries. Larry then walked out. His magazine filled with exactly eight blanks, and beneath them real bullets, Larry was ready to go. He gave a nod at the security guard and headed out, onto the real task for the day.

• - -

Larry went straight from the Infirmary to the Orca, which was towards the outskirts of the Colony. He arrived a few minutes early, the engineers had already left, but his scheduled block of time with Monica hadn't started. Larry took a look inside the ship, making sure things were in place. In the Cargo Hold, everything was in place, just as normal, which was perfect. Larry moved around a few crates, which were quite heavy when they weren't in zero gravity. Looming over him, one of the cryo-stasis chambers, at least 6 and a half feet. A large glass face taking up most of it, with a few levers at the side, the big slightly nightmarish machine was bolted into the wall. Larry heaved a crate above his head, balancing it on top of the thing. Even with ESSO-3's relatively benign gravity it was heavy; he could only imagine lifting the crates on other worlds.

Just as Larry finished, he strolled out the door of the ship only to be greeted by Monica, in her environment suit, who marched right past him boarding the ship. She gestured at him with her hand to come follow.

"Good morning," Larry said dryly.

• -   -

The dim clouds and hazy light blue morning sky faded into black, as Larry once again brought the Orca with its four roaring vertical engines up and out of the atmosphere. Flicking controls, making slight engine adjustments, it was all starting to become automatic for Larry. Monica sat still in her chair, distant, statue-like, gazing off. She kept this way as Larry brought them into orbit, and finally as Larry pulled them out of orbit, and they began heading off into open space, Monica spoke up.

"Not bad, Larry. Not bad."

"Not bad?"

"That's what I said."

Larry looked over at her, with as much of a poker face as he could manage. He was hunched over a bit, and there were very noticeable bags under his eyes. Monica seemed to react to this, cocking her head, and looking at him inquisitively.

"What?" Monica asked.

"What else could I improve on. Specifically."

Monica raised an eyebrow. She then shrugged. "I said you were not bad. Not as professional as I'd have done it, but not bad."

"What else could I improve on?" Larry repeated.

Monica gave an exasperated sigh. "You could've been....smoother. You were fairly smooth, but you weren't *smooth*."

"Smooth. Mhm," Larry said. "Why don't you show me next time what you mean by that."

"Sure, whatever you want," Monica replied.

Larry took them forward at a steady pace, the ship hurtling through black nothingness, with sunlight from the massive Sun leaking in from the left corner of the view. It was the same course to Gamma-2, the one they'd been preparing for, though they weren't going the full trip. Monica had also made Larry fly around ESSO-3 geography, or on other courses in other directions. But this was the primary set of skills, takeoff, get to orbit, head on through space, return and land. Over and over again, drilled daily.

As Larry lurched forward in his pilot's chair, he eventually saw Monica holding that revolver of hers. That little silver gun with a black handle, dusty but still retaining its luster. Compared to his factory-perfect standard issue, Larry had to admit, the revolver was a pretty weapon. Monica did her usual fidget, gently spinning the cylinder while inspecting it.

"Hey Monica, may I have a look at that?"

Monica gave him a puzzled look, "The gun?"

"Yeah."

"Sure."

They were cruising now, Larry took his hands off the controls. Monica delicately handed him the gun, like it was a sculpture. Larry took the weapon, mimicking her inspection, and pulling back the hammer ever-slightly. Monica hesitated.

"Can I see yours?"

"Of course."

Larry set down the revolver on the control board, taking out his gun and handing it to her, holding it so the grip extended out toward her. She took the gun eagerly.

"I wish I had one of these. Fast, efficient, modern, easy to operate," Monica said. "Too bad for Howe and his silly rules. That only you can use it."

"The weighting prevents someone from just grabbing my gun and using it against me," Larry replied.

"Right, I'm not saying that's wrong. I'm just saying they should've issued more. Or allowed citizens to earn them."

"I agree," Larry said.

Monica's lips curled à bit, into what Larry could only assume was a smile. "Thanks for teaching me to shoot."

"You're welcome,"

Larry waited a moment as Monica turned her attention away, and then remarked, "we'll both be sharp on the mission."

"...Right, of course." Monica said.

Just as she looked to be finishing up inspecting Larry's gun, Larry made a sudden move. Holding the controls, he yanked them to the left. The ship jolted suddenly. Monica almost dropped the weapon in her hands. There were two loud bangs from the back of the ship, the second following the first, something crashing into the wall. Monica jerked her head over her shoulder to look.

"What the hell? What happened?"

"My bad," Larry said, putting his hands up. "Slipped."

"Ugh, we must've forgotten to unload the cargo before take off. Weren't you supposed to remind me of that?" Monica said. She hastily set down Larry's gun, right beside the revolver on the control board, and got out of her seat. She was wearing magnet boots. Larry watched as she got up, planted on foot after the other, and trudged to the back of the ship. She was a bit unsteady at first. Larry watched as she made it over to the Cargo Hold, where there were floating crates still flying around a bit from the force of the ship's sudden jerk and recovery. As she entered the room not looking back, Larry made his move.

First Larry reached over and pressed the magazine release on his own gun, grabbing the magazine, an awkward thing in zero gravity, and meticulously pulling out the first six shells into his palm before returning it. Larry then picked up the revolver, its cylinder he had already left hanging out. He couldn't just drop the bullets out, thanks to the weightlessness, he had to actually pull each out one by one. Realizing how tedious this would be, Larry sighed, but there was no time to stop and consider. He firmly planted the revolver on the control board, picked out each bullet from the cylinder meticulously with his fingers replacing it with the rounds from his right hand. He did this six times, jamming his finger from moving so fast, and then closed the cylinder back into the revolver. As he heard metal stomping coming his way, he put the cylinder back out so it looked just the way he'd found it.

Monica fell back in her chair with a heavy sigh. She looked at Larry's gun, and then over at her revolver, and scowled. She grabbed her revolver from the control panel and put it back in its holster.

"Let's just get going, alright? Enough playing with these things like toys," she said.

Larry nodded. He put his own gun back in its holster, grabbed the controls, and resumed the flight.

• -   -

It was now late day, Larry came to the vehicle lot, nothing more than a row of buggies with charging stations. Most of the charging stations were empty, the vehicles were out in use right now. For the vehicles there, despite their imperfect tarps, dust coverings, regular cleanings and wipe-downs, they were still somewhat coated in debris. The only time windier than late day was nightfall.

Eric was leaning against one of the buggies, as he saw Larry he nodded.

"Afternoon Larry."

"Afternoon."

Eric lifted the tarp off the buggy and rubbed off some of the dust with his glove. As he did, the wind immediately began kicking up more to replace it. Larry gave it no more than ten minutes before that happened.

"This damn planet," Eric muttered. He looked over at Larry, who stood straight. "Ready to go shoot more things?"

"I guess so," Larry replied. "You nervous?"

"Of course." Eric smiled and shook his head. "You ever feel like a soldier, Larry? With all we've been getting ourselves into lately?"

"I don't feel like anything."

"Boy you're fun to talk to."

Larry was gonna drop it, but he decided to satisfy Eric's question. "I guess I do. Soldiers are usually killing other people, not metal, at least in history. But I've done both. So I am."

Eric thought for a moment. "Quint, you mean?"

"Yeah."

"You feel bad for that fella? I wouldn't."

"You kidding? He had it coming." They both laughed. But as

the laugh faded, Larry's face became solemn, his tone haunting. "I really did kill him..."

Their discussion was interrupted as Monica came up to them. She was grinning, her hand on her holster. "Ready for this, boys?"

"Let's get moving," Eric said. The three of them loaded into the buggy, Larry at the wheel, Eric at the seat next to him, Monica in the back. Larry revved up the electric motor, hearing that familiar underwhelming whine, and they head off. Eric directing Larry to where they needed to be, far from Main Colony.

• - -

They saw the disorderly piles of scrap spread out in the distance. On the horizon in the orange twilight glow, the shadows were very distinct. This camp was different, it almost looked abandoned. An empty, eerie, strange assortment of nonsense only the robots would understand.

As they drove closer, they saw there were a few robots. A few spiders, moving aimlessly about. And one larger one, which Larry made out to be a gorilla. But Larry saw what was missing that was there at the last camp. No rocket to be seen. The tall rocket ship was at the center of the last camp, almost like an Altar, and the robots had been frantically working at it. This one had no rocket, whether it was up doing some business at the Station, or just not included in this camp, who could say.

The most pleasant difference, Larry realized as they came close, no ringing. His ears were clear, harsh winds and tire scraping of course, but relatively speaking all was peaceful. Whatever nightmarish machine, communication, or whatever else caused the ringing, which was so loud it reached Main Colony miles away last time, was not here.

They pulled all the way up until they were a few dozen feet from the camp, and then Eric motioned Larry to stop. The tires rolled to a halt, and Larry, Eric, and Monica hopped out of the vehicle. Monica took the lead, with Larry and Eric together behind her, as they marched to the camp. Larry drew his gun, but Eric again motioned him, this time to wait.

Two spiders and a gorilla, dead ahead of them, meandering. They still looked like black silhouette figures. It was nothing but open rocky surface in front of the trio, not even a tall rock for cover. Monica drew her revolver, which looked like a tiny little thing in this vast open area. She stepped forward to establish her aim, and meet her enemy head-on. As she took one more step forward, in an instant, one of the meandering spiders twitched and shifted all its focus to her. Its four legs sprinted so fast and blindly it looked like it'd fall over itself. There it was, the first spider was charging right at her. Soon, another spider and the gorilla followed.

Larry and Eric stepped out to each side of her, holding their guns, but this was all Monica. The robots dead set on her, both arms holding her gun out. The wind careening into his helmet, Larry felt a chill down his whole body. He stood there, his hands pulsing with blood, looking over at Monica and back at the robots, itching to fire a shot. But he stayed his hand.

Monica first tried to get the spider while it was still far, firing her first shot. The flash of the shot illuminating her whole body in the semi-dark for just a moment. A loud bang, though the wind muffled it significantly. She looked forward, the silhouette, almost looking like a real spider from its shadow, still pressing forward. To its left, the other spider was only five feet behind it, the gorilla a little farther behind that.

Undeterred, Monica fired again twice. Two loud bangs, her gun pointed dead ahead. The robot still charging forward, nothing changed. Monica looked over at Eric, Larry couldn't see the expression on her face.

"It's the wind, I'm gonna wait until they're closer!" Monica shouted. They could barely hear her over the roar all around them.

Now as both spiders were closing in, Monica lined up her aim, firing one more shot at the first spider. No more than fifteen feet away. Nothing.

Monica screamed with frustration. Larry could see her hands shaking. She changed targets, firing a shot at the spider on the left. Nothing. She waited until the first spider was almost upon her, firing again. Nothing. It wasn't a silhouette anymore, it was two distinct pairs of wiry metal legs, the front two with a massive pair of blades, rushing forward.

Larry couldn't actually hear the clicks of Monica's empty gun, as she jammed her finger on its trigger; but at the same time, he *could* hear it as clearly as ever.

"No!" Monica screamed.

"Larry! Kill it!" Eric shouted.

Larry's gun was already up, following the oncoming robot in a straight line. Larry picked a point, the robot less than ten feet from Monica, and opened fire. Three crisp shots, two of them hitting the robot right in the small body, its soft spot. All four legs were intact, but the thing collapsed to the ground, falling right before Monica. Larry sighed with relief. Not only that he'd gotten it, but that before the heat of battle he'd remembered to take the last two blanks out of his magazine.

There was still another spider charging at Monica from the left. This time Eric stepped up, running towards the thing with his shotgun. As the spider changed its focus, locking onto and starting to run at Eric, there was no more than seven feet between them. Eric opened fire, a thunderous blast from his shotgun. He pumped it with his left hand and fired again. The spider was stopped dead in its tracks. The nearly point-blank blasts took it down, ripping through its legs and body, tearing it to pieces.

Monica stood still, watching. Eric almost looked like a cowboy, tearing apart the robot with confidence. Larry came up to her, everything still rushing, his ears, head, and body. He put a hand on her shoulder. She looked at him, confused and slightly wild-eyed.

"Come on, reload your gun, there's still more," Larry said.

The gorilla was coming at them, hurtling forward with momentum. They had also caught the attention of the last spider, of the three they'd originally seen. It hopped off a pile of scrap, junk and parts rolling down onto the ground, and it began running at them as well.

Monica snapped back into focus, dumping out the empty rounds, taking out six more and planting them into her cylinder with efficiency, the way Larry had taught her. Larry waited until she was finished, and then the two of them ran forward.

What happened next was a blur. The massive, heavy gorilla pounded forward at them. Though it had no face, only two pairs of husky assorted metal legs, shoulders, and a body, the thing inexplicably looked nothing short of blood-thirsty. As the distance between them closed from both sides, Larry and

Monica stopped dead in their tracks, raising their guns
together, aiming down sights.

Just as he was ready to shoot, green light filled his vision.
Larry was confused for a moment, before realizing what was
happening and being extremely grateful for the visor he wore.
The light was harsh, headache inducing, and made him want to
squint, but that was all. Pushing through it, Larry fired a shot,
piercing the device on the gorilla's left shoulder. He heard two
loud bangs right next to him, as Monica fired twice at the
gorilla. She finally hit, getting the gorilla on the leg and body.
They each fired two more times, and the monster of a robot was
finally brought down. It fell to the ground, still twitching.

One last spider was heading at the pair from diagonal left.
Larry and Monica turned to face it. As they did, Eric caught up
with them. Eric watched as Larry and Monica tore that robot
apart too. With a few decisive shots. Monica fired one last shot.
Then all they heard once again was the roaring wind, and the
three of them stood, panting.

"Let's go see if there's anything else here," Eric said. They
walked forward into the camp. It was empty. Piles of junk with
no real boundaries, the occasional half-built machine, of who
knows what intended purpose. There were lights in the camp,
dim red lights, like those back on the Station. Some lights were
completely invisible of course, infrared. Larry vaguely remembered this from the first camp, it was such a rush he had hardly
noticed the red tint.

They all looked around quietly for a while. Then, as they
stood near the center of the camp, Eric got their attention.

"Monica, what was that?" Eric said. He laughed, but not in a
pleasant way. Harsh, and cold.

"I..." Monica tensed up. "I just choked. It won't happen again."

"It took you six shots to finally hit something! I can't rely on that. I thought you said you were ready."

"I know. I know. By mission time I will be ready." Monica said.

Eric now turned to Larry, who was standing next to her. Eric shook his head slowly.

"I trusted you to train her, Larry. What are you, incompetent?"

Larry sighed. "She's got reloading down, Eric. I saw it. And she picked up in the second half of the fight. She just needs more...target practice."

"Fine. Get it done. I want another shooting demonstration from her in a few days. We're out of camps so just do it at the next best thing, the Range. You'd better get her mission ready, Larry. I'm gonna need you both as shooters."

"Understood," Larry replied.

Larry, Eric, and Monica made their way to the buggy to head back. There was nothing more to talk about, making the ride back tense and awkward. Larry mostly kept his eyes ahead while driving, but he occasionally looked back at Monica. She no longer fidgeted with her gun, or gleefully spun the cylinder. She no longer sat upright and dignified. She sat hunched forward, staring out into the distance. Looking back at the empty camp. On an empty planet.

18

L arry was on his morning route to work, ready for the big day ahead. Eric's mission report this morning made him do a double take, "THREE HOURS UNTIL MISSION TIME PEOPLE GRAB YOUR GEAR PACK YOUR SHIT FINISH UP AND GET GOING GO! GO! GO!" Larry almost never wasted time in the morning but today he was extra efficient. And yes, the message was in all capitals. Howe might've been rolling in his grave at the loss of military-style formality. Rolling around on the cold metal floor he was very slowly decomposing on, due to thin air, orbiting in space.

Larry got to the Water Treatment Plant. On his right, the familiar structure at the top of the hill. That same rushing river below him. With chunks of ice flowing down it. The place was busy with workers at this point, Larry could hear shouts and machinery going. He turned to his left, where most of the rest of Colony was, and saw someone else walking the same route, maybe two dozen feet from him. As he looked the person in the eyes, it was David.

"Larry!" David called out. David cut across and jogged to catch up with Larry. David reached his arm out, and Larry went to shake it, until noticing he was holding something.

"Monica's visor. If you could get that to her when you see her, that'd be great."

"Sure, will do." Larry replied.

David handed it to Larry. David then turned and stood, facing the horizon, the early morning sun just peeking over the tall mountain range in the distance. Larry did this as well, taking a deep breath.

"I'm ready for this." David said.

Larry looked over at him inquisitively. From David's face, he appeared very present.

"Oh yeah?" Larry said.

"Oh, I'm terrified, don't get me wrong. But I'm ready to do my job."

Larry nodded, looking back out at the distance. "You're a lot like me."

"Huh? I'm nothing like you." David replied. "I mean... not in a bad way."

"What do you mean?"

"You're bold. Reckless, even. Ready for a fight. I just think of that night mission where you and Stephanie came, with the robots. You hid behind..." David began laughing "You fought them hiding behind nothing but a buggy tire!"

They both laughed. They laughed for a whole minute. Larry sighed as they settled down, until he heard nothing but the soft howling of the wind. Even the workers at the plant had

stopped being noisy for a moment, and for that moment everything felt still.

"Stephanie, Eric, Monica, you guys are all like that." David
went on. "Frankly, I prefer to just sit back and work comfortably. I'm not one for thrill."

"I suppose..." Larry said.

"Yeah."

"No." Larry said. "No, I am like you. Howe, Eric,
Stephanie, and Monica, they all wanted to be in charge, in
some capacity. Sure, maybe they'd take orders if that's the
position they're in, if leadership weren't accessible at the
moment. But they've all chased the prize. Obsessed with it,
honestly."

"They all want to be in control?"

"Exactly." Larry said. "And that's not necessarily a bad thing.
It's not bad to be competitive. But I appreciate a guy like you,
who just wants to do his job. No need for ego."

"Yeah, you have a point." David replied, nodding in agreement. "You have a point."

"But who knows, maybe I'm wrong," Larry said. He cleared
his throat. "Alright, I'll go get this visor to Monica."

"Great. I don't know if you're aware already, Stephanie wants
to show you and Monica one last thing before the mission."

"About the ship?"

"Yep. She's at Engineering."

"Then I guess, we'll go see Stephanie." Larry said. "See you
on the mission, David."

"See you then." David replied.

Larry went off, heading for the Shooting Range. He looked
back and David was heading off in the other direction. The
ridiculous combat knife hanging from David's hip. Then again,

as melee weapons were not standard issue, it was, at least, a unique tool.

• - -

Monica was already there at the Shooting Range, firing away at targets. She was using the moving targets the engineers had set up. A target set up on a little rolling pair of wheels. The target itself was made from leftover gray fabric material from construction, with a target design painted on it. It already had a few bullet holes in it. Larry watched as Monica traced carefully, her arms steady. She fired a shot through the dead center of the fabric.

"Good Shot!" Larry shouted.

Monica took a deep breath, and grinned. "Yes. It was." She then did the reloading motion she and Larry had practiced so many times. Clean and efficient, she loaded six fresh rounds into her gun, and raised it as if to fire again, in one motion.

"You're ready." Larry said.

"Long as I don't choke again." Monica replied.

"You won't, trust me."

Monica raised an eyebrow, but then nodded. "Yeah, I've practiced enough now. I'm ready," she said, holstering her gun.

"Here, take this," Larry said, holding out the visor.

Monica took it. "Good. Anything else?"

"Stephanie wants to see us both. Something about the ship."

"Gee, I'm thrilled." Monica said dryly. "But, I wanted to get to Engineering anyway, so yeah I'll come."

"Alright, let's head over."

Monica went and took apart the moving target, and she and

Larry cleaned up the Shooting Range. They then began their walk over.

. -   -

Engineering, the main workshop and what was essentially a hub, for many small groups working on their independent projects, was very crowded. The building itself was a solid structure, housing projects from weathering and erosion, but most work took place in the large tents outside. Larry and Monica walked past the tents, seeing several groups of engineers busy with all their equipment laid out. There were also plenty of engineers at the workshop building itself, or moving things back and forth between it and the tents.

On this particular occasion, out in the distance from the tents on open ground, the massive Orca stood. The ship stood dozens of feet taller than the actual building in its vicinity. Having not spotted Stephanie yet, Larry began heading over to the ship. But Monica turned and went over to one of the small groups of engineers, inside the tent to their right. There were three engineers with their tools in hand working, one of them saw Monica and stood up. She hugged him. They talked briefly, and then hugged again. He wished her good luck as she went back over to Larry.

Larry simply waited, and then continued walking as Monica returned.

"Don't you have anyone to say goodbye to?" Monica asked. "We're about to put our lives at risk."

Larry shrugged.

As they approached the Orca, there were three more engineers at the base, working together. And then one engineer separate from the rest, tinkering, by themselves. And a security guard, keeping his distance. The group was at least ten feet from the loner.

"Eric definitely informed them of what she did," Monica said.

"Definitely," Larry agreed.

As they got close, Stephanie dropped what she was doing, stood and went right up to them. There was a bounce in her step, and as she got close, Larry could see she appeared excited.

"Welcome! I've got something to show you," Stephanie said.

"Back up, you're in my personal space," Monica said.

Stephanie made no reaction and held her smile. "Larry, you never updated me. Did they work on her?"

Larry caught his breath. "What are you *talking* about?"

"The moving targets. Did they help her aim?"

"Oh right. Yes, yes they did."

"Excellent. Now follow me."

Stephanie led them to the front of the ship. It now included two large metal tubular objects bolted on the sides, each a dozen feet long. Each had a large open latch with a bundle of wires, leading into a hole of a removed plate from the ship. Larry looked inside one of the tubes, there was a wide rounded head of an object staring back at him.

"By far our biggest, most expensive accomplishment these past two weeks. My design. Heat seeking missiles," Stephanie said.

Monica was peering through both tubes and looking them over, even running her hands on the ship. "Woah... how'd you do it?"

There was no response. Stephanie watched Monica but said nothing.

"How do they work?" Larry asked.

"Ah, glad you asked," Stephanie replied. "They're analog. Once activated, the missile uses infrared lights to steer itself to whatever heat source, no computers involved. Just good old fashioned machinery. A lot like those used during the Cold War, 20th Century. Which-"

"20th Century, I'm sure Howe would be excited at that," Monica remarked.

"Which saved us loads of time and resources." Stephanie finished. "Make sure the ship is pointing more or less *at* whatever you're firing at. The more of an angle you're shooting from, the more likely the missile won't be accurate. Face what you're gonna blow up."

Larry nodded. "How many missiles do we get?"

"Three. We were thinking four, but we're having a serious mechanical issue with the last one, I don't know why. We're trying one last time now to get it working, but don't hold your breath."

"Got it."

"Here, follow me inside the ship. I'll show you the new controls we added," Stephanie said. They followed her.

As they got to the control board inside, it was the usual layout of buttons and switches Larry was now familiar with, but as he sat in the pilot's chair there were two additional buttons to his left and right. These buttons hung out from the wall attached to loose wires, bolted down to the control board, but hanging up almost at Larry's shoulder height.

"Makeshift buttons, can you guess what they're for?" Stephanie said. "Each fires one missile from its respective side. You have two missiles on your left, one on your right. Don't forget."

"Got it."

"Here let me try it," Monica said. Larry got up and she took the seat, and grabbed onto the two triggers. She nodded approvingly, and stood back up. "Alright. This is good, fine addition to the ship. I think we're well-briefed now. Let's go find Eric."

"Let's go," Larry agreed. "Stephanie, you should come with us."

Stephanie sighed. "Might as well."

The three of them made their way off the ship. As they got back outside and started to walk off, Larry saw from the corner of his eye the security guard moving to catch up with them. Larry waved him off. The other engineers looked up at them too.

"I'll keep watch of her," Larry said, tapping the gun on his hip. The engineers, satisfied, returned to their work.

• -   -

In a setup much like the tents by Engineering, four scientists were outside behind Hydroponics of all places, running last minute tests. There were two scientists behind a blast shield standing back, watching the other two from around ten feet away. The other two were leaning over a table setting up chemicals, out in the middle of the open rocky area. Propped up behind the table was a sheet of metal. Those other two scientists were of course Eric and Ken.

Larry, Monica and Stephanie came up behind the blast shield. The two scientists stepped aside out of their way, one of them Larry noticed, eyeing Stephanie in a very unnerved way.

Monica waved her arms. "Hey leader, we're ready to go, hurry up!"

Eric looked up from his work at them. Larry could faintly hear Eric laugh, and then he turned to Ken and nodded. "Demolition Test is a go! Three....Two....One!"

Eric and Ken jogged back to the blast shield, Eric laying down a wire on the ground as he went. Once all five of them were crowded behind the blast shield, Eric held up two ends of the wire to his face. He pushed them together.

For a brief second there was nothing. Then a thunderous boom as a cloud of white smoke shot out, spewing dust and small rocks everywhere. Monica jerked back in surprise. Larry stood firm but his hands shot to his ears. Eric clapped his hands together and shouted "Haha yes!"

There was no table left, and the metal plate flew back several feet.

"That metal was bolted to the ground," Ken clarified.

"Very securely," Eric added.

Larry and Monica gathered themselves. Stephanie was standing unphased. She looked over at Eric and pretended to yawn.

"Wow, you made something blow up. They've been doing that since when, the 1300s?"

"How's that fourth missile going," Eric replied. "Oh and by the way, maybe keep your mouth shut since I almost considered giving you handcuffs for this mission. I only didn't cause it's a safety hazard."

Stephanie scoffed. But then muttered, "Yeah, yeah you can trust me."

Eric turned to Larry and Monica. "She showed you the missiles?"

They nodded.

"Well, I'll pack up my stuff. Larry, head to the vehicle lot so you can grab a buggy to load onto the ship. Then we should be ready to go."

Larry nodded again, and turned to head to the vehicle lot alone. But first, Ken extended out his hand, and Larry shook it.

"I'll accompany them to the ship, but probably get going before you arrive. See you after the mission, Larry."

"See you, Ken."

• -   -

To get to the closest vehicle lot, Larry had to walk all the way back the way he came and a bit further. He was noticeably stiff. It didn't make sense why, of all days today, he'd slept pretty well. Maybe the toll of all the running around, the combat, he'd been in recently. He wasn't sure. Another buzz of adrenaline would get him going again, though, he knew that. Wouldn't be anything to worry about.

Still made for a painful walk. Passing by that familiar lengthy tarp, housing crops. The wind only gently rattled it this time. Then an open stretch of rocky land. Then the tents with the engineers, barely noticeable. And another open stretch all the way to the vehicle lot. The near silence in his ears was unnerving, like before it made everything feel still. So still that it felt fake.

And coming up on the vehicle lot, picking out a buggy that was charged and ready, wiping some dust off the exposed part of its tires that its cover couldn't reach. He wished when he turned it on it would give a loud rev, not a quiet electric pur, that did nothing to alleviate the empty silence. Larry stopped for a moment, crouching down, leaning his helmet on the buggy. He took deep breaths. There he stayed for a moment until he gathered himself. He was ready to go.

• - -

The crew was all set to go. At the Orca right by Engineering, which Stephanie had been working on only a short time ago. Stephanie, Eric, and Monica were nowhere to be seen, so Larry assumed they were already on board. And as he drove up in the buggy, looking through the ship's front glass for just a moment, he saw Monica at the pilot's seat. He curved around the ship, still a good 20 feet from it. Behind it he saw the ramp set up leading into the ship, and David and the two medics, Devin and Jose, standing there, ready to guide him. Larry drove all the way around, and pulled up a good ten feet behind the ship, the buggy not yet oriented properly.

Larry looked back at them. "Tell me when, David!"

"You know what you're doing?" David shouted back.

"Yeah. I've seen this before."

Larry placed his hand on the shoulder of the passenger seat, rotated the car around, and began carefully backing up. David gave a few micro-adjustments, which Larry made, but for most of it Larry was on point, not needing direction. The buggy climbed up that ramp, 45 degrees upward. And just as before, it glided through the ship's opening with just a few inches to spare on each side.

Larry was now inside the ship. David and the medics went in the same way, through the back. They were in the Cargo Hold now, the boxes having been removed. The buggy took up almost the whole space, but not all of it. The four cryo-stasis chambers, two on each side, those 6 and ½ foot tall very confined machines, were there. One could just narrowly fit around the buggy and still use the chambers. David, Devin, and Jose sidestepped around the big bulky vehicle, to the Cargo Hold's entrance.

Monica at the pilot's seat peered back, and she closed the opening to outside at the back of the ship. And for a moment, as she hadn't yet turned on the lights, the Cargo Hold was actually dark. Only natural light from the front window lit the ship.

Larry climbed out of the buggy and made his way around to join his crewmates. Stephanie and Eric were already seated in the long row of seats, across from each other. David and the medics still stood by the Cargo Hold. Devin looked at Larry as he came around.

"Jose and I have been on rescue missions before, don't get me wrong. But usually those involving natural accidents, not....robots."

Now that Larry was up close, he could see Devin was pale. Maybe it was just the lighting, but it looked that way to him. Devin, who was the shortest one there by a good few inches. Had to be one of the shortest at the Colony. Even disregarding Security, the average height of the men and women of ESSO-3 was definitely above that of the general population. Healthiest candidates only, the criteria didn't just apply to mental health.

"They're deceptively quick, and aggressive. Prone to sudden movements," Larry said. "Just keep your eyes and ears peeled."

"I'm staying by you, or her," Jose chimed in, pointing to Monica. "Give myself some protection. I'm too young to die."

David chuckled. "You are pretty young, Jose. But you think the rest of us wanna die either?"

His tone leveled as he said it. David's joke fell flat. There was an awkward silence, and David cleared his throat. Things felt somber. Larry turned to the two medics.

"I'm sorry about what happened to Grace."

"I miss her," Devin said quietly. "She was just, so...." Devin's voice broke. "She was a good friend."

"She was an inspiration," Jose agreed.

"We're not going to die meaningless deaths," Larry said. "We're going to get through this mission. And I'll protect whoever I can."

The other three gave silent agreement. They walked over and took their seats one by one. All of them besides Larry taking their seats in the right row, Eric's row. Larry didn't look at the others, he knew what they were doing. He only looked over at Stephanie. And she stared at the ground. Head down, shoulders hunched, a blank face. Looking well below eye level. The attention only changed when Monica addressed the crew.

"Alright everyone, strap in. We're going to Gamma-2."

19

Their tiny ship, so massive back on ESSO-3, but beyond insignificant out here, was gliding through the open black nothingness all around them. Out the window one could see mostly stars, with a small dot of a destination in the distance, and the Sun creeping in from the left view. Gravity was gone, ESSO-3's orbit had been broken, and the Crew of Seven all sat still, biding their time, as their pilot took them through the route. They were getting close.

"Last time Larry and I were here during our fly-by, we came across a hellish cluster of structures," Monica said. "We may have to stay in orbit and revolve around the planet a bit to see, but keep your eyes peeled. That's our destination."

Eric, who had been delicately fiddling with the fingers of his robotic arm, cleared his throat. "Larry."

"Yeah?"

"You like to name things. You named the camps. What are we gonna call this one?"

Larry answered without hesitation. "The City."

"Perfect. Off to Robot City everyone. Capital of RobotLand."

Devin chuckled at this.

The ominous Gamma-2 with its maroon hue came into view. A smooth and glassy surface at first. But as they approached, the details became clear. First, the massive craters all over the surface. And then, soon enough, dozens of tiny scattered dots, looking unnatural and wrong. The Robots' structures. There had to be hundreds in total.

The Orca came into orbit. They were still hundreds of miles above the surface, but with virtually no atmosphere in the way, it was all very apparent. All the major features could be made out. Not that there were too many distinct ones, just mountains, valleys, craters, and plateaus.

"Keep your eyes peeled for the City," Monica said.

But there were no signs of it yet. No major clumps of the artificial structures, nothing as big and obtrusive.

"I'm gonna head about the orbit until I spot something." Monica said.

She rotated the ship around so that Gamma-2 was to the left of their view, and throttled the ship forward. They flew directly into the thin reddish hue of the horizon, matching the curvature of orbit. Larry watched the planet's surface recede below them, looking out for the City.

"It'll be closer to the north pole," Larry reminded them.

Sure enough, as they had crossed no more than halfway around the planet, they spotted it. It was jarring. Had to be dozens of structures, but all very sprawled and spread out. A dense clump in the center of it. Monica still moved with the curvature of orbit, but brought the ship down, closing in. The closer they got to the City, the more they could see just how disjointed it was. It stood on a straight run of plateau that was miles long and wide.

The ground got closer and closer as the ship gradually dipped down, until they were only several miles above and before the City. At this point, the flimsy atmosphere did begin to put up a fight, as debris was kicked up against the front of the ship. Most of it was too small to even notice, save for the sounds of little rocks bouncing off the ship. And the turbulence of a slight wind resistance rocking the ship gently. Monica shrugged this off and pressed forward.

There were no clouds to block the view. Only that dim red haze dispersing as they approached the ground. The City was in clear view now. A bizarre layout, all sorts of shapes. Tall thin towers for buildings. Large open nets of repeated buildings, rectangular structures, irregularly shaped structures. Squinting, Larry could make out cables laid down all over the place. But very close to the center, what could not be missed, a massive telescope. Peaking out at an odd angle, higher than everything else, like a beacon of the City.

Eric's eyes lit up. "It's so much larger than the ones on the Station!"

"And it's facing the right way now, isn't it? I mean we're on the side of the planet facing the Sun," Devin said.

"Gamma-2 hardly rotates," Monica clarified. "Maybe once every... 40 ESSO-3 days. We're fine on that, don't worry. We weren't going to show up only to have to wait twelve hours to see whatever it is they're looking at."

"Also means the Robots constructed this telescope to monitor the same region of sky for a very long period of time." Larry added.

"They're watching something, alright. This is our chance." Eric said. "Take us in, Monica."

Which was redundant of him to say, as Monica was already doing that. But just after Eric had said it, Monica reacted to something else. Larry saw it now too. In the corner of the front view, somewhere in the distance above the City, a tiny bright flash. A flash that was moving towards them.

"It's coming right at us!" Monica said.

"Missile? They do have defenses." Eric said. "Expecting us. Or someone else."

"What? That was pretty damn fast." David chimed in. "What do they have, radar? Did they detect us? Send some kind of encoded transmission that we're supposed to-"

"Doesn't matter," Stephanie interrupted. She spoke sternly. "Monica, listen closely."

"Yes?"

"Don't fire yet, we need to overcompensate to make sure this works. Wait until I tell you."

"Got it."

The small ball of fire ahead of them was closing in and growing large. Whatever the actual warhead looked like, it was impossible to tell as it was a blur. It crept up from the bottom right corner into the center view. It grew from a tiny dot into something big in just several seconds.

"Now!" Stephanie shouted.

Monica took a hand off the controls and clamped her thumb on the makeshift left button. They couldn't hear the launch over the Orca's roaring engines, but a few seconds later they saw their own ball of fire shooting forward from the left corner of view. At first it just shot straight out, but as the two objects in the sky got close to each other, they both made sharp diversions. At once there was a huge burst as the two objects obliterated each other.

Everyone but Stephanie cheered. But even Stephanie still had a smug smile of satisfaction. David gave a massive sigh of relief. Devin and Jose looked at him, equally relieved themselves.

"Man that was too close." David said.

"Excellent work!" Eric said. "Great job guys."

"Not over yet," Stephanie said.

And she was right. Within seconds, out of the same bottom right corner of view, another tiny, almost innocuous looking bright flash. Eric's excitement disappeared immediately, and David's apprehension returned.

"Alright, you two know what to do," Eric said.

"No." Stephanie said. "We have to turn around now."

"What? We're so close to the City!" Eric shot back.

"No, she's right." Larry said. "Turn around now and land. I can drive us to the City. But if we run out of our missiles we're screwed."

"Quick, do it now." Stephanie reiterated.

Monica compiled without a word. She made a harsh maneuver, rotating the engines all the way forward, mid-flight, until the ship almost stalled. The whirr of the machinery rose above the sound of the engines themselves, as she pushed the rotation mechanism to its limit. She began landing immediately, the engines, having rotated fully, were propelling the ship down and backwards. All while she kept the front facing forward, so they were still facing the incoming missile.

Even as the Orca was receding, the missile was rapidly catching up. It was practically upon them when Monica finally fired the second counter-missile of her own. Shooting out from the ship, it almost immediately collided with the incoming missile, blowing up right in their faces, creating a shockwave that rocked the ship.

The monitor that had annoyed Larry so much during his training was flashing bright yellow, but Monica was still in firm control. The maroon rocky features and mountains of the planet came into full view. The ship was still flying back, but they decelerated to a steady crawl. They touched down abrasively on Gamma-2's surface.

• -   -

The crew waited a very long few minutes, but there were no signs of any more incoming missiles. They were on the ground now, a few miles from the City. Monica had turned her chair to face the others, catching her breath. The crewmates unstrapped, standing up and stretching out.

The first thing Larry noticed was how he bounced out of his seat. It was an uncomfortable feeling. He lifted a knee, and felt like he would bring it up so fast it got knocked out of its socket. Larry thought back to the very first time he had touched down on ESSO-3. He didn't fully remember it, but this must have been what that was like, except even more.

Eric noticed everyone else feeling it out. "The gravity. We'll take a few moments outside before leaving to get accustomed."

"If anyone needs magnet boots..." David started.

"Absolutely not, that'll just slow everyone down," Eric said.

Larry wandered past the others to the Cargo Hold. He laid a hand on the buggy, the big mass in front of him that took up the whole room basically. He reached over and ran his hand on the thick tire. He stood and watched the others when he was done.

They were all facing Eric now. Monica was just putting away her revolver, which she had inspected once again. Stephanie had her toolkit in hand, which had been thoroughly searched a number of times before the mission. David, Devin, and Jose were also now standing and facing Eric. It was a tight space but they had still formed somewhat of a semicircle.

"Alright, you were all briefed this morning, but in case you forgot, or lost it while shitting your suit when those missiles were coming at us, I'll reiterate," Eric said. "We're about to enter a combat situation. For some of you, this is your very first combat situation. It will be chaotic, it will be unpredictable. But whatever you do, stick to protocol."

"We're really about to do this," Devin whispered under her breath. She laughed quietly. No one responded.

"Here's the plan. Larry over there is gonna drive us in. We will drive until we reach the giant telescope. Should be very hard to miss. Once there, we will use the explosives we brought to blow our way in. Hopefully we won't damage anything sensitive while doing this, a more tactful option unfortunately did not present itself.

Once inside, keep your head down and eyes up. The robots can come out of nowhere at times. Stay close to one of our shooters, Larry or Monica, at all times. I will be, with my shotgun, the last resort shooter, should anything get close. Remember your roles. Remember your training. We get in there, find the telescope, find out what the Robots are monitoring, and then get the hell out of there. Any questions?"

There were none. They went and got their supplies. Eric grabbed his shotgun, the medics got their equipment. Nothing more was to be said. They loaded their supplies into the buggy, climbing around and over it carefully. Stephanie and David went outside briefly during this to set up a cheap, collapsible ramp they had brought along, for the buggy to unload. Soon, once that was taken care of, everyone took their seats in the vehicle, and was ready to go. They opened the circular docking opening, and Larry drove them out.

• -   -

The buggy's tires once again scraped against rocks, now on its second foreign world. Larry had to watch the ground very closely; slight bumps threatened to hurtle the whole vehicle upwards. It was definitely only a task for those comfortable behind the wheel.

All around them was a dome of thin red haze, a sky so thin they could see the stars and blackness of space above it. It felt wrong. It was like a strange hybrid of day and night. Like looking through frosted glass. It made Gamma-2 feel unreal, like a simulation world that hadn't finished rendering.

They were driving across a large open plateau of maroon colored rock. It was littered with large open craters, but they were spaced out enough that Larry had no trouble avoiding them. Around the sides of the plateau, rock formations like canyons, towers, and mountains stood off in the distance. On this vast open space was their little vehicle, heading to the City.

While Larry kept his eyes forward, as always, no one spoke. Eric, to Larry's right, held his shotgun in his lap. He stared out ahead just like Larry. Behind them, Monica had her gun in her hands. David, Devin, and Jose sat poised, ready, glancing around. Even Stephanie sat still and was composed. In between them, a few packed crates. The crates were filled with bundles of sticks of the explosive material, each beige stick loaded and wrapped in wires.

The Outskirts of the City were very quickly approaching. For a little while it appeared empty, but then Larry saw movement. At the very edge of the City, which they were coming up on, it was mostly piles of parts. It led into a wide field of what were presumably solar panels, a messy and disjointed array, spanning a few hundred feet in each direction. A mesh of cables were laid all over between the panels. This array was made up of over a dozen rows, and after passing a few piles of scrap the buggy drove through two of these rows. It was wide enough for the vehicle, and it would've been wide enough for two, but not three.

There had been a few spiders digging around in the piles of scrap as they passed, but all off in the distance, spread out enough that it wasn't an issue for Larry to drive right through. The Solar Panels Array was completely empty. Up ahead, at the edge of his view, the prize. The telescope peaking out, surrounded by structures in the distance, it was a straight shot to it. As he drove by row after row of solar panels, it was so unnaturally repetitive, it felt as though there were walls closing in around them.

The buggy came to a clearing as it passed the last rows of solar panels. Here there were now plenty of robots in view. None in their direct path, but all spread out over the distance. Little movements here and there. They saw mostly spiders for now, but couldn't clearly make every individual out. The clearing opened up to a much more - almost urban - interior. To their left, a massive structure. It was at least three stories tall, and it was mostly an intricate layering of steel pipes, curving all around a few central cylinders.

"Refinery, probably. For their raw minerals," Eric said under his breath.

The others in the back of the vehicle all looked out. Monica leaned out to see it, and with a quick glance Larry could see the look of awe on her face.

In the gaps in that structure, they could see glimpses of where the pipes lead behind it. Dozens of feet behind it was machinery, actively mining the ground below. There were only brief flashes of its visibility through the Refinery as they drove, and most of what Larry saw was machinery. But he also caught the movement of something big. Something much bigger than a spider was out there. He could hardly make out its shape.

"Do you guys...." Larry muttered.

"What?" Eric asked.

"Don't know what I saw, but I'm glad it's off in the distance," Larry replied.

To their right were several smaller structures. It more resembled a camp from back on ESSO-3. There was a machine as tall as a building, which looked like a mechanical crane. Some piles of scrap laid about, but only a small amount. A tall tower, mostly of thin mesh. Wires on the ground, in between all of it.

"Maybe the radar they used on us? Communication?" David asked

Beyond them, rows and rows of copies of the same familiar machine.

"Prism-computers," Stephanie said.

Another identical copy of the Communication Tower came up, this one had a spider crawling around on top of it. The spider's limbs were sprawled out, its two blades doing surprisingly surgical work, appearing to be handling a pipe. At the base of the tower, which they didn't notice right away, a gorilla stood.

"Eyes down!" Eric shouted.

The crewmates complied, ducking their heads. There were murmurs once they realized what Eric had spotted. But the gorilla, though appearing to stare them down, made no sudden moves as they passed.

"This is getting tense, Eric," Monica said.

"I know. We might get out of the buggy soon. But you should keep going Larry, we're almost there."

The buildings on their sides began to narrow, as they could now see the telescope coming up in full view. Dead ahead of them, at the center of it all. It was peaking out at the top of a small cylindrical structure, only one story. No windows or features of course, just a small minimalist Observatory to house the giant telescope; perhaps maybe data it collected as well.

On their left, the Refinery still stretched out, almost all the way to the Observatory itself. To their right, more and more small structures tightly packed together. More and more visible movement and robots jittering about, at less of a distance. Larry kept his foot jammed down on the pedal, the buggy was shaking as they moved and its tires couldn't spin any faster.

"We're spotted! Something's following us." Monica shouted.

Larry looked to his left and saw what she meant. At the very top line of pipes of the Refinery, a single spider was aggressively sprinting forward, angling ever-slightly towards them, and almost matching their speed. It moved on two sets of pipes, its legs gripping and slipping repeatedly on the thin surface. It looked absolutely unstable, but the spider did not fall.

Larry heard the click as Monica cocked her gun.

"Wait!" Eric said.

"Don't shoot, you'll alert them," Larry agreed.

Larry had been in the exact same seated position for so long that he could feel his leg tingling. His whole body felt a bit numb, and as if he were coming out of it. His hands felt as though they could drift off the wheel at any second. But he held firm.

A screech pierced the air around them. The extremely thin air. It sounded like a quiet whisper because of that, but Larry was immediately alert. Closing in from both sides, there were robots suddenly running out from places where they hadn't even seemed to be. It was all in Larry's peripheral, and all in a very short moment of time, but they were absolutely being swarmed.

Larry slammed the brake. The tires came to a screeching halt, and the front of the buggy was almost lifted up into the air. Two spiders, one from the left and one from the right, fell and landed just a dozen feet in front of them. They hadn't fallen, so much as they'd been propelled through the air and floated in a straight path to the ground. There were so many things happening, sounds coming from behind him, the others' voices, so much going on that Larry had to tune out. The two spiders in front clamped on the rocky ground as they landed, dust kicking up everywhere. Larry drew his gun.

Both coming right at him, Larry picked the one on the left. Larry blasted several shots through its legs and body, disabling the creature. It slipped, stopped in its tracks, and toppled to the ground. The other spider was almost upon them, but Eric had his shotgun ready. He blasted the spider with three explosive shots, it went down after the second. Larry turned the wheel sharply, preparing to drive around the two dead robots.

He heard a shriek. It snatched his attention. An ear-piercing shriek, that came from a person. He had no idea which one.

"Drive!" Eric shouted. Larry did so immediately. He maneuvered around the two dead robots and drove ahead at full speed. Robots still closing in on them from all sides, including from the front.

As Larry jolted forward, he heard a loud thud behind him. He quickly glanced back. David had landed on the crates.

"What happened?" Larry and Eric both asked.

"He was hit!" Monica responded.

"What's happening... I... I can't see!" David cried.

"David, let me see." Devin started. She went to get out of her seat, but as the buggy rocked, Jose stopped her, muttering "Not now."

"Was he blinded!?" Monica said.

"He was wearing a visor!" Eric said.

"Must've been a defect." Stephanie said. "You *rushed* us Eric, gave us too many tasks. Gave us non-essential tasks. This is the price of foregoing efficiency."

"Am I'm blind! I...I'll never see again!? Eric!" David cried.

The enclosing robots were now upon them. Several spiders and a few gorillas charging them from the front. Larry couldn't see behind him, but assumed the situation was much the same. Larry made a sharp left, hugging the left side of the path, which was still the Refinery.

"Above! Above!" Monica shouted.

Larry had just enough time to turn and glance at what was falling straight at them.

•-   -

A spider landed in their vehicle. Larry slammed the breaks.

He instinctively leapt out of the driver's seat, hurtling out several feet from the low gravity, landing onto the open ground. He sprinted away from the buggy. He turned around with his gun raised as soon as he could.

Four imposing wiry metal legs. It took up almost the whole buggy. Two of them with their pair of blades swinging wildly. Four people in white environment suits outside of the buggy, and they were scattered, all rushing away in different directions. Eric was still in the passenger seat and had his shotgun raised. Somebody's body was under the Spider, it had been crushed, possibly worse. Larry could only see the helmet sticking up. Larry identified Stephanie with her toolkit, heading directly away from him. Two others headed off towards the Refinery, he couldn't recognize them. But when he saw the fourth person heading to his left, stumbling and falling, he knew who it was.

Larry ran straight to this fourth crewmate. As he sprinted around the buggy, he saw Eric battling the Spider from the corner of his eye, as it reached its stringy limbs and tried to swing at him. Larry ran right past and got to the stumbling person, who was on their knees, and about to be overrun. Robots were coming out from every direction.

Larry got over and put his arm around the person for support. He got to his feet.

"Who?" David asked.

"Larry. You're safe. We need to go."

Larry led David forward. There was a Communication Tower right in front of them; It was the only cover within reach. Larry wanted to utilize the bounce in their step, but David was unstable and had no bearings. To compensate, Larry had to walk slower instead. They marched toward the tower, but there was not a lot of time to get there.

Larry could hear the crunching and pounding of rocks beneath the crowd of encroaching robots. At least five robots on his right, a handful on his left, all focusing on just him and David, as the others had split to engage the rest of the crewmates. That was at least a dozen robots coming right at him alone. Larry kept marching forward.

But he also heard footsteps running right at him from behind, much nimbler and lighter. He couldn't turn around to see it, but soon enough another crewmate in their white suit had come up, and was supporting David on the right. Together the three of them were able to move faster. Larry saw from the corner of his eye, this new crewmate, carrying a toolkit. They were also holding one of the crates by its handle.

They came up to the tower, took a turn and went around it. As they got behind it, they set David down so he sat leaning against the structure. They very briefly panted and caught their breath.

"I helped. Now you'd better protect us, Larry." Stephanie said.

Larry nodded, having already drawn his gun again. He took a quick sweeping count. Six robots from his now left side, four spiders, two gorillas. To his right side, seven robots, all spiders. Larry got started firing away.

Larry emptied a whole magazine into the crowd on the left. Shot after shot, the sounds muffled by the thin air. He hit several of them, but only managed to bring down one spider. Larry reloaded as fast as he could. "It's too many to shoot." Larry said.

"I could use the explosives," Stephanie said.

"Are you sure?" Larry said.

"Yes. We have to. I'll wait till they're close enough, and no closer."

"Okay."

As Larry unloaded more shots, Stephanie reached down and opened the crate she had brought. Inside it were three neatly wrapped bundles of beige sticks. She also opened her toolkit and brought out the detonator device. She hooked the device onto her belt. She then grabbed two bundles of explosives in her arm, and had the last one in hand ready to throw.

As Larry turned to the right side crowd to soften them up, he noticed that the buggy was gone. He stopped briefly to use his earpiece, and kept firing as he talked.

"Eric, do you come in?"

There was a pause. "Yes. Larry, who are you with?"

"Stephanie and David. You have the buggy?"

"Yes, I had to drive off to get out of there, there were too many of them. Where are you now?"

"Big tall Communication Tower, right where we stopped. You can't miss it."

"I'll come around to you."

"Got it." Larry said. He stopped for a moment to reload. He was burning through ammunition. "Have you come in touch with Monica?"

Eric grunted. "Yes, but not in a while. She's with Jose. In the...Refinery. It's a labyrinth in there, so I'm coming to you first. You should try to reach her."

"Okay."

"Larry, above us!" Stephanie shouted.

Larry looked up. There was a spider crawling rapidly down the Communication Tower. Larry aimed straight up and fired shots right into it.

"Wait!" Stephanie tried to warn him, but he had reacted too quickly. The spider's body came tumbling down at them. It was slow enough that they were able to dive out of the way. Except for David, whom the body narrowly missed. David jumped.

"What was that!" David cried.

"No time to explain, you're safe though!" Larry said, as he got back to his feet. But they had lost time. Three spiders and a gorilla were coming from the left side. Four spiders from the right side. And they were just dozens of feet away.

Stephanie threw two of the bundles to her left. She threw the last one to her right. She waited until the left side crowd was on top of the explosives, and used the detonator.

A huge explosion went off in front of them, sending dust, rocks, and shrapnel in all directions. Stephanie and Larry both dropped to the ground instinctively. Metal legs, blades, and plates flew out everywhere.

Disoriented, Larry got to his feet. His ears ringing, which he was almost accustomed to by now. And his vision blurry. He made a broad sweep. The crowd from the left had been all but disintegrated, torn to bits. The Communication Tower, though still standing, was unstable and leaning slightly. To his right, three spiders still charging forward, as if nothing had happened. He was so dazed that this hardly shocked him into action. Further right, in the distance there was a vehicle moving towards him, the buggy. Behind, Larry could only take a quick glance, but there was plenty of movement from the array of prism-computers. They had probably attracted more attention.

Larry had to act fast. Without thinking, Larry sprinted away from the Communication Tower, away from everything, towards the array of prism-computers, into the wide open. Nothing but empty rocky surface and faint redness for hundreds of feet in front of him. Larry struggled forward firing shots in the air. The three spiders were drawn to it, closing in on him within moments, away from the others.

"What are you doing!?" He could faintly hear Stephanie shout.

Everything was faded. There were still too many to shoot. He was almost out of bullets, he couldn't see or think straight. Larry simply ran into the hazy redness. It engulfed him. He ran until he could feel that the robots were upon him. And he tumbled to the ground.

He faced up. One spider out in front sprung at him. All he could see was this blur of motion coming at him. He was about to let it have him. But something changed. Over everything else he could faintly hear the scraping of tires.

Larry sprung to his feet, dodging the attack, and ran desperately to the sound. His entire body ached madly, it was burning, but he pushed through it. He pushed through, completely ignoring the constant pounding of metal on rocks behind him. He ran several more feet before falling face forward into the ground. He caught himself with his hands before his helmet got hit. He felt as the buggy drove right past him, his body still on the ground.

Larry finally looked up, and saw the buggy about a dozen feet from him. Eric was standing on the driver's seat; A tall white figure pelting down the spiders with bullets. There was already one spider body right beside Larry, still twitching. The second spider had gone down just as he looked. And the third one, poised to jump onto the hood of the buggy, Larry drew his gun and assisted Eric in tearing it to bits.

As they finished Larry laid back down on the ground to catch his breath. The pounding in his head began to subside.

Eric brought the buggy over to just a few feet from him, got out, and walked over. He reached out his organic hand and pulled Larry up. Both men were panting.

"You are so damn lucky to be alive," Eric said.

Larry nodded.

"Come on, we have to go find Monica. Now."

Eric and Larry went back to the buggy. As they got there, Larry went for the driver's seat.

"You sure you wanna drive after all that?"

"It's second nature to me," Larry replied. "Let me do my job."

Eric gave no argument. He got into the passenger seat, and fed more shells into his shotgun. Larry set his hands on the wheel, took one more deep breath, and drove them back to the Communication Tower.

● -   -

As they arrived, David still sat leaning against the big structure. It was too faint to hear, but he looked to be whistling to himself. The carcass of the robot that had fallen from the tower was in its same spot just a few feet from David, almost completely motionless now. Stephanie was knelt over, her arms buried in the body of the thing, and she appeared to be dissecting it.

Larry pulled up to them with the buggy, and Eric got out.

"What in God's name are you doing, Stephanie?" Eric said.

Larry looked more closely, and saw she was using David's huge combat knife, with the ornament wooden handle, cutting through the thing's wires. Her toolkit was open beside her, its contents in disarray.

"Using this knife to dig out my tools which were stuck under this big dead robot." Stephanie replied. "For once your bravado came in handy, Eric."

"We need to go. Take what you've recovered and leave the rest." Eric said. "Larry, make sure she gives up that knife as soon as possible, okay?"

"Definitely," Larry said.

"If you wanna be efficient," Stephanie said to Eric, "Go help David back into the buggy."

Eric did just that, and Stephanie wrapped up her dissection, packed the disorganized toolkit, and got in one of the back seats. Within a minute the four of them were ready to go.

"Please, please let her still be there..." Eric muttered. He used his earpiece. "Monica. Monica, come in. Monica!"

But there was no response. Eric tried again.

"Jose, Come in."

Nothing on the other end but silence.

"Monica!" Eric shouted at the top of his lungs. He slammed his robotic fist on the hood of the buggy, startling David who felt the vibration.

"No, no, no! We took too long! What was I supposed to do, I couldn't be in two places at once..." Eric's voice broke as he finished the sentence.

He buried his head in his left hand.

"I'm sorry, Eric." Larry muttered.

"We're not done," Eric started. "We'll drive through the Refinery. Take a good look. Until we find them, or their bodies. I don't *care* how long..."

"Eric." Larry said.

"I know."

"We can't stay out here."

"I know."

"We have to get David to safety."

Eric sighed. He lifted his head and sat back up. He gave one more slam on the hood, and grimaced. "Let's go."

They drove back. They drove parallel to the path they'd come. Past the Communication Towers. Past the Mechanical Crane, and other small structures. Without much atmosphere, there was no howling wind. Mostly silence. Movement of more robots out in the distance, no confrontations, just a subtle threat just out of reach.

They returned to the Outskirts, and the vast Solar Panels Array. They drove back the row adjacent the one they'd come. Row after row of solar panels, unnatural repetition, walls closing in on them. Again and again.

"Devin," Larry said. "What happened to her?"

"Killed. Spider landed right on her, crushed her bones. Cut her up. Body fell out during the chase actually." Eric gave a brief, empty chuckle. "Man, you're lucky you didn't have to see that."

Eventually they left the Solar Panels Array. Passed a few piles of scrap, and soon they were clear of the City entirely. Just open plateau from there. Mountains on the sides, and in the distance, but this flat stretch of land was all that mattered. Stephanie took out her tracker, but it wasn't needed.

They found the Orca. There was their ship, standing in place. Not a speck of dust to be seen on it, thanks to the nearly non-existent winds of Gamma-2. It was exactly the way they had left it. They left the buggy outside. The crewmates got out, made their way around. They returned to the ship, just as they had left it.

20

Larry and Stephanie stood aside as Eric led David past the rows of empty seats, to the Cargo Hold. Eric kicked aside a pair of magnet boots left in the aisle, making a loud thunk. For just that second everything wasn't silent. Once at the Cargo Hold, Eric, his arm still around David, stopped and gazed at the ominous cryo-chamber looming before him.

"You agree to undergo cryo, David? If there's a chance for treatment we'd best...preserve..."

"I know," David said quietly. "I agree to it."

"Alright."

Eric pulled the lever on the side of the cryo-stasis chamber, the glass lid popped open. He helped David clumsily remove his environment suit, and carefully laid himself in the chamber. He put the straps in David's hand and allowed him to fasten himself in.

"It'll be over in an instant David. Stay strong."

David sighed.

Eric shut the lid. He pressed the Freeze button, gasses came down, the glass fogged up, and David was soon no longer visible. Larry and Stephanie now joined him, they left the Cargo Hold, and took their seats in the aisle the two of them across from him.

Eric gave a bitter laugh.

"So that's it then. Monica, Jose, Devin. Gone, right?" Eric said.

"Unfortunately," Larry replied.

"Mission failed. Mission failed." Eric scoffed. "God, why did I ever think this was a good idea? To send us out here, unprepared, completely in the dark, to get killed."

"There was no way we'd be fully prepared," Larry said. "We were dealing with things totally new here, uncharted territory. That was a risk we knowingly took."

"You were probably running off the high from the success of Howe's mission," Stephanie chimed in. "Now you know better."

"Only *you* would call a mission where we lost half our crewmates a success, Stephanie." Eric said. "You truly have no conscience, do you."

"But we gained knowledge, Eric." Larry said. "Without the Station mission, we'd have never learned what we've learned about the Robots."

"Knowledge is not worth sacrificing lives."

"Knowledge of our enemies could *save* lives down the line."

"Then we truly have failed." Eric said. "Because the most important knowledge of all, perhaps for our whole species, the knowledge of what else is out there. To not mince words, Alien Life. We had a chance at it, and we failed, and lost three good people."

Stephanie stood up. "I know I'm the last person you want to hear it from, Eric, but the most efficient course of action is returning to ESSO-3. We're spent."

"I agree with her," Larry said. "I'll fly us back home. We get David medical attention. And if we want to come back, and try and finish the Mission, we gather up more security officers, some medics...."

"No." Eric said firmly. Larry and Stephanie both gave him cold, judging looks. But Eric did not back down.

"Eric..." Larry started.

"I said no. I'm not leading any more people to their deaths. Not under my command. I don't care if they volunteer. Sit your ass back down Stephanie."

Stephanie scoffed, but obliged. "Then what do we do, huh?"

"Look, you two are right about one thing. We're on the verge of perhaps the most important knowledge we can come by. We have to finish the Mission." Eric said. "We have to. So we're going to finish it ourselves. Just the three of us."

"What?" Larry said.

Stephanie laughed. "You've lost it."

"I am not afraid to die," Eric said. "Stephanie, you care for no one. Larry, you've got no one to care for. And we're three of the most skilled officers around. We're finishing this."

Stephanie and Larry both looked at each other.

"If you try to send me to my death, I am more than willing to fight back or kill." Stephanie said.

"And if you return to ESSO-3 alone, Ken's instructed to immediately apprehend you. You're very lucky you're an asset to the team, we made provisions Stephanie."

"Don't send me to my death," Stephanie replied.

"You'd better have a plan," Larry said.

"That can be discussed. But it will be the three of us, alone," Eric said. "You will do your jobs. Understood?"

"Understood," Larry said.

"You've dragged me this far," Stephanie said. "A cripple, a security grunt, and an engineer. Great."

"Larry, you remember back on the Station mission, after you, me, and Grace got separated. We moved through a chamber with spiders, and got through without fighting a single one of them?"

"Yeah. We snuck right through. We kept quiet, and the robots couldn't hear us even when we were closeby."

"Exactly. Whatever the robots have, they don't have good hearing. So we're going to try and do the same thing out here, sneak our way to the telescope."

"But this is a wide open area, and there are a lot more robots here,"

"True. But the same principle applies. We'll take a more roundabout route. We'll go from cover to cover. And we'll minimize use of the buggy. Avoid attention at all costs."

"Well we are light on our feet, and we now know more of the area and what to expect," Stephanie said. "It's still suicidal, but not purely idiotic."

"Once there," Eric said, "We use what explosives we have left. Hopefully we can minimize the attention that draws. Get in the Observatory, see what we're looking at, see if we can approximate where it is in the sky, and get out. Once we have that, we can analyze safely back on ESSO-3."

"Alright Eric," Larry said. "I'm with you now. Let's do this so nobody else has to."

"Are we ready?" Eric asked.

"Ready," Larry said.

Stephanie shrugged.

"Let's do this," Eric said.

Eric sprung to his feet, Larry and Stephanie stood as well. They had already left their equipment, Eric's shotgun, the explosives, in the buggy outside. All the crew of three had to do was gather themselves, ready themselves, prepare to go. Eric set up an automated message, to notify Mission Control if nobody returned to the ship after several hours. A rescue team would have to be sent to get David, and Eric's message would notify them of the City, its missile defenses, and the Orca's location. But this, Eric mentioned repeatedly, was the last resort. They would be back to disable this automated message.

With everything in place, Larry, Eric, and Stephanie left the ship. Back onto the surface of Gamma-2.

• -   -

Whatever time had passed did not show in the features around them. The red haze, the sky of frosted glass, a window to the empty space vacuum and stars above. The rocky features around them, from distant mountains to surface pebbles, perfectly preserved. Larry caught his breath. The soreness from all the exertion was seeping in, but the job wasn't over yet. He sighed as he took the driver's seat of the buggy, Eric again riding shotgun. Stephanie in the back. They got going, the engine giving a nearly inaudible whir.

"This place makes ESSO-3 look pretty," Stephanie said.

As they got going down the same open plateau of rock, Larry, for once, relaxed at the wheel. The bumps and intermittent craters were a lot easier when Larry had seen them twice already. He slouched, let his shoulders down, lightened his grip.

"Makes ESSO-3 look like paradise," Larry chuckled.

"Calm down there buddy," Eric said.

Eric sat more relaxed as well, his legs crossed, his shotgun in his lap. An arm leaning on the side of the buggy.

"ESSO-3 could make for a good vacation spot, if you melted the ice." Larry said.

Eric looked over at Larry. He glanced back at Stephanie. "Did you spot any leaks in his suit?"

Stephanie was busy arranging the crates at her feet. This would have only taken a minute, but she was playing around with different orderings.

"Figured I wouldn't mention it since I spotted leaks in yours too," Stephanie replied.

"So clever."

The plateau began to narrow before it widened again, and as they approached the Outskirts of the City, this was very noticeable. Larry was driving further to the right this time, and he was much closer to the edge.

Eric steadily tapped a robotic finger on the side of the buggy. Larry caught himself easing on the pedal, and pressed firmly. He drifted past a crater, coming so close that pebbles kicked up from the tires fell into it. No one in the buggy was phased.

They finally came upon the Outskirts, piles of scrap coming up this time off to their left. Larry made out the figure of a single spider in the distance. It wasn't moving.

"Here we are," Eric said. "Showtime."

Larry slowed the buggy.

"Hold on, we can get closer," Eric said. "But turn. Veer sharply."

Larry nodded and cranked the wheel. The buggy gradually made its way around, even more rightward. As it curved, Larry kept his eyes peeled to the left. So far, nothing stirred.

Back to the very large, and hundreds of feet wide, Solar Panels Array. Larry's curve took them to the outermost row of panels. Out that far the large cables laid on the ground in between were less densely packed. It was more just a few cables that snaked. As Larry crossed over just past the corner of the outermost panel, he was just over a dozen feet from the edge of the plateau. Past that edge was a straight drop into a crevice, spanning miles. Beyond that, jagged ominous mountains. Though moving down the line, this gap the buggy headed through widened considerably.

Larry straightened the vehicle out. They passed rows and rows of panels, but this time peering in from the outside. This time there were a few robotic figures within the Array, passing in and out of view. Too far to make out whatever work these robots were doing

As they passed the last row of panels and emerged from the gap, the three crewmates now came upon the City from a new angle. Off to the left were the majority of buildings, a Mechanical Crane, a Communication Tower, a damaged, leaning but still standing Communication Tower. Past that of course, but not in full view, the Refinery. Just as they had left it. Dead ahead of them, several dozen feet, was a maze. A maze of prism-computers, with some semblance of shape, almost but not fully aligned in rows. And in between these two clusters, save for a few scrap piles, lots of open space.

As Larry drove forward, he scanned the surroundings left to

right. The robots had definitely dispersed. There was motion on the pipes of the Refinery, peaking out above the other buildings. The unstable crawling, up, down, and around pipes, like bugs in some bizarre nest. Larry noted four or five spider figures at least, but pretty clearly they were out of range.

The actual structures preceding the Refinery appeared mostly empty. Nothing crawling along any of the towers. Only one or two visible on the ground. The open space rightward passed the structures, the route Eric had driven down when rescuing him, before proceeding to Stephanie and David, it was empty. Not even any dust kicked up, of course, the lack of wind. Larry and Eric both glanced at one another.

"I don't see many. Where could they have gone?" Eric asked.

Larry shrugged.

"Resources?" Stephanie said. "Repairs? They just fought a battle."

"Ah, that's true," Eric said. "Hard to believe we diverted the whole Colony, though."

"Of course."

"Yeah, look ahead," Larry said.

The maze in front of them was a complex. It led almost to the edge of the plateau. Tall metal boxes with lines of circuitry, standing like monoliths. Haphazardly placed. There were enough of them, Larry couldn't fully tell, but dozens, so that they formed a big block of a feature. With thin spaces in between them of only a few feet. Those long cables, like from the solar panels, laid on the ground, sprawling all the way back to the rest of the City. One cable, Larry followed, led all the way to the Observatory. That distant cylinder, one story, uniform, no windows, with a massive telescope peeking out the top. The big prize.

On queue, a gorilla strutted into view just 20 feet ahead of them, in a gap between two prism-computers. Its thick stump-like front legs, its long arched body, took up nearly the whole gap. Just as soon as it came in view, it disappeared back into the maze.

"You think we could drive around?" Larry asked.

"That open empty path between that maze ahead and the other structures looks tempting," Eric said. "But what if something from the maze spots us? Or, if we drift over to avoid the maze's view, we'd be close enough something from the City might spot us."

"Right. And I don't want to leave the buggy just yet, of course. Too far."

"Well, looks like there's no way around," Eric said. "We'll have to get through the maze."

"But we'd have to do it on foot, right? Buggy won't fit. And it certainly draws attention."

"Go through the maze on foot," Eric said. "Spot when it's clear for the buggy to go around. Once we're sure the coast is clear, no robot is looking that way, the buggy will have to make a sharp turn around."

"Meanwhile the spotters would have to sneak through without alerting anything. Just like when we were on the Station."

"Just like the Station," Eric agreed.

Another robot, a spider, passed into view, further to the right. It appeared to be facing them, but it didn't react. Larry shuddered, and thought to back up the buggy, but didn't.

"Ok. We need to make a break for it, now. Once we get in the maze it'll be easier. You two ready to run?" Larry said.

"Hold it, you're the ones with guns, Larry," Stephanie said.

"You and Eric go. I'll bring the buggy around."

Larry hesitated. But looking at the maze, there were no robots currently in sight. Larry willed himself into action. He leapt out of the driver's seat and made a break for the maze. He saw Eric in his peripheral going with him.

The bounce in his step helped him cover the ground rapidly. Larry took big strides, focused on the first prism-computer dead ahead of him. Fifteen feet, ten feet, six feet. There was no time to look around. Larry kicked a rock sticking out of the ground at the last minute, and stumbled into the wall in front of him. But he caught himself, arms hugging the edges of the big computer. He stood hugging that computer and got his bearings. It covered above his head, and to his left and right, but not comfortably. He wasn't exposed, but he felt like it.

Larry looked to his right, and there was Eric one row over, awkwardly hugging the wall just as he had. He took a quick look over his shoulder, Stephanie back at the buggy was already in the driver's seat.

"Ready for the fun part?" Eric said. "Peak on three."

Larry nodded.

"One...Two..."

On three they both peeked out right. Larry saw in front of him, almost an entire clear unobstructed view, two parallel rows. One prism-computer off at the end was diagonal, partially blocking the view, but he could still see to the end. No robots.

"Clear!" Larry shouted.

Eric replied a moment later. "Clear. Don't shout, I'm on earpiece."

"Right."

They both advanced. Now Larry turned to the side of the big computer, hiding from the horizontal line of space. Right in his face were several wires and a few flashing nodes. Red light, or invisible of course. Larry hugged that wall, before peaking out cautiously. He saw a straight open view all the way through. He even caught a glimpse of a Communication Tower off in the distance. He then hurriedly cocked his head to check down the vertical row again, and then made his move, shuffling to the front wall of the next prism-computer of the row. Eric followed suit.

"I'm exposed, and I'm getting whiplash," Eric said. "We're doing this every row?"

"Presumably," Larry said.

They advanced like this for another two rows. As Larry clung to the fourth prism-computer of his row, he heard Eric gasp. He wanted to see what had happened, but fought this impulse and instead slid over to the left wall of his cover and hid. He had a prism-computer right in front of him in the horizontal row, and his vertical row was clear for now.

"What is it?" Larry asked.

"Spotted one to our right. I'm good now." Eric said, breathing heavily. He then added, "Shit, there's another. Move left."

Larry and Eric both shifted down and left multiple rows. But there was no coordination. Instead, they scurried. They ended up with Larry two rows ahead of Eric.

Larry peaked and found a spider in his vertical row. It was in no hurry, but it soon wandered out of view. Larry was now having to peak many angles just to make sure he was safe. It was straining him. Eric was crouched behind his box, straining even more. He was about to make another move.

"Wait, Eric. Time to spot. You stay there, try and track those couple robots you already saw. I'll forge ahead."

"Ok," Eric breathed.

Larry drew his gun and kept moving. There were four robots that they knew of so far in the maze. Unless they had double counted, he was going to assume not. They seemed to be focused on something off in the far corner, away from him and Eric. Repair, construction, who knew. What was important, was for Larry to make no errors. Eric just had to stay in place.

Larry made a run down a few rows. As he did this, he caught a glimpse of a spider not facing him. One of the ones from before, he was sure of it.

When Larry made it about two-thirds the way through the maze he stopped. Eric's part of the maze, back towards the beginning, was the most crowded now for sure. Nothing he could do about that.

"Eric, you copy?"

It was a low voice that replied. "I haven't moved, These things are gathering near me, Larry. You better get in position."

"I'm in position," Larry replied. "On your mark."

"Ok... One, Two..."

For a moment there was no response. Then, "Clear! Now Stephanie!"

Larry waited with his back to a wall, his hands gripping its smooth edges. Almost at the leftmost end of the maze. He could see out ahead of him another glimpse of the City. Still just part of a Communication Tower. The leaning one, he thought, but he wasn't sure. Clearing most of the maze, he'd covered virtually no real ground.

It mattered little, soon enough he saw front tires creeping into view. An instant later, back tires. The buggy nearly passed right by.

"Stop Stephanie." Larry said.

A few seconds later, the buggy backed into his view. The white figure at the driver's seat lined up with him and stopped. She was a good distance from him. She beckoned.

Larry peaked one last time over his left and right shoulders. When he knew he was clear, he sprinted. As he cleared the maze, he made a sharp cut. Stephanie turned the buggy and drove to him. They met halfway. Stephanie stopped only for a moment as Larry got in.

"Head around back," he said.

"I know," she replied, grunting as she cranked the wheel. She took them in a wide curve around the maze, going until they arrived parallel a good 20 feet behind it. She then slowed and drifted down the rows so Larry could see. Right away Larry spotted Eric, pressed against a prism-computer, who had moved a few rows up, but was still deep in the maze. They drifted a few more rows down, and soon spotted a spider moving across the opposite way.

"Eric, we see you, we've cleared the maze. You just need to make it through." Larry said.

Stephanie backed the buggy up so Larry could see Eric once again. He was moving down rows frantically.

"Keep waiting, don't leave," Larry said.

"You know we might have to," Stephanie replied.

Larry said nothing.

They watched as Eric quickly but methodically matched Larry's pattern, peaking and shifting down rows. He knew to stay to the left. Larry leaned over to peer into the adjacent row, and sure enough, the spider he had spotted was creeping over. The outline of four wiry unnatural legs moving across, about to reach Eric's row.

"Eric, coming up behind you. Move left," Larry said.

Eric reacted immediately. He ducked to the left out of view just as the spider's front legs came into view. All the way at the other end of the maze, the spider crawled over to a computer. It delicately laid its front legs on the machine, dipped its head and interacted with it. Larry squinted and saw as it plugged in. Its body twitched slightly as it did. Meanwhile, Eric had shifted over two rows, into a vertical row that was too obstructed for Larry to see.

Larry had to wait a solid minute. He kept his gun out just in case, but there was nothing he could do. Aside from that one spider, he saw no movement in the rows in his limited view. When he glanced back at Stephanie, she gave no tells, she simply had a blank face.

"Eric, how you doing?" Larry said.

"I think I'm almost clear. I'll start sprinting soon. Stay put." Eric responded.

Stephanie inched forward so they could see a few more rows. Sure enough, they found Eric, and soon he was sprinting down a clear row. The robots must have been on the right, and left sides of the maze, but there were none in the middle right now. Larry could feel Eric's adrenaline just by looking at him. The man with the metal arm hurried, until finally he cleared the maze completely. Running up and leaping into the back seat of the buggy, climbing in with both hands.

"Time to go," Eric said, as he landed in his seat.

"What happened to your shotgun?" Larry asked.

"I dropped it, almost got spotted in the maze. It's gone now."

Stephanie wasted no time. She cranked the wheel one last time to take them in a wide turn away from the maze. Following this turn, they could curve widely around and end up at the

Observatory. No more obstacles in the way. It was an open path, and it was far enough from the rest of the City to not have to worry about being spotted. Larry cocked his head and kept his eyes peeled at the City. They had cleared the leaning Communication Tower and were now well on their way.

"I'm taking the buggy all the way there." Stephanie said.

"Absolutely, we'll have more than enough leeway." Eric replied. "You both know what to do. There will be no time to waste."

● -   -

The Observatory was surrounded by structures, but they were less densely packed than some other areas. Most of the buildings around it were more generic, probably either for storage of some resource, repairs, or who knows what. There was a launch pad nearby though, and what was unmistakably a rocket. Just like Larry had seen at the very first camp on ESSO-3.

But as they arrived just outside the Observatory, this and everything else around was none of their concern. The imposing cylindrical structure, likely made of some synthetic material given its strange texture, and almost tarp-like quality, was right in front of them. They could see the massive telescope above, balanced on a light mechanism. They were here.

Stephanie stopped the buggy. She hopped out and went to the back. Eric handed her a crate and her toolkit, and Eric himself grabbed a crate. Eric stepped out, and the two brought the crates to a few feet from the Observatory's wall, and set them down. They opened the crates, revealing those bundles of beige sticks, and planted them accordingly. Larry got out as well, and took a quick look around just to be sure they were safe.

This quick look revealed something uncanny. As Stephanie and Eric were kneeled over, busy with their task, Larry was standing and facing the City. He saw the Refinery, which was so lengthy it almost ran to the Observatory itself. And something was cutting across from it. A pair of spiders accompanying in the distance. But not just them.

Bipedal. Massively long legs. Not wiry, but thick, plated, filled out and with joints. Easily taller than the Observatory, a good 20 feet, maybe more. Carrying a sleek metal torso, mostly of thick pipes. A long neck, and arms extruding out, again thicker and with joints, and long enough to hang below its waist. Pulleys on the arms, to support not fingers but a more primitive claw, and a few drills as well. Its shoulders had two large cylindrical pointers, undoubtedly appropriated from the gorilla's design. But these weren't the scale to be blinding lasers. Maybe instead they were mining lasers. Corroborated by the huge load this thing carried on its back, no doubt supplies from the mine, related to the mining machinery Larry had spotted last time. And its head? No other words could do this peculiar shape justice. A HammerHead.

Stephanie and Eric came up to him, breaking his fixation.

"You're gonna need to back up farther than that buddy," Eric said.

"Let's go," Stephanie said sternly.

The three of them gathered behind the buggy. Stephanie had the detonator in hand. Beige bundles out in the middle of the open, ready to blow. They looked away as Stephanie counted down, and hit the detonator. Just a second later, the explosives went off.

21

U gly. It was extremely ugly. As the dust cleared, and the cloud of smoke dissipated, Larry peered his head up from the buggy. His ears were very grateful for the thin air muffling the sound of the blast. Stephanie and Eric had already gotten up and were making their way inside. This massive block of a structure, this landmark, the Observatory, now had a hole blown through its strange mesh wall. A big hole.

Through that hole was the ugliness. As Stephanie and Eric reached the hole, and Larry came up to them soon after, they could all appreciate it. Thick wires covered the place. Cables, more like. Hanging down from above like vines, and sprawling across the floor. Not only was it like looking through a spider web, it made the mere five or six feet between them and the apparatus of the telescope virtually obstructed. It was hard to even get a close look.

"You have to be kidding me," Eric said.

"Interior design. Another thing the Robots need to work on," Stephanie remarked. She eagerly brought out the combat knife.

"Larry, how the hell does she still have that?"

Larry tapped her on the shoulder and held his hand out. "I thought you guys were here to interpret. Might wanna use your wrench for the more delicate equipment."

"Right, of course," Stephanie snickered. She placed the knife in Larry's hand and brought out a wrench from her tool-kit. "Well?"

"Let's go," Eric agreed.

Stephanie shoved the first cable out of her way and got going. Eric used his bare hands, his robotic one for the heavier cables. They both took careful steps inside. Together they steadily cleared a path through. It took them a few minutes to get all the way through.

"Larry, you coming?" Eric asked, grunting as he worked.

"I'm keeping watch out here," Larry replied.

"Ah, smart."

The two reached the main apparatus of the telescope. The thick aluminum cylinder protruding from the center of the room, all the way to well above the roof of the building. Passing the buzzing instruments and machines, it was set up on a mechanism that allowed it to rotate. With the cables cleared, Larry could see these pulleys in action, making a slight adjustment. Tilting the telescope no more than a degree.

"Is it adjusting itself... autonomously? The precision, it's incredible!" Eric said.

"All that computing power has to be going somewhere," Stephanie said.

"Stephanie, even for you, this has to evoke some feeling of wonder."

"Of course. It's fascinating. Exciting."

"Terrifying, too, what these things are capable of. But we'll worry about that later."

Eric bent down and cleared the way to take a look through the massive thing. When he did, he went silent.

"Stephanie. Come look at this now."

Stephanie, who had been inspecting the mechanisms of the telescope, complied. She swapped places with Eric. She was mesmerized as well.

"What is it?" Larry asked, facing them for a moment.

"Alien Life," Eric replied.

Larry frowned. "What do you mean? A ship? A station?"

Eric shrugged.

"It's... hard to tell," Stephanie said. "This isn't the best view."

"That's it? You just found...something?" Larry said.

"I can't even believe this is real," Eric muttered. "Like I knew we might find something, but..."

"How do you know it's not Robot? How can you assume that?" Larry said.

"We know," Stephanie said. "It's obvious."

Eric and Stephanie swapped again, so Eric could gaze through the telescope once more. Stephanie stood still, looking off into space.

Larry cleared his throat. "Shouldn't you guys be doing some... analysis? Approximating where it is in the sky?"

"Right, absolutely," Eric replied. "Let's get on it."

Stephanie brought out some equipment, and together she and Eric got going. Meanwhile, Larry turned away from them, and took stock of the rest of the City around them instead. The maze of prism-computers off in the distance, it was far enough away. And there was little activity happening there anyway, so they were safe. The open plateau around them was all clear as well. But looking back at the City, their original route to the Observatory, past the Refinery and such, the ominous HammerHead he'd spotted had crossed out of view. Now it came back into view, it was hanging around the wrong side of a Communication Tower, straight in the distance. He had no idea what it was doing, it was hardly moving.

Larry looked over to the buggy, tiny in comparison. Ready to take them out of there at any time. "Guys, there's something new out here. It's massive. I suggest you hurry." He heard shuffling from the Observatory.

"I hear you man. We're finishing up here." Eric replied. He spoke now to Stephanie. "This is big. This is so big. This knowledge can't die with us."

"I wasn't planning on dying. Let's pack up shop," Stephanie replied.

"We need to get back to the ship. We need to relay this information to Ken," Eric said.

A minute later, Stephanie and Eric made their way back out the entrance they'd blown in. Stephanie had packed up her tools. Together, they made their way with Larry back to the buggy. As Eric got in the front seat, he stopped. "Wait... shoot. I don't have my shotgun. Well Larry, you're the only one armed. Are you gonna shoot, or drive?"

"Drive."

Larry cranked the wheel and took the buggy around. He was taking them straight back, through the open clearing between the maze and the rest of the City. As they made their turn, Stephanie and Eric finally saw what had made Larry agitated. Dead ahead, off in the distance but very much in their path, doing work on the leaning Communication Tower. The bipedal, long-legged monstrosity. The HammerHead. And a few spiders around it.

It stood hunched over, claws wrapped around the beams of the tower, reaching all the way to the top of it, adjusting them. Intricate pulleys that composed the giant's arms squashed and stretched to do the movements. Red lasers from its shoulders soldered the broken beams. Its bizarre head focused on the task, but occasionally spinning around slightly in its socket.

"What in the world..." Eric started.

"You're heading right at it!" Stephanie shouted.

"We've got to," Larry said. "We can't go around through the City. That was a deathtrap last time."

The buggy's tires careened through the rocky surface, pelting up dust. The debris it did kick up practically floated. Larry was heading top speed straight for the monstrosity.

"Okay, Okay. We'll just ask the big guy to excuse us!" Eric said.

"Yep." Larry replied.

Buildings were passing by to their right. On the left, the maze coming up on them. Whatever attention they attracted from there, now on their way out, was the least of their concern. Just the towering legs of the HammerHead, with its wide stance, took up a decent portion of their path. Larry began veering left to avoid it.

The HammerHead was still occupied with its repairs on the Communication Tower. But its spider escorts, now three in number, perked up and rushed at the buggy. One came from under the tower, two from behind the giant. They weaved around its stocky legs on both sides, the left one cutting out in front.

Larry waited until this pack-leading spider was almost upon them. Timing it just right, when the thing was about to leap in the air, Larry turned sharply. The spider flew right at them, and right past them, narrowly missing as it tried to latch onto their rear.

"Jesus!" Eric shouted.

Larry tried to reach for his gun. But his right hand shot back to the wheel as the second spider came on them. It was coming diagonally however, it would not be easy to dodge.

Stephanie had dug through one last crate in the back. She held a beige bundle and the detonator in her hands. She tossed out the bundle of explosives out to their side and jammed her finger on the detonator. Larry heard the loud boom but had no idea where it had come from. There was no time to react.

The explosion caught both remaining escort spiders' attention for just a moment. Larry made another sharp left and was able to clear them. He kept curving off to the left away from the robots. There was movement in the maze, which they were now passing, but it did not concern him.

As they cleared the area, Larry was finally able to glance back. One giant HammerHead busy with its task. With legs that luckily didn't crush them. A couple of confused spiders jittering about the open area. And a maze teeming with a few robots. Sights Larry was very happy to be leaving behind. Larry looked back at the road, and they were now soon returning to the Solar Panel Array. Going around the long way once again, they simply had to follow the route back. No more robots in their immediate vicinity.

"You know how many times I've had one of those things

right in my *face* today?" Eric said. He sighed with relief. "Looks like we're clear now. Let's never come back to Gamma-2 ever again."

"Oh, so you were planning to?" Larry said.

Eric grinned. "You were damn right. This place makes ESSO-3 look like paradise. Home, sweet icy home."

• -   -

Navigating back for the final time had been light work. It still looked like no time had passed around them. The environment, its red haze, its homogeneous rocky features, the sky peering right into the stars above. The wrongness of this whole world. Gamma-2 was like limbo. Eons could pass and it could stay in this exact state, watching a changing Universe as a passive spectator. It felt both like years and instantaneous, the time they spent there, and the crewmates of the Gamma-2 Mission were more than ready to leave.

Back at the Orca they wasted no time. As Larry backed the buggy into the ship, sealing the hatch behind him, Eric and Stephanie had already boarded. Eric stood hunched over the control board, firing up the ship's computer. As the screen flickered on, he first disabled the auto-message they had set up for in case they didn't return. Then, Eric immediately sent off a message to Mission Control.

Larry, after climbing over the buggy, made his way down the aisle of seats and joined Eric and Stephanie at the controls. After they finished the message, Larry took his pilot's seat. The other two strapped in. Larry had trained enough to make a smooth takeoff, especially in this light atmosphere. He fired up the powerful engines, set course just as he was taught, and took them back to ESSO-3.

• - -

It was a long flight back through the black vacuum of space to ESSO-3. From this perspective, the massive Sun of the system was at their back, and it took a while before ESSO-3 came into view, so they were truly gazing out into nothingness. It felt like a long flight back, but in actuality it was a short one. Larry was antsy for answers his crewmates hadn't yet provided. Still, Larry appreciated the safety, relative comfort, and quiet that came with it. They all needed rest.

Coming up on the dark blue sphere with gray clouds, and massive glaciers visible from space, Larry took them back into the atmosphere. The Orca touched back down near the Colony itself, in a wide open plain of gray rock on the outskirts of the Colony, somewhat close to a Quarters Area.

After they landed, Larry took the buggy outside. This cleared room in the Cargo Hold for Eric and Stephanie to address the first matter at hand. Eric pulled the lever of the currently active cryostasis chamber. He cringed as he did so, looking away. Gasses were pumped behind the glass screen, and its fog dissipated. There was David, peaceful, but empty eyes wide open. He began to wake.

"Hello? Anyone there?" David asked.

"It's us man," Eric replied. "Mission success. We...did it. We returned."

"Oh. Oh good," David laughed. A quiet laugh. A sad one.

"We're gonna get you some help. Here, come with us."

Eric unstrapped David and assisted him in getting out of the machine. David stumbled as his feet hit the ground. Eric kept his arm around him. He had Stephanie take the other side. The three of them steadily made their way down the ramp, as Larry watched from his driver's seat.

"Windier," David said.

"Huh?" Eric asked.

"The wind. That's ESSO-3 wind."

"Ah. You're right," Eric said.

They helped David into the backseat of the buggy. This time all three of them sat in the back, leaving only Larry in the front. When they gave him the clear, Larry began driving. He drove with a single hand on the wheel, and rested.

"Hey," David said, in his soft voice. "Is Larry here?"

"I'm here," Larry replied.

"Good. Would've hated to lose you."

It was quiet for a while, and then David spoke up again.

"Remember when you fought those robots, alone, from behind a tire?"

"I remember," Larry said. His voice broke.

"Yeah," David chuckled softly. "That was somethin' to see."

• -   -

As they entered the Infirmary all attention was drawn to them. The place was back to its normal state, engineers gone, security gone, it was just busy doctors and medical equipment. Two doctors met them and took David, quickly ushering him to a cot at the far end of the room. Special equipment was already set up at that designated cot. Ken had been chatting with the Head Doctor, the new one who had been instated, and now both of them came to Larry, Eric and Stephanie.

"It's a good thing you messaged us when you did," The Head Doctor said.

"Is there anything you can do for him?" Eric asked.

"David was wearing his visor when he took the injury, correct?"

"Yes, but what does that matter? It was clearly faulty."

"Some protection is always better than none. Vision loss always varies from case to case. If you preserved him in cryo soon after the injury, even better. There's a chance we could treat, even reverse his blindness."

"But right now it's up in the air?"

The Head Doctor nodded solemnly.

"And the others? Monica? The medics?" Ken said.

Eric shook his head.

"Horrible. I'm so sorry that happened," Ken said.

"Well we'd better get to business I guess," Eric said.

"Alright," Ken said. "So what exactly did you guys find?"

"We reached the planet, and fought our way to this Observatory. Artificial Observatory monitoring the sky. From there we..." Eric collected himself. "Actually, let's fill you in on the robots first."

"They have a full blown colony on Gamma-2," Larry said. "Fully functioning, solar powered, almost like a mirror ESSO-3. Showcased some major construction feats. But I wouldn't call it a military threat, per se. It was self-sustaining, but I saw little evidence of weapons or some organized army. Well, missiles, so there were weapons, but defensive ones."

"Okay, we definitely have to keep an eye on that," Ken said. "We know how quickly these robots develop. Or we *don't* know, I should say, that's the issue."

"It was bleak, but it could've been worse. Our small crew held its own," Eric said.

"The robots are still in ways primitive," Stephanie said. "They don't seem fully coordinated, they're a bit sporadic."

"Okay. You guys will be sure to update our records on the robots after this. Sounds like there's a lot to document," Ken said. "Now tell me about the other big discovery. Alien life? A Station?"

"It could've been a Station, or a massive ship we saw, we couldn't know," Stephanie said. "Hard to describe. It was very unique looking."

"We know approximately where it was in the sky. High orbit, around the Sun," Eric said.

"I see," Ken said. "How the Robots pinpointed it, this thing, that's what I'd like to know. What in the world kind of image processing..."

"All that computing power has to go somewhere," Stephanie said. "Recognizing threats, that's a pretty good evolutionary goal."

"They can follow ships millions of miles away," Eric laughed. "And they can't hear us sneak by them in a maze."

"Hold on," Larry said. "The robots plug into their computers. We see it every time. What if they themselves aren't smart, but whatever AI they built, is...directing them."

"That's... startling," Ken said. He cleared his throat. "But we'll have to talk about it later. Eric, what's your plan with the Alien Ship? Or Alien *Object*, let's say."

"Okay, okay," Eric said. He took a moment to think. The Head Doctor had left them and attended to other duties. Larry, Stephanie, and Ken had their eyes on Eric.

"Okay, I didn't want it to come to this, but... We have to go."

Ken's eyes widened. All three of them reacted to what Eric just said.

"You can't be serious," Stephanie said.

"We just got back," Larry said.

"We have no idea what we're dealing with," Ken said.

"I know, I know it's terrible," Eric said. For a second his lip curled, a nervous grin, but then he was all business. He took a deep breath. "Look, we have no idea how long this thing, this Alien Object, is going to be where it is. We know right now its position because Stephanie and I deduced that."

"Okay," Ken said. "That's true."

"And we know it'll take hours to get within range of the Sun, traveling at top speed."

"Right," Larry said.

"And there's no way in hell we're going back to Gamma-2, to take another peek at the Observatory. Or ask the friendly robots how their magic mechanical telescope tracks such a comparatively tiny Alien Object. Here on ESSO-3 we're low-tech. The best we have available is our primitive astronomer, who is bound to lose sight of the thing eventually."

"Sure," Stephanie said.

"Now may be our only chance to run a Reconnaissance Mission. Go in, find out whatever we can about the Aliens, and then get the hell out of there."

"Wait, think about this Eric," Ken said. "Isn't it hasty, and reckless to alert the Aliens to our presence?"

"Yes, I hear you, but they're already in the same system as us Ken. The cat's out of the bag. A human colony on the habitable planet? They're bound to find us. It's just a matter of whether we learn about them first, or they show up one day."

"And think broader. This Colony could go down. We have

over a hundred brave people here, it'd be devastating. But what if these Aliens find the real prize? The Home System, where 99.9% of Humanity lives? We are obligated to warn Humanity however we can, even at our own expense."

"I... alright Eric. This isn't a game. But I trust your judgment," Ken said. "What should we do to prepare for this Reconnaissance Mission? Gather up another crew?"

"I'd rather get back to my prisoner accommodations than be a part of this suicide mission," Stephanie said.

"Oh believe me Steph, I'm glad to put you back to that," Eric said. "No, Ken, no more crew. I know nothing about what I'd be getting them into. I'm going myself."

"Eric," Ken said. "You sure? Taking on that risk. Not to mention putting the Colony's leadership in jeopardy again..."

"You're a smart man Ken, you can run things around here. And Larry?"

"Yep. Need a pilot?"

"Precisely. It'll be you and me man. Two-man Crew. One more Mission. Let's get this done."

"Let's get this done," Larry agreed.

There was murmuring from the doctors around them. Eric gathered himself, and took one more moment to think.

"Stephanie, you said you had a fourth heat seeking missile prepped?"

"We never ironed out some kinks..."

"Well iron them out. You have two hours at best. That, plus the missile we had left over, would make for two missiles at the ready for the Orca."

"The rest of you," Eric continued. "Well, you know what to do."

They split up. Larry escorted Stephanie back to Engineering, returning her to her security detail as promised. Ken went to coordinate his Rescue Team, as they might yet be utilized. Eric returned to his office, rapidly sending off instructions to any personnel he could assign last minute projects. A short, rushed Mission Prep was underway. Just a small window of time until Larry and Eric would venture off again, for one last time.

22

S everal workers cleared from the Orca, and now it was just Eric and Ken standing off to the side, making way for the buggy. Larry pulled up to the front of the ship and parked, allowing two engineers from the back to haul out a large object, their arms trembling. A heat seeking missile. Larry stepped out and gave them a hand, and together the three of them brought the missile to the large metal tube on the starboard side that housed it. They carefully lined the heavy thing up, and slid it in inches at a time. Larry waited as the engineers secured the missile properly. After a few minutes they finished their task.

Larry walked with the engineers back to the buggy. As they got there, one of the engineers waved him off, taking the driver's seat. Larry bent over and grabbed a small device from the passenger seat. He turned and walked away, and the engineers drove off. Larry came over to meet Eric and Ken, who stood impatiently.

"What have you got there, Larry?" Eric asked.

Larry held out the detonator in his hand. "From Stephanie. Said she couldn't get the missile's circuitry fully working. Or something like that. But worse comes to worst, you can set it off manually with this."

Ken and Eric looked at each other. Ken shrugged. Eric raised an eyebrow.

"Ok then... long as it works," Eric said.

"A little dangerous to have on board, this detonator, don't you think?" Larry said.

"You're telling me," Eric said. "Whatever, just be very careful with that thing, okay?"

"Yeah."

Ken cleared his throat. "Larry, I've got a little last minute safety briefing for you. I'm sure Monica taught you this stuff, but..."

"Go ahead," Larry said.

"Alright. Now as you know, by the time you get near the Sun we'll be hours away. But the moment you send us a distress call, on protocol we'll drop everything and have a ship take off. We've got a great pilot, security, a medic, a fully equipped Rescue Team. So don't be hesitant to give us a call."

"Got it."

"Now, in the event your ship sustains damage," Ken went on, "Worst case scenario, the hatch between the Cargo Hold and the rest of the ship can be triggered from the control board. Close it immediately, you may be able to prevent catastrophic air leakage."

Larry nodded.

"And finally, in the event you need to land for repairs, and let's say you don't have the means to get all the way back to ESSO-3, well..." Ken said.

"Gamma-1?" Eric said.

"Eh, I'd say Gamma-2 is your safest bet. Obviously avoiding any dense areas of robotic structures."

"Great, the last place I wanna go. I'd rather haul ass all the way back to Home System frankly." Eric laughed.

"Or go down with the ship," Larry added.

"You got that right," Eric said.

"Yeah, okay. You guys know what to *actually* do, when the screwing around is over," Ken said. "But that's it. Time's wasting."

"Agreed," Eric said.

"Alright. Good luck you two. We're all behind you," Ken said.

"No worries Ken. We'll be back in no time." Eric replied.

With that, Larry and Eric disappeared into the Orca. Moments later, the thrusters activated, and the ship took off into the atmosphere. The Reconnaissance Mission had begun.

• -   -

"You're not even gonna ask what I'm working on?" Eric said.

Larry, who had made all the major maneuvers of the course, was simply keeping the ship steady. A straight path to the destination. The solar mass that lay dead ahead of them. Past Gamma-2, which was at this point well behind them. They were headed for a spot in high orbit, their waypoint technically several degrees away from the Sun. But until they were practically on top of the waypoint, it made no difference. It looked the same as if they were headed straight for the Sun. And when they got there, they may as well sink right into it, like the microscopic speck they were.

"I know I know, big mission. You like to stay quiet, in your little private zone, or something."

"Correct." Larry turned and looked at him. "What are you working on, Boss?"

"Please, don't call me Boss, I am your scientific companion," Eric said. He stretched. "Your fellow workman, honestly."

The monitor on the control panel, rudimentary as it was, was filled with lines of characters. Eric was able to type with both hands, though the right hand usually stayed locked in place, fine motor skills not being its strong suit. His left hand could adjust and reach for faraway keys. Back on Gamma-2 Eric had set up an automatic distress signal, a routine communications procedure. This project was far more complex. As Larry gazed over the screen, he saw plenty of 1's and 0's.

"First Contact, we're on our way to go meet this ship. Or station. Or whatever it is, right? I figured I'd prepare a little greeting," Eric said. "A simple message written in Binary. I'll wait for your call to send out the transmission."

"What kind of message?" Larry asked.

"Well, it's not like the aliens are gonna speak English," Eric went on. "But math is the real universal language. So I set up a few simple math concepts. 1+1 = 2, the Pythagorean theorem... a prime number here and there, all in binary. Hopefully, they get my message, respond with some math of their own, we could get a dialogue going."

"You're assuming there are aliens, on board the thing."

"There could be nothing conscious aboard that heap in orbit, far as I'm concerned. Or maybe it's manned with a full crew. All I'm saying is in the event there are aliens on board, and they perceive my message, it could help. A contingency."

"Honestly, Eric, I have reservations," Larry said. "I want to scout this thing out, definitely, but not necessarily to make contact."

"I hear you. We want to provide as little information about ourselves as possible. But going in the dark is just unproductive. We're not just going to hover around this Object and then leave. Let's at least try to establish a dialogue, so that we can learn."

"Alright. You have a point. We can go through with that."

Eric resumed working away at his program.

"Oh and Eric, maybe leave out a prime number or two. We're almost there."

• - -

The Sun, though getting bigger and bigger in front view, was now veering off to the right of them. A sign they were getting very close. Larry kept his eyes trained on the black vacuum of space ahead of him, pretty soon a visual would emerge. And it did. A tiny dot, almost indiscriminate, had come into view, and was gaining size.

Eric's eyes widened, as he looked up from his work and noticed. Larry kept his course.

"No more time," Larry said.

"And no turning back now." Eric finished.

Larry kept forward only a few minutes longer. Soon enough he eased the Orca's engines into a full stop. They arrived.

Hundreds of feet In front of them, and below them, was an imposing structure suspended in space. It was at least as large as the Robot Station from ESSO-3, probably much wider. But a much more definitive shape. The whole thing was bright silver, mixed with black. An elliptical centerpiece branched out to a massive surrounding ring. As Larry watched, the ring made a constant slow, lumbering rotation around the centerpiece.

"Incredible...Artificial Gravity," Eric said. "Like on the Transport Vessels. The rotation of the ring gives it centripetal force, all around. Anyone walking inside the ring would have gravity simulated for them. This looks a lot bigger, and heavier, than any example I've ever seen though."

Beyond the ring, there were two extensions to other wings of the structure, irregularly shaped, but with smooth walls. The Robot Station had been jagged, with loose parts everywhere. This structure was smooth, rounded out, and deliberate.

"How many of the Orca could fit in that thing, Eric? Lengthwise."

"Hard to say. Lengthwise? Any way you slice it, I feel like an ant. Bring her in closer."

Larry did just that. He also brought the ship around, so they were facing the Station from an angle. It hardly mattered, the ring section was uniform all around. The whole thing was so smooth, it was as if it were made of clay. As they got closer, the ring, though its width was the most impressive, was definitely tall as well. Multiple times the Orca in height.

"I think we can safely say... well it looks like it's a Station," Larry said.

"How many humans could that thing hold? Thousands? Jesus." Eric said.

Larry brought the ship back out, so they could view the whole structure. There were no lights, no moving parts, nothing to indicate activity on the Station. Just cold, hard, lumbering silver.

"Well," Larry said. "It's very big."

Eric shook his head. "Ugh, we're not learning anything out here. No signs of life. No apparent weapons. We need to find out more. You alright with me sending my greeting, Larry?"

"Go for it."

Eric added one last line to his program and sent it. A radio signal filled with encoded mathematical patterns, sent out to the giant, ringed, almost ghostly space station, in high orbit of the Sun. Eric waited eagerly.

"Okay, so if they deduce the math, which they should be able to if they're intelligent," Eric said. "How can we then move from math to communicating coherent ideas?"

He looked at Larry, who shrugged. "How should I know, man? It was your idea. I'm no linguist."

"Yeah, I'd kill to have one of those right about now. How come we didn't send linguists to ESSO-3?"

Without a word, the look Larry gave Eric made him scoff. "Yeah okay, I was being rhetorical."

Several minutes passed. No response. Nothing but maddening silence. No sign of anything in the Station, which just kept on its lumbering rotation. Larry looked to Eric, whose determined face said it all. They would wait hours if they needed to.

Fiddling with the control board, something brought Larry's attention right back to the front view. The ageless-looking Station had not changed, but there was something else. A small bright flash, in the corner of their view. Another, in the opposite corner. And a few more flashes, popping into view. Growing in size, coming at them.

"Missiles! Incoming!" Larry said.

"I see them. This is it Larry! Hang on!" Eric said. He

grabbed Larry by the shoulders, startling him. "I knew we were gonna get ourselves killed! But we sent information to the Colony. And now we can say the Station's weaponized. We've done our job! We've done our job!"

"No need for that talk, I've got our heat-seeking missiles ready! I'll wait till the incoming missiles converge, take out as many at once as possible. Then I'll do evasive maneuvers!"

"*Two* missiles Larry!" Eric laughed wildly. "Two missiles! We're a speck! In the sky! With two little missiles! What's that gonna do? There are things out there in this vast unknown much bigger than ourselves Larry, much much bigger, and today we're about to die to one!"

Larry waited with his hands clasped around the makeshift triggers, his thumbs poised to launch their missiles. Eric held the manual detonator for the missile that was last-minute. Their front view was filling up with bright flashes now. Several of them.

"We could've stopped at Gamma-2, quit while we were ahead," Eric said. "Been satisfied knowing there was something out there, not what it was."

"No we couldn't. You wouldn't have stopped. You'd never pass up the chance," Larry said.

"I don't think you would have either."

The bright flashes were mere moments away, converging on the ship. But, as Larry's thumbs were nearly going to squeeze the triggers, something strange happened. The bright flashes, several of them now, went out one by one. Each one exploded, bright white plumes taking their place. No sound of course, in the vacuum, but the bright flashes were destroyed. The missiles had still been hundreds of feet from the Orca, and yet, they all went off nearly simultaneously. Larry eased his hands off his missile triggers, the incoming missiles had caused no damage. There was momentary silence.

"What was that?" Eric said.

"They didn't kill us," Larry said. "And they aren't firing any more at us, not that I can see."

"Defects?"

"That was obviously deliberate," Larry said.

"Yeah you're right. They all went out well before they touched us," Eric said. "What in the world does that mean?"

They waited a few minutes before there was another bright flash, only one this time. Larry still braced himself, ready to counter it. But as the incoming missile got within hundreds of feet of them, it blew up suddenly, not even touching them.

"I think I see the game they're playing," Larry said.

"Careful. Let's not make any assumptions." Eric said.

"Should we fire back?"

Eric thought for a moment. "Yes, the manual missile. Blow it up before it reaches them."

Larry fired the manual missile. It flew out of the ship at high speed. But once it cleared the ship, it looked like an insignificant dot sinking towards the giant ring. It took a little while, and it was difficult to tell how close the missile was to impact.

"Okay, blow it early to be safe," Larry said.

Eric used the detonator. A small, but sizable explosion went off above the giant ring. It was significant enough to be seen, but did not size up to the overall massive Station.

"Okay, that was a little pathetic," Larry said. "Hopefully they don't realize we aren't loaded with weapons."

"I mean, we're rather small," Eric said. "Maybe we don't want to be perceived as a threat. Whatever it is, I think you should take us in closer."

Larry lowered the ship and brought them in towards the ring again. The powerful engines of the Orca, though relatively tiny out here, were good enough for covering distance.

As they got closer, Larry still couldn't notice many details from the smooth silver surface of the ring. It looked the same all over. No loose parts, no insignia or painted designs. Just pure solid metal. However, as he was pulling in this time, he saw a bright blue flash of light off to the right of him. He soon realized this wasn't a moving flash, rather it was a beam of light. A beam of light flowing straight up and out into the vacuum. A good eighth of the way down the entirety of the ring from them.

"What's that? You see that?" Larry said.

"I dunno, a beacon? You should go check it out."

Due to the rotation of the ring, this beacon was actively curving away from them. Larry brought the ship around and followed the curvature of the ring, steadily gaining on the beacon. Soon he got close enough to see it clearly.

"There, up ahead," Larry said.

Beneath this strange blue beacon, in the middle of the ring, an irregularity. One that could only be described as a large, extruded set of metal beams, in the shape of a curved triangle. It was wider and bigger than the Orca, but not by too much.

"What in the world." Eric said. "It looks like... docking, right?"

"Yeah, I think so." Larry said.

"It's too big."

"Actually, I think it's not. We can adjust the docking clamps to fit that shape. Just about. All-purpose docking, just as Quint showed me."

"If you say so." Eric said. "Close the hatch to the Cargo Hold just in case."

"Good idea," Larry said.

As they were talking, the blue beacon had shut off. The docking port was moving constantly away from them, thanks to the ring's rotation, but regular movement was something Larry could work with. He used the thrusters to match the speed of the rotation, and allowed inertia to help him keep that speed. Once he had matched the ring's rotation, he used microbursts to line up the back of the ship with the oversized docking port. He could see on screen how close he was getting, and it took many careful adjustments, but eventually, Larry got the ship in place. He pulled a lever, and the docking clamps attached. Larry lifted his hands from the controls. They were now gradually spinning in line with the Station.

"We're hooked," Larry said.

"Okay," Eric said. "Open the Cargo Hold hatch."

Larry reopened it. No rush of air, no vacuum. In that room, the four cryo-stasis chambers were still there. It looked a lot more roomy without a big buggy taking up almost all the space. Most of all, he noticed the back wall with the circular docking opening. At any moment, he could open up the ship to this total unknown.

"Okay, pause." Eric said. He turned his chair to face Larry. Larry faced him. Eric took a deep breath. "Larry, this is insanity. We reached this Station. They sent a missile volley at us, I thought we were dead. They didn't kill us, when they could have. And now they've led us, with this beacon, to dock on their Station. Why?"

"I frankly have no idea," Larry said. "They at least didn't shoot us on sight. That's a good thing."

"Yes, that proves they - or it - or the residents of this Station, have restraint. That's established. The question is what do we do now?"

Larry thought for a moment. Everything was still around them, save for the constant, unnerving rotation of the ring. "Board."

"Board?"

"You said so yourself. We weren't learning anything hovering around the Station. So we went in for a closer look," Larry said. He was emphatic. "And as soon as we did, we could've been killed. But we're still alive. If we've taken blind risks on our lives, all the way up to this point, we may as well just do the big one, and board. High risk, high reward."

"Larry... but they never returned our communication. We're really going in blind. We have no idea what's on board that Station. With the Robots, we at least had a general grasp of their technology, and where they came from, but with this..."

"It's too late for all that. We did communicate with the Station. Just now, with our weapons exchange. If we can learn anything more about these Aliens, we have to try."

"Okay, that's true."

"And one other thing Eric."

"What?"

"I have to go."

"Why?" Eric said, rising aggression in his tone. "That was never the plan. You were just supposed to fly me here. Larry, this is the end of the line, let me go in, you fly back to ESSO-3."

"Eric, the Colony is yours. You're the leader. And the Head Scientist. I'm just a guy who shoots things."

"You're more than that."

"Let me go."

"No."

"I'm the only one who can fire my weighted gun. Do you really want the person going in to be unarmed?"

Eric sighed. "Alright. You have my trust Larry. Find out what you can, get the hell back here. Go board the Station."

Larry made his way down the ship to the Cargo Hold. He briefly considered magnet boots, and decided against them. There was no more preparation to do, he was at the docking opening, Eric would just have to open it for him.

"If you fly back without me, and aren't confident in landing on ESSO-3, land on Gamma-2, away from large robot clusters. Thin atmosphere so it's more forgiving. You can contact the Rescue Team from there, like Ken said."

"It's not gonna come to that Larry. Good luck."

Eric opened the hatch. Larry boarded the Station.

• - -

He had no idea how long he'd been staring at the bronze plate in front of his face. As Larry's eyes began adjusting, he realized he was staring at the floor. His arms and legs, once he remembered he had them, were sprawled out against said floor. Larry took a deep breath, and got to his hands and knees. On a mental count to three, he pushed himself up and got to his feet. He stumbled a bit, his head rushing.

Now he remembered the source of his disorientation. All around him it felt a weight pushing down on him. The pressure created a sensation in his inner ear, uncomfortable to say the least. It'd been a while since he'd felt anything stronger than ESSO-3 gravity. This gravity was no doubt stronger than base-line level.

Larry looked around. He was in a wide open tunnel, plenty

of space all around him. The lights were dim. The walls were strange, there were pipes and wires running down them, usually in an organized fashion. The materials that made up the walls were an amalgamation of metals. He had already noticed bronze floorplates, and it made up parts of the walls too. Steel seemed to be the primary material. There was also lead.

As Larry glanced back, he finally fully established where he was. Just a few feet from the docking port he had entered from, which was on the floor. He heard slight static from his earpiece.

"Larry, you still there?" Eric said.

"Yeah, yeah I can hear you," Larry said.

"Good. Stay in touch. I'd hate to lose signal in there," Eric said. "What's it look like right now?"

"Tunnel. Lots of metals. I'm making my way down."

Larry marched down the long hall. For a few minutes he could just keep going straight, everything was eerily the same. He knew he was in the Giant Ring, so the floor should be curving as he went. And it probably was, but it was so subtle Larry couldn't notice it.

"Gravity's brutal," Larry said. "I'm getting used to it. But it's a workout."

"If that's the case, don't go out too far," Eric said. "Make sure you can make it back to the ship without passing out."

"You're forgetting something Eric, I'm in great shape," Larry said.

"Well don't push yourself buddy."

Larry got a bit farther before stopping in his tracks. He saw up ahead the wall in front of him. Just solid bronze and metal plating. Dead end. Which made no sense, he hadn't seen any branching offshoot tunnels yet.

As he stood in his tracks, he heard movement. Metal clang-
ing, it was fast and irregular. He traced the sound to up above
him. He could vaguely hear it come from behind, then get
louder as it passed seemingly right over his head, then it went
forward. Immediately his hand went to his holster.

"Eric, I'm hearing movement."

"Movement? Back up. Get out of there."

Lastly he heard something like a hatch burst open. Dead
ahead there was nothing but a solid wall. But right before that
wall, from the ceiling, the creature dropped down. Larry drew
his gun.

• -   -

The creature was seven feet tall. It stood on two long legs. It
had a long, slender pair of arms. Beneath them was a short,
stumpy, second pair of arms. But the widest, thickest part of its
body was its torso, enwrapped in an exoskeleton. A curvy black
shell. The whole body resembled an overgrown, bipedal Beetle.
That was at least the closest thing Larry could conceive to fit
this lifeform's appearance.

But its head was the strangest. It was thick, it took up a
significant portion of the body. A thick skull, two dull green
dome eyes sticking out from it, one on each side. A defined jaw,
with what appeared to be a pair of pincers. Three horns at the
top of its head, two small ones protruding out to the sides, a big
one in the middle shaped like a fork.

Just in the seconds as the creature entered the tunnel, it was
distinct from a robot, in a way difficult to describe. Its movements weren't delayed, jittery, or reactive. They were smooth
and deliberate.

As Larry stood face to face with this creature, his gun drawn, but the creature's hands empty, neither one made any sudden moves. That was until the creature raised all four of its arms, bringing its two slender ones together. It began making gestures with its hands.

Its arms mostly stayed in place, the Beetle's fingers made the signs. Larry noticed how complex the digits of these two hands were. He couldn't tell how many fingers, but they were complex, it had opposable thumbs. The creature resembled a beetle, but its hands were closer to a monkey's. It was uncanny.

The Beetle's mouth made an ugly clacking sound to accompany the orchestra of non-verbal signs and gestures. Signs which Larry had no clue what to make of. One repeated sign, in which the Beetle held up a single digit on a hand, Larry tried to focus.

"Larry! What's going on?" Eric shouted.

"Quiet!" Larry responded.

The Beetle stopped signing. It cocked its head.

Larry kept his gun up and made no moves. The Beetle kept looking at him. Then it made a single voiceless gesture and turned its whole body away from him. It took a step forward. It looked back, gave Larry the same gesture, turned around again, and took steps forward.

"I... think it wants me to follow it," Larry said.

"What! What is *it*, an alien lifeform? Do not engage."

"It looks unarmed. I'm gonna follow, cautiously, and keep my distance."

"Well keep enough so you can make a run for the ship."

The Beetle looked back again, as Larry stayed in place. It repeated its beckon. This time, Larry tread cautiously forward, but he intentionally planted his feet on the ground after a few steps. The Beetle gave one last gesture, and then leapt back up the way it came. It disappeared into the ceiling.

Larry ran up to the end of the tunnel to see where it had gone. As he looked up, there was a wide open shaft, and at the front wall of that shaft, a row of bars. Larry tried to jump up to the first bar, but he was anchored down. He cursed under his breath. A jump like that, back on ESSO-3, would have been easy. But here on this Alien Station, things worked differently. Larry leapt up again, and he was able to grab the first bar, but only by his fingertips. They burned as he struggled to wrap his hands around the bar. And the next bar was just barely in reach.

Larry clenched his jaw. He had come this far, he wasn't going to let a little gravity stand in his way. Slowly, with tremendous effort, he brought himself up bar by bar. He climbed, it was just like the cave job. He brought himself up rung by rung. As he finally made his way to the top, he nearly collapsed on the ground.

As Larry got to his feet, there was more tunnel up ahead. But blocking his view and facing right at him was the Beetle. It waited a few moments, longer than Larry needed, and kept going. This tunnel was more of a corridor, branching off into other tunnels at the sides. The Beetle kept walking straight, and he followed ten feet behind it. As it walked the Beetle was center-heavy, so it hunched.

At the end of the hall they reached another climbing shaft. This one was not straight up, however, it was around a 60 degree incline. It was longer, so still a tricky climb, but not as brutal as the first shaft. For the first time Larry got to see the Beetle climb. All the awkwardness in its walk was gone, the creature scaled the wall with all six limbs with ease. Larry steadily climbed after it.

Along the next tunnel, as Larry glanced off to his right, he caught a glimpse of two other figures in a room. They were on opposite sides, hunched over, and looked to be working on the piping along the wall. Larry stopped for a closer look, and the Beetle leading him made its ugly vocal call. Larry decided to follow along. On the way, he described what he'd seen to Eric. He kept his voice low, and the Beetle would still look back at him occasionally, its beady eyes scrutinizing him.

"Horns, very big kinda green eyes, seven feet tall..." Larry listed details. Eric said nothing, so Larry assumed he was enthralled.

After a short vertical shaft, they finally arrived at a destination. Larry followed the Beetle into a large room dead ahead. The Beetle stood at the entranceway by Larry. The room Larry had been led to was unique, to say the least.

The room was made of steel and gold. It was sizable, but only about as big as maybe Larry's quarters back on ESSO-3. Including the one who had led him, there were four Beetles in the room. There was no furniture, only a pair of large, very curvy chairs set up, around a large solid block. He had no idea what the chairs were made of, but if he had to guess, a plastic or a polymer. Probably the most familiar, most human thing he had seen thus far on the Alien Station.

One of the chairs was occupied by the one Larry would refer to as the Leader. He had no idea what authority this one held, if anything, but it was the only one he'd seen with any form of apparel. It wore a gold headpiece that fit snugly between its horns. Next to the Leader was the Bodyguard, Larry didn't know what his position was. His acquaintance who'd led him here he dubbed the Escort. And off in the corner, the most mysterious one facing away with his fingers inside a bunch of tubes, seemingly connected or interfaced with a panel of nodes, he called this Beetle the Technician. All of these uncomfortable eyes, save for the Technician, were on Larry, and the Leader addressed Larry with the beckoning motion the Escort had used.

"I'm in a room with four of them. One of them I think is some kind of leader or officer," Larry whispered. "They want me to sit down."

"Four Beetles? Don't let them rope you in Larry, you have to stay near the exit at all times, ready to make a run for it."

"I know. I'm going in with caution. So I can get some insight."

Although as Larry walked over to take his seat, he didn't like his odds. He'd seen how quickly the Beetle scaled those rungs. Could he really make it back to the ship without getting seized?

Another thing Larry noticed that was immediately off-putting, was on the back wall when he took a closer look. Four long metal legs and a little body mounted on the wall, on display. Larry hadn't recognized it immediately. A semi-dissected robot spider. The Robots and the Beetles were no strangers.

Larry took his seat in a chair very oversized for him. The Leader faced him.

Larry was in a face to face confrontation with this grotesque, big-headed individual wearing a golden headpiece. The Escort had moved in from the door to watch, which made Larry's view of the situation slightly less bleak. He kept the exit in the corner of his eye continuously.

The Leader's face was impossible to read. No eyebrows, no

lips, nothing to indicate expression. Larry could be a specimen, an adversary, or a meal to this thing, he just didn't know. Whatever it thought, it was examining Larry, and when it finished, it began right away with its strange process.

The others looked to the Leader, who had a brief sign exchange with the Escort. The Escort also made a few vocal clacking noises. When this was done, the Leader reached below the block of a desk and pulled out an item in its left hand. This little gray item was shaped like a gun, a cylinder base, a trigger a finger wrapped around, a thin barrel. The Beetle waved this object around for Larry to see. It pointed it straight up and pulled the trigger.

After a heavy click, a gust of red hot fire left the barrel, hitting the ceiling. This brilliant stream gave the whole dim room a red tint momentarily. The other Escort and the Bodyguard signed and clacked amongst themselves. The Technician looked up from his work.

As the Leader released the trigger and the flame subsided, the Beetles' attention was on Larry. Larry had no facial recognition to go off of, but his brain, going off very little, imagined them sneering at him. Especially the Leader, his cruel demeanor, he looked to be taking delight. Of course Larry knew these feelings were primal, not rooted in objective observations.

The Leader made an aggressive clack noise. Everyone's attention was still on him. The Escort also seemed to try and get his attention, he had no idea why.

"The Leader just showed off some kind of weapon, a Flame Gun," Larry said. "Now they're all looking at me."

"Hmm... seems like a weapons demo," Eric said. "Like what we did earlier with the missiles between the Orca and the Station."

"Yeah I think you're right. Should I show my gun?"

"No, don't show them anything," Eric said. "The minute they know what you're packing, they have insight as to whether or not they can overpower you. You can show them the gun, but don't fire it."

Larry reached and brought out his pistol. He waved it for all the Beetles to see. But as they watched him intently, he holstered the gun without ever firing it. The Beetles communicated among themselves. Larry expected them to try and coax him, or repeat the demonstration. Instead, the Leader proceeded.

Next, the Technician came over with equipment in its hands. The Beetles had four arms, but their secondary pair of arms were much smaller, and had no recognizable digits. So they really only had two hands. The Technician laid his fancy equipment on the table. Small handheld machines, some with flashing lights, and various switches or nobs. Larry didn't notice any screens on these devices, though so far to him that didn't mean much. He had no idea what they did.

The Leader pushed the devices off to the side and laid his hands on the table. It leaned forward, Larry gave his attention. The Leader tapped both of its arms once. Then waited. Tapped once more. Then waited. Tapped twice. Waited. And finally tapped three times.

"Eric, I think it's giving me some kind of Morse Code. Or Binary, or something. Here, listen to this."

Larry had no idea how to ask the Leader to repeat itself. He decided doing nothing was better than giving a miscommunication. Luckily, the Leader repeated itself without needing prompting. The Leader did its tapping sequence once again.

"That's not code Larry, it's math! The Fibonacci Sequence. Maybe they did get my transmission..."

"How do I respond? What's the next number..."

"Five."

Larry brought his hand to the table and made a fist. He brought both hands, deciding to mirror the Leader. He knocked, slowly and deliberately, five times. The Leader turned and communicated with the Technician.

Meanwhile the others were still focused on Larry. The Leader took one of the devices it had pushed to the side. A strange little box with lights on it. He held it out across the table, his long slender arm fully extending. Larry carefully reached a hand over, thinking it wanted him to grab it, and the Leader pulled back. So Larry pulled back as well and made no sudden moves.

The Leader held out the device at a distance. He ran his hand up and down a few times, from Larry's head to his waist. When he finished, he handed the device over to the Technician, who eagerly returned to his work station.

"What's going on Larry. More math?"

"I don't like this at all Eric. I think they just scanned me with some device. It felt invasive."

Larry shrunk back in his chair. Every time he spoke to Eric, even softly, he felt their eyes on him.

The Technician was off in the corner, busy with whatever he was doing. The Leader hovered over the two other devices the Technician had left. It took him a moment before selecting the next one. Another equally peculiar handheld device. It inspected this one, but then left it on the table.

It looked up and made a small clacking noise, which got Larry's attention. It brought out its entire lengthy, stringy left arm and laid it flat on the table, facing palm up. It kept its arm in this position, and made more noises at Larry.

Larry looked around, as everyone was watching him. They all expected him to do something. Larry once again mirrored the Leader, but he wanted to keep his trigger finger free, so he laid his left arm out palm up on the table.

As soon as he did this, the Bodyguard grabbed the device the Leader had selected with one hand and walked over to Larry. He reached his free hand to grab Larry's arm, while bringing the device down on Larry's hand. At the same time the Leader demonstrated retracting all but one finger in the extended hand.

The Bodyguard was about to grab his arm.

Larry recoiled back immediately, before the Bodyguard could grab him. He stood up and backed away from the table, towards the corner of the room. Larry drew his gun and pointed it at the Bodyguard.

If there was any reaction of fear in the Beetles they did not show it in this instance. At least there was no indication. The Bodyguard made no sudden moves, and neither did the Leader. All they did was stare at Larry. Massive unblinking dull green domes, watching his every move. The Leader then turned to the Bodyguard and communicated with him.

As they did this, Larry noticed something. On the Bodyguard's hip, he couldn't tell whether it was strapped on or what, was another gun-like item. Different from the Leader's weapon, but only slightly. Maybe another Flame Gun. Did they all carry them? Images of being violently burned to a crisp while helpless in the corner filled Larry's head. A very real possibility. The true danger of these creatures, at least in capability, was apparent to him in this moment. They could kill him if they chose to.

"Eric, I have to leave now. I'll explain when I get back. Be ready to take off."

"Alright Larry. Don't hesitate."

The Leader and Bodyguard were still discussing, in their cryptic hybrid language. Larry moved forward with his gun raised. He switched off between pointing at the Leader and then the Bodyguard. They were looking at him again, and they did nothing.

As Larry sidestepped around the empty oversized chair, the Bodyguard backed up to give him space. Clearly it understood what was going on. But it did not reach for its Flame Gun, and Larry questioned nothing. He turned, now he had the Escort to his back. So he adjusted himself to move out diagonally, and keep all four Beetles in sight. He was shaking while he did this. It was too many targets to keep his gun on. If any of them sprung at him, there was no way he could fight them all off.

Larry finally reached the exit, and backed up to the Vertical Shaft he had entered from. The Beetles did not move from their spots. But he didn't trust the Technician off in the corner, who he could now hardly see. Everything was too dim, too unpredictable.

Larry turned his back for a split second, and dropped down the shaft. He dropped like a stone, making a hard thud as he hit the floor, almost falling over when he did. At this point the heavy gravity had worn him out. But he still had a run to make. Larry sprinted down the corridor. Bronze plating, steel, lead pipes all around him. But no Beetles in sight, fortunately for him.

Larry ran down these empty halls. He made his way back

down the 60 degree shaft. Climbing down it quickly was no easy feat. Then he had to run down another tunnel. When he finally got to the original vertical shaft, it was too large for him to just drop down. He'd break an ankle, or his whole leg, surely. Larry made the instinctive decision to just climb down.

He turned around, reached his leg down to place his foot. That unnatural gravity tugging at him to fall over the edge. Larry made his climb down, almost slipping but not stopping. Until he let go with three or four rungs to go, and landed in the same spot where he'd seen the first of these Beetles. The first one, presumably any human being had ever seen.

Once again, it was a long empty stretch. Larry heard crawling, and he heard movement from the walls around him. At this point he wasn't sure if it was just his mind playing tricks on him. It didn't matter. Larry sprinted down one last long hall, his gun raised, until he reached the original docking port, almost passing it without notice.

"Eric, open the door now..." Larry panted.

Eric complied, and Larry returned to the Orca.

• - -

"I think I can take over now," Larry said.

Their front view showed nothing but black empty space. Eric and Larry switched seats, so Larry could be the one piloting them back. They had been flying for a little over 40 minutes, and there was no sign of any sort of pursuit. It was safe to say they had cleared the Station. They were headed back on Larry's plotted course now, returning to ESSO-3.

"Ah, very good. So, are you ready to tell me about it?" Eric said.

"Yeah, guess I am," Larry said.

"Giant Beetles, huh?"

"That's the closest thing I could think of to what they looked liked," Larry said. "They were big, tall, excellent climbers, and very capable."

"They were clearly intelligent, weren't they?"

"Oh yeah. I couldn't tell what they were doing exactly. And they've probably been here, in this System, for a while. Who knows how long."

"Well, safe to say they didn't show up last week, sounds like."

"Exactly," Larry said. He took a deep breath.

"How do you feel?" Eric said.

"Good. I did it man. We learned about their technology. Their physical forms. Barely scratched the surface, but that wasn't the Mission today. Two hours ago we didn't even know for sure there were aliens. All that putting my life on the line, and others' lives, it actually came to something."

"Yeah, it feels damn good. This one's on you Larry, outstanding."

"Thanks. So many chances for them to destroy both of us, though."

"Yeah. If they wanted to, they easily could've"

"Right, but that doesn't mean they're friendly," Larry went on. "I had to leave because their tests, whatever First Contact ritual they were doing, got way too invasive."

"Perhaps they were just as curious about us, as we were of them"

"Perhaps."

Larry gave one last solemn remark, before remaining quiet for the rest of the way back.

"Humanity is about to have something big on its hands, in the near future."

Eric nodded. "But for now, we celebrate our newfound knowledge. Whatever the future holds, well, we'll do what we've always done. Play our part."

23

It was exhausting work, but for Larry, piloting colonists and supplies back and forth between ESSO-3 and the Transport Vessel was a fine way to spend his last day. Most people might be bothered, having to work while most of the others had the day off; and once finished getting bussed, they were probably celebrating without him. Truly relaxing for the first time in forever. But Larry didn't mind.

Larry sat in his pilot's chair on the Orca, having landed back on ESSO-3 for the umpteenth time. Even among the other pilots, his shift of course ended up scheduled to finish last. Although the coordination was good, as Larry peered out his front view, he could already see the last buggy kicking up its trail of dust in the distance, heading towards the ship. Larry would still have a good few moments to stare out at the ominous mountains, the gray rocky plains, and the brilliant sheets of ice of this surface one last time.

It wasn't a bad way in which Larry spent the past few weeks, not bad at all. Returning to a regular work schedule. Unfortunately the cave job was redelegated, as was his former driving job, but that was the temporary nature of ESSO-3 gigs regardless. Assistant Defense Coordinator, now that was a good job for him, and a relevant one these days. The occasional surveillance of Gamma-2, well of course, they had to keep those deadly, bizarre little metal creatures under close watch. With no more camps in the immediate area to worry about, the Colony could take a proactive approach to defense. And of course, assisting Ken in his various little projects was a treat.

Plenty of fruitful positions Larry had been able to serve before his final task, a glorified shuttle pilot on the last day. But now he was here, finishing up for the day. As the final few colonists arrived, he allowed them to load their buggy into the Cargo Hold, and haul a few extra crates onto the ship. Larry realized the other thing that made him feel better about finishing last, Eric had to as well. Eric, as Master Coordinator, or whatever silly title he had given his position, had to stay on ESSO-3 until this last scheduled departure. So did Ken. So Eric and Ken, after finishing their work, took their seats in the Orca's back row, along with a couple other workers with unfortunate scheduling.

Eric sighed as he sat down, already taking off his helmet and stripping down parts of his environment suit.

Larry chuckled. "Wouldn't it be easier to wait till after we board to take off your suit?"

"Just take us into the damn atmosphere already, Larry."

Larry obliged. He powered up the engines and took them into the atmosphere. And soon enough, back into outer space.

"You know, it's a good thing we requested solid building materials so often, hopefully most of our structures will still be standing if Humanity decides to set up shop on ESSO-3 again," Ken said. "You know, revitalize the Colony."

Eric cleared his throat. "It'll be a long time before this System is fully safe again, I'll say that. And who knows, decades from now, Humanity might have more livable options by then, than a frozen wasteland."

"ESSO-1 and ESSO-2, those are where I wanna know more about," one of the workers said.

"Hey man, we could find a place even better than that. Outside of this damn ESSO program altogether," Eric said.

"You're way too much of an optimist," Ken said. "Then again, who knows."

Eric laughed. "All I know, is how irritated the whole Agriculture Department was about having to uproot. I told them I'm sorry guys, but everyone else is working within our timeframe just fine! This Withdrawal has to be done on schedule."

"Those guys are intransigent," Ken agreed.

Larry docked the Orca, one last time, on the impressive Transport Vessel. The scope of the Transport Vessel was hard to describe. It was a grand ship, and the Orcas were like its lifeboats. At the moment, it housed all personnel of the ESSO-3 Colony.

Larry, Eric, Ken, and the remaining workers boarded, unloaded the Orca, and went their separate ways to do tasks. There was still work to be done before beginning the Interstellar Journey. Shipwide diagnostics at the very least. Most of which could be done from the parts of the ship gifted with Artificial Gravity. Those rotating ring segments, now eerily resembling to Larry his experience onboard the Alien Station, at the mercy of the strange, bizarre, uncanny beings he had the pleasure to meet firsthand. Though these rings were not on the same scale.

The best part of being on board the Transport Vessel was an escape from the gloominess of it all. Just the color scheme, ESSO-3's dark gray and purple sky, the blackness of space, or even the red haze of Gamma-2, that still left a vivid impression in Larry's mind. Here onboard many things were bright and white. When he first boarded one of these vessels, ages ago, the color had given off an unpleasant vibe of medical sterility. But here, coming back, it was familiar and comfortable.

And things were so spread out and sparse back on the ESSO-3 Colony, Larry barely saw people. Here he could bump into people around every corner, or in every corridor. Especially when most people spent their time in the Artificial Gravity segments. It was jarring, at first, how often Larry ran into other people. Even the residences weren't singular.

Rediscovering his favorite nooks and crannies of the Transport Vessel would be for another time. For now, having worked all day, Larry had one place he wanted to go, and that was the Bridge. Larry put on a pair of magnet boots and came to the Bridge, one of the parts of the ship in freefall.

The Bridge was a cozy spot. It was a bigger version of the Orca's cockpit, some chairs, some monitors, level floor. It was more of a workstation. But taking up the whole front wall, a grand view of outer space beyond them, everything that was out there. And standing there in the middle of the room, watching that grand view, was Eric. In his deep black, skin tight indoor outfit. He stood with his hands behind his back. Larry came up beside him to watch that same view.

"Real pretty, isn't it?" Eric said.

"Yeah."

The stars around it as well, but the real focus of their view was ESSO-3. From this distance, all its features faded away, into just a dark blue, nearly purple glow. A rich, saturated glow. All their time spent, all their troubles and worries, all their fantastic discoveries, on this little dark blue sphere. A little island, far away from anything else. Its serene, dreamy glow.

"Shame we had to pack and leave," Larry said.

"You just say that cause we're out here," Eric said. "That planet is a feral beast. But, from a distance, it looks nice."

"Ha, yeah. Our progress though."

"I still have my reservations, I had from the beginning. I'm still making peace with the decision. Much as I'd love to stay, keep expanding, keep growing, defend our land. Hold our own. Much as I'd love to do that, things were heating up. Robots, that were a constant, evolving threat. An Alien presence, that we still know virtually nothing about. Our situation just wasn't sustainable."

"Now with this Withdrawal, you'll have a lot to explain Howe's superiors. Your superiors, now."

"Absolutely," Eric said. "But there's one thing I'm certain of in that regard."

"Oh yeah?"

"I worked with Howe for a long time. Especially as a senior officer. Not always up close, but still," Eric said. "And I'll say this. As corrupt and narrow-minded as Howe was, he would've made the exact same decision, for this Withdrawal, as I'm doing now. I just know it."

Larry nodded.

"Besides, I don't know if you've read up on your American History. I wouldn't want ESSO-3 to have ended up like old Roanoke, Virginia."

"I have no idea what you mean."

Eric frowned.

"So how about when we return to Home System? What then?" Larry said.

"Well, our service is up. I don't care if we haven't fulfilled our damn contracts. I terminated every single one on the computer systems, this is final."

"You'll have quite a case to make to those superiors."

"So we'll make the case. Besides, we'll likely be hailed as heroes Larry. What we discovered out here? We did our duty, went beyond it in fact. They'll send us our separate ways."

"We may as well hope for the best."

"We have a good case Larry. A very good case. We'll get the best," Eric said. His tone was unwavering.

"How about Stephanie? What's to be done with her?"

"I am absolutely thrilled to do that paperwork," Eric said. "At the end of the day, we're not Military. I bet she'll be tried as any other civilian murder case."

"Two counts."

"And definitely premeditated," Eric said. "Good luck to her."

"And you? What's your plan when we get back, after sorting out the case?"

"Contacting the family members of the deceased. The Company will likely handle it, but I'm more than happy to help. Oh and after that... resume my science career, get myself a nice new place, the sky's the limit."

"Are you gonna try to contact your ex-wife?" Larry asked. "I'm sorry, that was insensitive."

"No, it's alright. Frankly, I'm not sure. I've moved on with my life. But, I think I would still like to contact her. I think it's worth doing."

Larry nodded.

"Enough about me, how about you?" Eric said. "A single, young guy? What are you gonna spend that big fat salary on? And don't say you don't know."

"I do know."

"Bullshit."

"I'm serious."

"Well?"

"I'm gonna use it, in any way I can, to get back out here."

"You're kidding?"

"Back out to the Frontier. I'm not kidding," Larry said.

"Why? Still trying to escape your problems? I remember what you said about not wanting to think about things."

"No. it's different this time." Larry spoke with vigor. "Look, I know I'm low-level. I know I don't have all that much to offer in fields like science. But I'm not just going to be some drone back home. Out here, I made a difference. I *helped* people. I took a position few others wanted to take. I protected great people, who did great work."

"So yeah, I'm going back out here. Maybe to a different colony, if they need people, but that's what I'm gonna do. Once more, with a purpose. It's a *feeling*, this time. You know? And while I'm at it, I might even work on having an actual social life next time. Really push myself."

Whatever condescension, or even just teasing Larry expected in Eric's response when he looked at him was not there. Eric smiled.

"I'm gonna miss these little talks we've had."

"Yeah," Larry said.

The two quietly stared out at their planet one last time. Eric laid a hand on Larry's shoulder.

"Probably time for your nap, if you know what I mean."

"May as well get it over with. Worst part of the trip."

Larry left the Bridge, Eric stayed. Larry wandered all the way to his residency, the ship's halls mostly empty now. Larry finally got to the looming empty chamber that awaited him. Not as ugly as the industrial chambers back in the Cargo Hold of the Orca, those looked nightmarish. This one had a nice polished metal finish. It was laid out on the ground, not standing upright. But it was still the same lonely, aimless little place. Just like home. Larry laid down in the contraption, and watched the nitrous gasses fill all around him. He closed his eyes. It was peaceful.

THE ADVENTURE CONTINUES...

Thank you for reading my debut novel Rocky Frontier. I hope you enjoyed it! Please leave a review and tell me what you think. The sequel, Deadlock, is on its way. Be sure to join the mailing list to be notified for Deadlock, and any future projects I'm working on.

Deadlock, Coming Soon

Made in the USA
Monee, IL
09 March 2022

92584818R00173